DON'T EVER GET OLD

DON'T EVER GET OLD

DANIEL FRIEDMAN

Minotaur Books

A Thomas Dunne Book ✄ New York

A THOMAS DUNNE BOOK FOR MINOTAUR BOOKS.
An imprint of St. Martin's Publishing Group.

DON'T EVER GET OLD. Copyright © 2012 by Daniel Friedman. All rights reserved. Printed in the United States of America. For information, address St. Martin's Press, 175 Fifth Avenue, New York, N.Y. 10010.

www.thomasdunnebooks.com
www.minotaurbooks.com

ISBN 978-0-312-60693-0

First Edition: May 2012

10   9   8   7   6   5   4   3   2   1

For my father,
Robert M. Friedman

ACKNOWLEDGMENTS

Thanks to my agent, Victoria Skurnick, for her excellent advice and for her perseverance as an advocate for this book. Without her help, *Don't Ever Get Old* probably would have been longer, slower, and unpublished.

Thanks to my editor, Marcia Markland, and to assistant editor Kat Brzozowski, for their passion and dedication, for putting up with my dumb questions, for praising me more than I deserve, and for bringing this object into existence or, in some cases, into electronic pseudo-existence.

Thanks to Susan and Skip Rossen, Stephen, Beth, David, Lindsey and Martin Rossen, Jenny Landau, Sheila Burkholz, Scott and Rachel Burkholz, Carole Burson, David Friedman, Claire and Paul Putterman, and Rachel, Andrew, and Matthew Putterman, for their support and encouragement. I'd especially like to thank Dr. Steve Burkholz, for helping me get my medical jargon more-or-less right.

Thanks to my grandparents, Buddy and Margaret Friedman, and Sam and Goldie Burson, and to my great-aunt Rose Burson, whose stories and experiences helped to establish the framework for Buck Schatz and his milieu. Y'all have been my inspiration and so much more, and I hope this makes you proud.

Thanks to my brother, Jonathan Friedman, for putting up with me, and for being my first reader.

And thanks to my mom, Elaine Friedman, for everything.

DON'T EVER GET OLD

In retrospect, it would have been better if my wife had let me stay home to see *Meet the Press* instead of making me schlep across town to watch Jim Wallace die.

I'd known Jim since back when I was in the service, but I didn't consider him a friend. So when Rose interrupted my programs to tell me she'd just got a call from the hospital and that Wallace was in intensive care and asking for me, I said I'd have plenty of time to see him at his funeral.

"You have to go visit him, Buck. You can't ignore a dying man's last request."

"You'd be surprised, darling, by what I can ignore. I got a long history of being ignorant."

I capitulated, though, after I lodged my token objection. I saw no point in fighting with Rose. After sixty-four years of marriage, she knew all my weak points.

Jim was downtown at the MED, too far away for me to drive. It was getting hard to remember where things were and how they fit together, so my world had become a gradually shrinking circle, with the house in the middle of it. But that excuse wouldn't save me; Wallace's daughter, Emily, offered to come and pick me up, even though I'd never met her before.

"Thank you for doing this, Mr. Schatz," she said as she backed her car out of my driveway. "I know it must seem weird that Daddy is asking for you, but he's nearing the end, and they've got him on a lot of stuff, for the infection and for the pain, and for his heart. He's sort of drifting back into the past."

She was a couple of years past her fiftieth, I guessed; the flesh around her jawline was just beginning to soften. She was wearing sweats and no makeup and looked like she hadn't slept in a long time.

"He's not so coherent all the time, and sometimes, when he looks at me, I'm not sure if he knows who I am." She stifled a sob.

This was shaping up to be a real swell morning. I made a grunting sound that I thought might seem sympathetic and started to light a cigarette.

Her face kind of pursed up a little. "Do you mind not smoking in my car?"

I minded, but I let it slide.

Visiting people in the hospital was a pain in the ass; I knew going in that they wouldn't let me smoke, and I always worried a little that they wouldn't let me leave. I was eighty-seven years old and still buying Lucky Strikes by the carton, so everyone figured I was ripe to keel over.

Jim Wallace was in the geriatric intensive care unit, a white hallway full of filtered air and serious-looking people. Despite all the staff's efforts to keep the place antiseptic, it stank of piss and death. Emily led me to Jim's room, and the glass door slid shut behind us and sealed itself with a soft click. Norris Feely, Emily's overweight husband, was sitting in a plastic chair, staring at game shows on a television mounted on the wall above the bed. I thought about asking him to switch it over to my talk program, but I didn't want to give anyone the impression that I was willing to stay for very long.

"Pleasure to meet you, Mr. Schatz," he said, without looking away from the screen. "Pop has told us a lot about you." He extended his hand, and I shook it. His fingers were plump and sweaty, and he had more hair on his knuckles than he did on his head, but his nails were manicured and coated with clear polish, so they stood out like little pink rhinestones stuck onto some hirsute, misshapen sausages.

A weak voice from the bed: "Buck? Buck Schatz?" Wallace was hooked up to an IV, a heart monitor, and something I thought might be a dialysis machine. He had a tube in his nose. His skin had taken on a waxy yellow pallor, and the whites of his eyes were brownish and filmy. His breath came in slow rasps and smelled like disease. He looked horrible.

"You look good, Jimmy," I said. "You'll beat this yet."

He let out a rattling cough. "Reckon not, Buck. I suppose I'm not too long for this world." He waved a feeble hand, a mostly unsuccessful attempt at a dramatic gesture.

"I wish things were different," I said, which meant that I wished Jim had been kind enough to die without bothering me about it.

"God, how'd we get so old?"

"If I'd seen it coming, I'd have got out of the way."

He nodded, as if that made a lot of sense. "It means so much that you're here."

I didn't see why it was so important to Jim to share his final hours with somebody who thought he was kind of an asshole. Maybe he found comfort in familiarity.

He pointed a quivering finger at Norris and Emily. "Go away

for a minute," he told them. "Gotta have some old war talk with Buck, in private."

"Dad, the war was sixty years ago," said Emily. Her nose was running, and her upper lip was damp with snot.

"Don't tell me when's what." Jim's eyes seemed to slide out of focus for a moment, and it took him a couple of deliberate blinks to regain his bearing. "I know what I need to say, need to say to Buck. Get."

"Daddy, please." Her voice trembled as she spoke.

"Maybe I'd better go home," I said hopefully. But Jim had gotten hold of my wrist, and he was hanging on with surprising strength.

"No, Buck stays," he wheezed as he jabbed a finger in his daughter's direction. "Privacy."

Norris draped a protective arm over Emily and guided her gently out of the room. The sliding door clicked shut behind them, and I was left alone with the dying man. I tried to pull my arm out of his sallow claw, but he held tight.

"Jim, I know you're a little confused, but the war was a long time ago," I said.

He sat up a little, and his whole body shook with the effort. Those sunken yellow eyes were bulging in their sockets, and his loose jowls twisted with anguish. "I saw him," he said. Phlegm rattled in his throat. "I saw Ziegler."

Hearing that name was enough to knot my guts up. Heinrich Ziegler had been the SS officer in charge of the POW camp where we were stuck in 1944 after our unit got cut off and over-run in southern France.

"Ziegler's dead, Jim," I told him. "Shot by the Russians during the fall of Berlin."

"I know he wasn't so good to you, Buck, when he found out you was Jewish."

Without thinking, I rubbed with my free hand at the ridges of scar tissue on my lower back. "He wasn't so good. But he's dead." I was sure this was true. I'd gone looking for Ziegler after the war.

"Probably dead. Probably by now. But I seen him. Forgive me."

He was still hanging on to my wrist, and I was starting to feel nauseous, either from what Jim was saying or from the stink coming off him.

"What do you mean?"

"I was working as an MP, manning a roadblock between East and West in 1946, and he rolled up in a Mercedes-Benz."

"No." I felt a lump rise in my throat. "Not possible."

Jim's stare was fixed on the wall, and he didn't seem to hear me. "He had papers with a different name, but I knew him when I saw him," he said. "Lord help me, I let him go."

"Why?" My mouth had gone dry. Side effect of all the damn pills I took. I swallowed, hard. "Why would you do that, Jim?"

"Gold. He had lots of those gold bars, like in the movies. I remember, the whole back end of the car was riding low from the weight of them. He gave me one, and I let him get away."

"Son of a bitch."

"We didn't have no money. Never had none growing up. And we wanted to buy a house. We wanted to start a family."

I didn't say anything. I tried to wrench my arm away from him, but his grip held. One of the machines next to his bed started beeping louder.

"Forgive me, Buck," he said. "I'm going over, very soon. I'm scared to die. Scared of being judged. Scared I'm going to hell for the bad things I've done. I can't carry this weight with me. Tell me it's all right."

I tugged my arm a little harder. I had to get out of there; I was going to be sick. "Forgive you? You knew what kind of a monster

Ziegler was. You saw the things he did to our boys. You saw the things he did to me, for God's sake. All a man's got is his integrity, and you sold yours, Jim."

I gave a sharp yank, trying to extricate myself from his grasp, but he hung on, looking at me with pleading eyes. I gave up on getting away and, instead, leaned in close to him. "If there's a hell, the two of you belong there together."

He must not have liked that, because his whole body convulsed, his back arched, and the heart monitor started screaming. Two doctors and a nurse ran into the room, and through the open door, I could see Emily in the hallway with tears streaming down her face.

"He's coding," shouted one of the doctors. "We need a crash cart."

The other doctor pointed at me. "Get him out of here."

"I'd be happy to go, Doc, if he'd just let me." Jim's hand was still wrapped around my wrist.

But the doctor was already pounding on Jim's chest and squeezing the respirator bag over his mouth. The nurse came over to me and pried the clenched fingers off my arm. She pushed me back, out of the way, as the doctor hit Jim with the electric paddles. Jim's body jumped. The doctor with the paddles looked to the nurse.

"Anything?" he asked.

"No."

The machine was still wailing.

"Gonna hit him again," said the doctor, turning the voltage knob on the defibrillator.

"Clear." The body seized up again, but the line on the monitor had gone flat.

The other doctor kept working the oxygen bag. I rubbed at my wrist; purple bruises were blossoming out from where Jim had squeezed. A couple of years back, my doctor put me on Plavix, a blood thinner, to keep me from having a stroke. The stuff made me bruise like an overripe peach.

I pulled out my pack of Luckys and flicked at the silver Dunhill cigarette lighter I carry around, but my hands were shaking so much, I couldn't get the damn thing to spark.

"You can't smoke in here," the nurse told me.

"He don't look like he minds much," I said, gesturing at Jim.

"Yeah, well, his oxygen tank probably minds, mister," she said, and she swept me into the hallway. The sliding glass door clicked shut behind me.

Norris was leaning against the wall, his face a slackened, puffy mask; Emily was pacing the floor, crying.

I touched her arm.

"There's nothing more you can do for him," I said. "But I need a ride home."

2

Emily Wallace-Feely looked like she needed somebody to hug her when she dropped me off at the house. I was sorry her father had just passed, but I certainly wasn't going to touch that woman. Her eyes were red-rimmed and her nose was still running. Catching a cold would be unpleasant and dangerous; any kind of illness might send me right back to the place I had just left.

I wished her the most sincere condolence I could manage while staying as far away from her as I could. I was very glad to get out of her car; happy to be away from the hospital's artificial atmosphere.

Memphis in early March was still cool and breezy in the mornings. High temperatures would hover in the seventies for a few more weeks before the Tennessee summer kicked in and things got hot and damp. By July, I'd sweat through a T-shirt walking to the curb to fetch the newspaper.

As I shuffled up the front walkway, I noticed, with considerable annoyance, that the lawn was greening nicely and the perennial bulbs in the flower beds were pushing tentative young shoots above the loamy southern soil. Seemed like last time I'd looked, it had been February and the yard had been brown, which suited me better.

Back when I could push a mower, I used to take care of the grass. It was something that Rose and I could do outside, together; she maintained the flower beds. Our yard was the best on the block, and we took a lot of pride in it. But since I had heart by-pass surgery in '98, we'd been paying some kind of Guatemalan refugee to handle that stuff. He was a hardworking, fastidious man, and his crew did a good job. I hated his goddamn guts, and I carried a deep resentment against the lawn. The Guatemalans had replaced me, and the indifferent grass had gone right on turning green in the springtime.

I used to talk to the lawn, cooing and whispering as I mowed and edged, fertilized and aerated. Working my key in the lock as Emily backed her car out of the driveway, I whispered something that might have been "Ungrateful."

I went into the kitchen, scrubbed my hands with hot water, and washed down a multivitamin with a glass of orange juice and a cigarette. Rose was cleaning up the breakfast dishes.

"How's Jim?" she asked.

"Dead." I handed her the juice glass, and she topped it off. "I'm going to see what's on television."

As I was settling into my comfortable groove in the sofa cushions, the phone rang. Rose was running the sink, so I answered it.

"Hey, Pop."

It was my grandson, Billy.

"Well, if it ain't Moonshine," I said. Billy lived up in New York, where he was a student at NYU School of Law. It was very prestigious and unconscionably expensive.

"It's Tequila. People call me Tequila."

Billy's full name was William Tecumseh Schatz, after the

great Civil War general William Tecumseh Sherman. Our family held the general in high esteem. My great-granddad Herschel Schatz came to America from Lithuania in 1863, after his family was killed and his village was burned in a pogrom. Union recruiters handed Herschel his conscription papers as soon as he got off the boat, and he rode south with General Sherman to raze Georgia. Every Schatz man since learned at an early age about how fine a thing it is to be born in a country where Jews get to swing the torch.

My late son, Brian, saw fit to give Billy the great man's name, but the kid went away to college and joined a fraternity, where "Tecumseh" became "Tequila." So he was known, forever after, as Tequila Schatz. Everybody was just so proud of him.

"How come you got to call yourself that?" I asked him.

"For the same reason you call yourself 'Buck,'" shouted Rose, from the next room.

"Oh, hush up. Nobody asked you," I yelled back at her.

"So, are you doing okay?" Billy asked. He was always asking about our health. It was annoying, but then again, so was most of the stuff he did.

"I'm still here," I assured him. "Had an eventful morning. Your grandmother made me go over to the hospital to visit my old war buddy Jim Wallace, and he died while I was there."

"I'm so sorry," Tequila said.

"Don't be. I was pretty sick of that guy. I've known Jim over sixty years, and he ran out of interesting things to say while Truman was still in office. And, as it turns out, he was a skunk. At least I don't have to feel bad that he's gone."

"What did he do that you're so upset about?" Tequila asked.

I took a long drag on the cigarette. "Why do you care?"

"You're my grandfather. You know, I love you."

"Oy."

He was always telling me that, I guess, because he never said it to his father. Every time he said good-bye to me at the end of a visit, he would kiss me on my face, even though he was, by most definitions, a fully grown adult man. And the discomfort was in no way ameliorated by the fact that every time he kissed me, I knew he was thinking that I might not last until his next trip home. For my part, I thought the same thing about him; young men are as fragile as the rest of us, but they aren't smart enough to know it.

"I don't see what's wrong with loving my grandparents."

I sighed and lowered my voice. "Wallace told me that the Nazi guard who beat me up when I was a prisoner escaped Germany alive, with the trunk of his car packed full of gold bars. Wallace took a payoff to let the guy go."

"That's got to mess with your head."

"Don't tell your grandmother about this. It will just upset her."

"I'll keep quiet," he assured me. I could have done without his patronizing tone. "So after all this time, why did Wallace tell you about this Nazi?"

"He wanted absolution, or something. Also, I think he expected me to track the guy down; set things right."

"Why would he think you'd do that?"

"Probably because I was a homicide detective for thirty years. You knew that, didn't you?"

He waited a couple of beats too long before: "Yeah, of course, Pop."

Most people who knew me going back, people like Wallace, still thought of me as police. But I was retired before my grandson was even born. I suspected he just thought of me as old.

"So what are you going to do?" he asked.

I thought about that for a second. "I'm going to watch Fox News for a while, and later, I am going to work a crossword puzzle while I sit on the toilet."

"Right, but what are you going to do about the Nazi?"

"I'm not going to do anything. When you have the option to do nothing, you should always take it."

"Don't you regret not taking back the dignity he stole from you?"

I coughed in a way I thought might sound derisive. Regrets were for suckers. The world was full of used-up men, sitting glassy-eyed on park benches staring at nothing or sinking into upholstered chairs in retirement home lobbies, and every one of them was mulling his irrevocable missteps. Wasted chances. Bungled opportunities. Busted romances with fickle women and pear-shaped business deals with crooked partners.

I took pride in not being one of those sad cases. I was grumpy more for sport than out of necessity. I married the greatest lady I ever met, and I had a distinguished career with the department and retired to a detective's pension. Ideally, I wouldn't have had to see my son die, but getting old meant outlasting things that ought to have been permanent.

The revelation of Heinrich Ziegler's possible survival did not incite me to vengeful fervor. The war was a long time ago, and fervor required a lot of effort.

"Whatever he took, I don't miss anymore," I said. "Dignity is something we all have to learn to live without, and revenge don't take much away from men like me and Ziegler. Every other kind of way we are apt to shuffle off this mortal coil is at least as ugly and coming almost as soon."

I paused for a second; I had that dry mouth again. I stubbed out the cigarette and took a long gulp from the juice glass. Never easy to confront the reality of the geriatric ICU and the place that comes after. Never easy to recognize what I might share with the doped-up, piss-soaked Wallaces of the world.

"If Ziegler is still alive, there ain't much pain I can add to the sorrows he's facing."

"I guess that makes sense," Tequila said. But I could tell from his tone it didn't make much sense to him at all. There was strain in his voice, and I imagined him wrapping the phone cord around his white knuckles on the other end of the line. Then I remembered phones didn't have cords anymore.

"Don't get me wrong; punishing him might feel good. But sitting on the couch feels pretty good as well. And the couch is in my living room, while Ziegler, if he's even still alive, could be on any one of several continents. I'm not sure they sell my Lucky Strikes overseas."

I couldn't bring myself to say it out loud, but even if I had been predisposed to doing things, I was facing mounting limitations. My quarry would be just as feeble, but, regardless, I wasn't sure I was up to the task of going on any kind of manhunt.

In the last few years, my stride had grown shorter and more labored. I could see a progressing decrease in my pace on the treadmill at the Jewish Community Center gym. I was down to a sluggish mile and a half per hour, and folks marveled about how I was still so mobile.

My skin had become dry and thin, almost papery in texture. If I jostled my arm too hard against a doorknob or bumped a knee into the bedside table, I could tear open and leak thin, watery blood all over the carpet. A couple of times, I hadn't been able to stop bleeding, and Rose had to take me to the emergency room. And it was easy to bump into stuff, because my eyes were failing. I needed a pair of glasses to see distance and a different pair to read. The fuzzy vision was, I guess, a minor blessing; it spared me from having to take a clear look at the mess of bruises and liver spots on my arms and cushioned the blow of seeing my collapsed and sunken features in the bathroom mirror.

"That treasure in gold bars sounds pretty appealing," Tequila said.

"Come on," I said. "You seriously think you're going to find lost Nazi gold? Even if he had gold in 1946, why wouldn't he have spent it all by now?"

"He's a fugitive. If he went looking to convert millions of dollars in gold to cash, or if he threw around a lot of money, he'd draw unwanted attention to himself. I think he'd try to avoid attracting notice, so he couldn't have run through all that treasure. And maybe he's dead, and the gold is just stashed away someplace, waiting for us to find it."

"Terrific. I can buy myself a Maserati and drive it to the grocery store at thirty miles an hour. I can go to a fine restaurant where I'll pay more and wait longer for food I can barely taste anyway."

"You were angry with Wallace because he let Ziegler go. If you don't at least try to find him, you're looking the other way, just like your friend did."

That stopped me for a second. The little prick had a point.

"There's no way I know of to find a man who was last seen in Germany in 1946. What do I do? Go to the police station and ask if anyone's seen a Nazi?"

"Sure. Why not?" Tequila said. "There's a whole lot of computerized record sharing these days between local police and federal authorities and even international agencies. If Ziegler's ever had a run-in with any kind of five-oh, he could turn up in one of those law enforcement databases."

There were no computers in the police station when I retired, and I had never learned how to use that set of tools.

"You really think so?"

"No," he said. "But even nothing can get boring when you do it long enough. It can't hurt to go ask, and then, at least, you can say you didn't just let Ziegler walk."

"Yeah, all right. I've got some time to kill before Fox News Sunday comes on, anyway."

Something I don't want to forget:

Historians consider the Chelmno death camp in Poland a minor extermination facility, because only a hundred and fifty thousand Jews died there. I visited in 1946, and there wasn't much left of it; when the Nazis closed the camp, they burned the manor house where they processed the victims and they blew up the furnaces they used to incinerate the bodies. Maybe they were ashamed.

It would make a better story if I said the acrid stench of burning human flesh still hung in the air at the Chelmno site. But it had been two years since the Nazis shut the place down, and it didn't look or smell like anything special. It was just a muddy field with some patchy grass.

There is a village called Chelm, which is famous in Yiddish folklore for the wacky misadventures of its population of idiot Jews. It would make a better story if the Chelmno camp were the same place, but it isn't. I checked. Chelmno is in the middle of Poland, near Lodz, and Chelm is somewhere to the east. The Jews of Chelmno couldn't have been all that smart, though. They let the SS load them into trucks and gas them with exhaust fumes, with carbon monoxide.

That was Heinrich Ziegler's job from late 1941 until the middle of 1942, when he got promoted for his zeal and efficiency. It would make a better story if I'd found him in the ruins of the camp, wrecked with contrition and self-loathing, waiting for somebody like me to come deal with him. But I didn't find anything at Chelmno. It was a waste of a trip, to tell the truth.

All I did was stand there for a little while, in that empty field in the armpit of Poland. I smoked a cigarette. I cursed a few times. Then I got on my motorcycle and went back to town to find someplace where I could get hammered.

I tried to kill Heinrich Ziegler, and I spent five weeks in a coma for my trouble. Later on, when I learned what he'd done to so many innocent Jews, the weight of my failure seemed almost unbearable. I needed to set it right.

Even after months of painful recovery, even after the armistice, my hands still wanted Ziegler's neck. He needed to pay for the dent in my shoulder and for the stripes on my back. And he needed to pay for Chelmno. So I hunted across Europe for the bastard with a pistol snug against my side and a serrated hunting knife tucked into my boot.

The Germans are a very orderly people, and the Nazis were very diligent about record keeping. In Berlin, I found documentation of every post Ziegler had held: accountings of his grisly work in Poland, dates and numbers in neat columns; matériel requisition forms from the prison camp in France where I'd met him; orders reassigning him to Berlin; carbon copies of the letter they sent to his mother after he got cut up by Soviet machine-gun fire.

Learning about his death gave me no solace. Ziegler had made me feel helpless, and helplessness was a kind of dirtiness. He had something of mine, and I needed to take it back from him. But I'd been robbed of my chance by forces beyond my control. And control was something I needed, but it was hard to feel like the master of my own destiny in the face of arbitrary slaughter on such a large scale. Learning Ziegler was dead just made everything worse.

For a while, I tried not to believe it, and I just kept hunting. I went to the places Ziegler had been and asked people about him. Sometimes, I asked hard. But the stories always matched up, always corroborated the records. So, at last, I relented and went down into Poland, to Chelmno, to bear witness to what he'd done there. But there wasn't anything to see.

So that's how my war ended: with a cigarette in a field full of nothing.

3

Police headquarters at the Criminal Justice Complex was pretty far downtown, well outside of my normal comfort zone, but I could stay on Poplar Avenue all the way there, so I went ahead and drove.

Crime was a growth industry in the city of Memphis, and the CJC did a brisk business in locking people up. That much had stayed the same in the thirty-five years I had been retired. A lot was different, though. The junkies and thugs getting ushered around the halls by cops seemed much younger, but bigger and meaner than I remembered from the old days. They also had a lot more tattoos than the ones I knew, and more of them were Mexican. The officers looked a lot younger than they used to as well, and more of them were black.

The changes threw my equilibrium a little bit, but I was counting on the power of progress. My detecting skills were state-of-the-art as of 1973, but I didn't have anything approaching an idea about how to use a computer to track down a Nazi fugitive.

I wondered if Tequila was right that we could find Ziegler

using the databases. I saw those things spitting out surprising and crucial information every week on the police procedural programs on television, but it always seemed like an expediency, a story device to get the cops to the killer in fifty minutes with commercials. Surely police work hadn't gotten that easy. If it had, the criminals would all be out of business.

I took a seat on a bench in the squad room, next to a handcuffed teenager who had tattooed some kind of tribal pattern on his face and neck in an unsuccessful attempt to hide his acne scars. I waited long enough to burn through three Luckys before a young officer asked me why I was there. He was a white kid, maybe twenty-five or twenty-six, but already overweight and balding. I asked to see half a dozen people who were pretty green when I left, people I thought might still be around. They had all died or retired, so I told the kid to send me to somebody in homicide.

"I'll call up there now and see if anybody can talk to you," he said. "What case are you here about?"

"Oh, I want to see if you folks can help me look some information up in the police computer, and maybe I could look at some old mug shots. I used to be a cop."

He picked up his telephone receiver. "You got a name, Officer?" he asked me.

"I'm retired detective Baruch Schatz."

"Baruch?"

"Yeah. It's Jewish."

He squinted at me. "Wait, you're not Buck Schatz, are you?"

"People call me that."

His authoritative cop frown broke into a broad grin. "Holy shit, man, you're a legend. I can't believe you're still alive."

I rolled my eyes. "Most days, neither can I."

The kid shouted to a black cop who was messing with the

coffee machine at the back of the room. "Yo, Andre? Guess who this old motherfucker is right here."

"Is that your new boyfriend?" Andre was a little taller than the kid at the desk, and in better shape, with close-cropped hair and straight teeth.

"This is Buck Schatz."

"Fuck you, you lying piece of shit."

"No lie. And fuck you."

Not everything had changed; cops still talked pretty much the same way they always had. Nobody ever tells a man with a gun to watch his language.

They paged somebody from homicide to come to see me, and while I waited, they asked me the same questions young cops always ask:

Yes, it's true that I hunted down a serial killer and brought him in on my own, while the rest of the department sat around scratching their asses. No, I didn't break his legs; I just smashed his nose with the butt of my pistol.

No, it's not true that Clint Eastwood followed me around to learn to be *Dirty Harry,* but Don Siegel, the Jewish guy who directed the picture, did call me on the phone to ask me some questions.

Yeah, it's true I once ventilated three heavies that a crooked city councilman sent after me. No, they were white men; that happened way back when all the crooked politicians in town and most of the thugs who worked for them were white.

For the record, it ain't true that I was the leading cause of death among scumbags in Memphis from 1957 to 1962. People used to say that, and it sounded good. But somebody actually counted it up once, and I was only tied for fourth, behind other scumbags, drug overdoses, and other cops. The tie was with car accidents.

"Damn, Buck. You used to be one hard-ass son of a bitch."

"Used to be," I said.

I shot the bull with them until the detective from homicide came out of the elevator.

"Shit," he said as he walked toward me. "You're really Buck Schatz. I thought these kids were playing some kind of prank on me."

He told me his name was Randall Jennings, and I shook his hand. He was medium height, early forties, white. Dark hair, graying at the temples. Rumpled suit. Yellowish sweat stains on his shirt collar. Mustache.

"You know, I always wondered what I'd say if I ever met you," he said.

"I'm listening."

"How'd a guy with so many enemies manage to live so long?"

I smiled, and I told Randall Jennings my favorite story from the war.

Before we hit the beach at Normandy, General Eisenhower came to wish us luck. I got close enough to shake his hand, and I asked him if he had any suggestions as to how I might stay alive to see my wife again.

When Ike looked at me, there was real sadness in his eyes, because he knew a lot of us wouldn't survive the next couple of days. And I'll never forget what he told me.

"Soldier," he said, squeezing my shoulder, "when you have nothing left to hang on to, you just hang on to your gun."

It seemed like good advice, so I followed it.

"That's it?" Jennings asked, unimpressed. "That's your secret?"

"That's it," I said. "But it's no small edge in the longevity game for a man to be able to put something persuasive between himself and anyone looking to do him harm."

He scratched thoughtfully at the stubble on his chin. "Now

the story we tell here is that the day Buck Schatz took his pension, he slammed his gun down on Captain Heller's desk and told the old man to shove that piece right up his fat ass."

I chuckled a little. "I told Max Heller to stuff my badge. The gun was not department issued. It was mine, and I hung on to it."

Jennings laughed at that. "So, what brings you to the CJC today?" he asked.

"I am trying to find a man I know from way back. I thought he was dead, but then I heard recently, maybe he's not. I wanted to see if you could look for him with your computer."

He raised an eyebrow at my request. "This guy killed somebody?"

"Not that I know of. At least not lately."

"Does he have a name?"

"That's my problem. I figure he's operating under an alias, but I don't know what it is. He'd have fake papers, good ones, under the pseudonym."

"So you want me to find you a man with no name?"

"Yeah. With your computer. I see on the television that y'all have access to all kinds of databases and satellites and DNA. Whenever the case looks like a dead end, the TV cops always find some impossible connection on the Internet. I thought you might be able to dig up a police report or a mug shot. Even a traffic citation would give me more recent information than I have right now."

"All right. Let's see what I can do for you."

We rode the elevator up to the homicide office. Jennings led me to his cubicle and sat down in front of his computer, and I grabbed a chair on the other side of the desk.

"This is Google," he explained to me. "It is the most powerful database in the world. You can find anything with this."

"They talk about that a lot on Fox News," I said. "I remember back when the only 'Google' was the sound a guy made when you punched him in the throat."

Jennings typed the words *man with no name* into the Google and stared intently at the screen. Then his face lit up, and I leaned toward the machine to see what he'd found.

"Okay, it says you're looking for this man here. He should be easy to find."

He angled the computer so I could see it.

I was looking at a picture of Clint Eastwood from *The Good, the Bad and the Ugly.*

"Ain't you two supposed to be friends or something?" Jennings asked. And then he laughed at me.

"Or something," I said, and I lit a cigarette.

The two of us regarded each other for a long, uncomfortable moment, and then Jennings spoke.

"I got some news for you," he said as his slack features tightened into a sneer. "These kids here may admire the Buck Schatz they hear about in stories, but I can see past your bullshit. I came up rough on the streets of this town. God knows what would have happened to me if it hadn't been for Max Heller."

"Aw," I said. I rubbed at my temples. "For Christ's sake." The young cops downstairs had been playing a prank after all, to put me together with Heller's protégé. Jennings hadn't even registered to me as somebody unfriendly. I wondered how I had missed the malice in his voice before. I used to be a hard man to fool.

"Don't talk to me about Christ, you Jew bastard." He pointed an emphatic finger at me. "I go to church. That's one of the things Max taught me to take seriously. He was the closest thing I ever had to a father."

It was my turn to laugh. "Feel sorry for you, kid."

"No." He stood up and leaned over the desk, a sign of aggression. I noticed, about then, that there was nobody else in the room. "You don't get to feel sorry for me. You look like a Mr. Potato Head. I feel sorry for you."

I didn't say anything. For fifteen years, Max Heller and I sat five feet apart, barely speaking, until he finally got promoted. I thought he was a careerist ass kisser, and he thought I was a loose cannon.

In the movies, we would have become unwilling partners for some reason and learned to respect each other. The reality was less exciting: we nursed a long-simmering mutual animosity, which never built toward much of a climax. Then I retired and mostly forgot about him.

"Forty years Max labored, doing fine, careful police work, locking up killers and closing cases, while you cruised around in a souped-up, nonregulation car, carrying an obscene nonregulation gun, shooting suspects, and getting your picture in the paper."

It was my turn to stand and point a finger at him. "I don't care what Heller told you. I was the best goddamn cop in the southeastern United States. This department pinned every award they had on my chest and then they made up new ones for me."

"Oh, don't I know it," Jennings said. "They tried to award me the Schatz Medal for Exceptional Bravery, and I refused to take the damn thing."

Nobody ever told me about that; I'd never even heard of this guy. I had not realized I'd gotten so far out of the loop.

"But while you were collecting your silly-ass crackerjack-box prizes, Heller was doing honest policing. You know he closed twice as many homicides as you?"

I grunted. Heller may have mentioned that once or twice. He jumped on open-and-shut cases like a cat on a ball of string, looking to boost his clearance rate. I always let him.

"When they passed him over for director, I never saw such a strong man so beaten down." Jennings gave me a mean, cold stare. "He knew he was through in police work. Six months later, he was dead."

"I never did anything to harm Heller's career," I said.

"You didn't have to. You represent everything that's wrong about this department and everything that's wrong with law enforcement. Max told me once that trying to be a cop in this town was like wading balls-deep into a river of shit, and you're part of the reason for that."

I sighed. "So I guess you're not going to do any kind of computer search for me, are you."

"Get out of my office," said Randall Jennings.

"Good to meet you, Detective," I said.

And that's how I found out I wouldn't be getting any help with my Nazi hunt from the Memphis Police Department.

Something I saw on the television that I don't want to forget:

"So many movies these days seem to feature overweight, out-of-shape male comic leads," said the television host. "Why do you think that is?"

"It's a side effect of a larger cultural transition regarding our conception of masculinity," said the guest. He was kind of a reedy guy. Beard, glasses. Jewish name. The floating text below his bulbous head indicated that he was a film studies professor at NYU. My grandson's school. That figured.

Moving around had become progressively more troublesome for me, so I'd decided that the best course of action was to leave the sofa as rarely as possible. I watched a lot of television. I liked the news and the talk programs. It was like having a conversation with someone I could switch off when I got bored.

"Explain further, Professor," said the host.

"Your traditional American masculine archetype is the sort of man you might refer to as a 'tough guy.' He works with his hands, protects his family, whips his slaves, exterminates the indigenous population. He does, in short, what tough guys do. In twentieth-century film, we see this figure embodied in the western or cowboy picture, beginning with Gary Cooper in *High Noon*. Later, we added urban analogues to the western hero, like the supercop or the modern vigilante."

"Well, what changed?"

"Society's expectation of men changed. More and more, we see the most powerful figures are the ones who spend their days working at computer terminals. And when America keeps two million people in prison, there aren't that many bad guys left on the street for tough guys to beat up."

I started digging in the sofa cushions for the clicker. I'd seen a fair number of regular, tough-guy heroes on Fox News, and lately, too many of them were coming home in flag-draped boxes.

"But the tough guy surely still remains prominent in our shared consciousness," said the host. "Audiences are flocking to the new hard-edged James Bond films. *Batman* is grossing half a billion dollars."

"Look," said the professor, smiling. "I liked *Jurassic Park,* but that doesn't mean dinosaurs still matter."

I changed the channel.

4

A couple of days after Wallace died, I awoke to the sound of Rose shuffling around in the bedroom.

"Good morning, Buck," she said when she saw me moving. "How are you doing today?"

I lifted my head off the pillow. It was twenty after seven. I had a full day of doing nothing ahead of me, and I'd overslept. "I'm still here," I said.

"I laid your suit out."

"I'm not wearing any suit. What have I got to wear a suit for?"

"The Wallace funeral."

"Oh, I'm not going to that. I already saw him."

She shook her head and laughed a little. She'd seen my obstinate routine before. "Just because you visited him in the hospital doesn't mean you don't have to go pay your respects."

"Yeah, but he died while I was there, so I went ahead and paid all my respects, to save myself a trip." I sat up and scratched at my armpit.

"We're going, Buck. Get out of bed and put your suit on."

"Woman, you're going to put me into an early grave."

But I got dressed. She knew I'd go. I always went. I insisted on driving, though.

There was a memorial service before the funeral, so we headed out to Jim's church in Collierville. It was one of those big new ones, made of vast sheets of tinted glass and fresh walls of white stucco. The place came complete with a food court, and it looked like a shopping mall.

The massive central auditorium had movie-theater-style seating for two thousand and packed in such a huge crowd on Sundays that the church hired off-duty sheriff's deputies to direct traffic in the parking lot. When we came for the memorial service, the lot and the sanctuary were pretty much empty, though. There weren't enough young mourners to be pallbearers, so Jim was carried by some Mexicans who were at the church to trim the hedges and mow the soccer field. Jim had lived long enough to bury most of the people he loved, and everyone else had forgotten about him.

The box they'd put him into looked unfinished and flimsy, like an arm might flop out if somebody jostled it a little too hard. There were a couple of small wreaths, but the flowers were sparse and anemic. Someone had gotten an old photo of the dead man blown up at Kinko's, to put next to the coffin. They'd run it off in black and white, on the cheap kind of cardboard. It was clear that whatever treasure he might have taken from Heinrich Ziegler, Jim had nothing left but his guilt when he finally died. His awful sin had left him wretched.

I couldn't forgive him when I saw him withering up in the hospital, but looking at that crummy casket, in that empty church, I pitied him. We walked up onto the stage and stood next to him. "Consider it square, I guess," I whispered to the box, as if it meant something. Rose squeezed my arm.

Emily and Norris were in the front row of the auditorium, right next to the stage where I had no hope of avoiding them. Emily was wearing black and crying. Norris was wearing a pink shirt and a blue tie. He looked like an Easter egg. For the occasion, he had tucked his gut into his unbelted trousers and tried to slick some wispy hairs across his shiny dome of a skull. He'd also gotten himself a fresh manicure. Rose hugged Emily, even though they'd only just met, so I couldn't avoid shaking hands with Norris.

"You've been so kind to Jim, and it's so good of you to be here," he said.

"It is what it is."

"Emily and I would like to have you and Rose over to our home for dinner later in the week."

"Yeah, it's real nice of you to offer, but we're not going to be able to do that." The thought of having to eat food those fingers had touched made my insides churn.

He ran the tip of his tongue over his upper lip. "Oh, I see. Busy, busy Buck. The game is afoot, eh?"

"I don't know what that means."

I eyeballed the rest of the attendees to avoid Feely's squinty gaze. There were two slack-jawed guys who looked like they might be Jim's relatives; the kind who lived close enough to drive and weren't smart enough to think of anything better to do. One had brought his wife and a fidgety little kid.

Also present: a few other old people, sitting alone and making no effort to speak to the family or anyone else. Maybe they were his friends, or maybe they were parishioners. Maybe they just saw the obituary in the paper and showed up, hoping for free food.

Rose and I took seats near the back, away from everyone else, and I lit a cigarette. Counting from when I flicked my lighter, it took a little less than thirty seconds for someone to come over to make me put it out.

"Excuse me, sir. I'm sorry, but we don't allow smoking in the church."

He was maybe in his mid-thirties. Clean-shaven. Light brown hair, cut short and neatly parted; wearing a blue button-down dress shirt and khakis. No tie. He had dimples, and when he spoke, he laid a friendly hand on my shoulder.

I scowled at him. "Take a hike, pipsqueak. Can't you see we're grieving here?"

"You must be Buck Schatz," he said. His hand was still touching me. "Emily told me about you. I'm Dr. Lawrence Kind."

"Oh," I snorted. "One of the doctors. You guys did a real good job on Jim."

He smiled at me. "My doctorate is in divinity. I tend the spirit, not the body. I certainly hope I did a good job for Jim, and that he was at peace in his final moments."

I started to say something about how Jim died, but I had an odd feeling that Kind was fishing for information. I took another long look at him. Maybe Jim had confessed to him about the Nazi and about the gold. This was a Southern Baptist church. Did Southern Baptists confess? No, I didn't think so. That was just for Catholics and Pentecostals. Or Episcopalians, maybe. There were so many types of goyim to remember.

Anyway, even if he wasn't the kind that confessed, Jim still might have unloaded his conscience to this preacher. If Norris's odd behavior was any indication, my old army buddy hadn't been too good about keeping his secrets buttoned up near the end.

And something was off about Kind. He had the kind of smile that flayed his face open, showing off spit-slick expanses of pink gums and lips and his tongue flicking between gaps in his small, crooked teeth. The preacher seemed smart, though, or at least like he thought he was smart. So I played dumb.

"This is your church?" I asked.

"I minister to the souls of this flock, yes." He beamed at me, and his reptile face filled with God's boundless love. I thought I felt a chill run up my spine, but it could have been just poor circulation.

"Well, you'll know where to find me an ashtray around here, then."

Kind frowned. "Buck, you can't smoke in here. I hope you're not going to make this difficult for me."

"Not having to care about making things easy for anyone else is one of the three best things about being old," I told him. "The other two are smoking and telling people what I think about them. I never go anywhere that I can't do at least two out of three."

"It's funny you should mention that," Kind said. "Emily is taking this very hard, and she doesn't feel she can compose herself enough to speak today, but it would be good if somebody close to Jim could say a few words. They think you knew him as well as, maybe better than, anyone else. I'd surely appreciate it if you could stand up during the service today and share what's in your heart about your friend."

"Doesn't seem like it would be a very neighborly thing to do, what with him being dead and all."

"Buck would be honored to speak, Dr. Kind," said Rose.

Kind looked at me. "So we can count on you?"

I sighed. "I guess."

"So happy to hear it." He lifted his hand off my shoulder and walked back toward the front of the auditorium.

"I hope he doesn't forget about my damn ashtray," I said to Rose.

"Behave yourself," she told me.

Kind stepped up onto the stage next to the coffin and grabbed his microphone. I figured he was probably used to playing to a bigger crowd.

"Good morning, all of you blessed children of Christ," he said. "I'm pleased to see you here, but I wish it could have been in happier circumstances."

He'd let me keep my cigarette, so I was happy enough. I'd have been happier if I didn't have to get up and give an extemporaneous eulogy.

"One of the benefits of a congregation like this one is that, together, we can have a real impact on the community."

I looked around. The crowd had swelled up to fourteen people, counting Dr. Kind.

"But one of the drawbacks to leading such a large flock is that I often don't have the opportunity to get to know everyone very well. With Jim Wallace, I missed that chance, and, now that he's gone, I am filled with deep regret. Jim's family tells me he was an easygoing man who found great pleasure in simple things, like a cold beer on a hot summer day, and crispy bacon with his breakfast. And God loves most those who find joy in everyday blessings."

"God loves people who eat bacon," I whispered to Rose. "How come nobody told the Jews?"

"And Jim deserved all those pleasures. He worked hard for many years in this community, and though he was never rich in material goods, he was rich in the love of his family and his many friends in the church and throughout the Midsouth."

All fourteen of them.

"One of those friends, Baruch Schatz, a man of the Jewish faith, has been close with Jim for more than sixty years. These two men served together in World War Two, and Buck came to Jim's bedside to comfort him in his last moments earlier this week. Such lifelong friendships are the greatest blessing the Good Lord Jesus Christ can bestow upon any of us. I believe Mr. Schatz has a few words to share today."

I stood up with a groan and walked to the stage. Kind handed me the microphone.

"I want to thank you, Dr. Kind, for that beautiful speech," I said. "You say you didn't know Jim very well, but I think you got to the essence of the man, especially with the part about the beer and the bacon. Not gonna be easy to top that."

"Just say what's in your heart, Buck," said Dr. Kind.

I considered taking his advice, but it didn't seem like a good idea under the circumstances.

"Jim lived a long life, and died an old man, and I guess that's something," I said. I realized I was still holding my cigarette.

"Um, Dr. Kind told me they don't allow smoking in the church, but I told him to take a hike."

Kind chuckled, failing to hide his discomfort. I wasn't going to make too big a scene in front of Jim's dozen mourners, but I was happy to let the pastor sweat a little.

"I always smoke at funerals, because, I figure, when the day comes that I'm the guy in the box, I don't want to be wishing I'd had time for one more cigarette. Actually, I have a lot of catching up to do in that regard."

I coughed.

"I quit smoking these in 1974. I figured if I kept on, the habit would kill me, likely as not. I wanted to see the year 2000. I wanted to see my grandchildren grow up. Now I've seen those things, and they were disappointing. Thirty years I wasted, breathing clean air. So, around the time my son passed on, I went to the store and bought a carton of Luckys."

I paused.

"Not sure what that's got to do with Jim, uh, I guess when you get to be my age, it's not always easy to follow a train of thought. Jim and I were in the service together. We were in a Nazi prison camp together. Worst thing that ever happened to me. I almost died in that place. Wouldn't wish Nazi prison on most people I hate, but I'm glad Jim was there."

"Because he sustained you during that trying time," said Kind.

"Sure, sure," I said. "You know, with his love of simple pleasures, like a cold beer on a hot summer day."

"Yes, exactly," said Kind.

"Of course, there wasn't any beer in Nazi prison."

Kind frowned. "No, I'd guess not."

"No crispy bacon, either."

"I wouldn't think so."

"Point is, Jim Wallace was my friend, and I'll miss him," I said.

"Thank you, Buck," said Kind, his voice full of warmth I knew I didn't deserve. Anybody who acted that nice had to be playing an angle.

I stepped off the stage, glad to be through with that. But when I got back to my seat, Rose didn't look too pleased.

5

Usually, there is a police escort for a funeral procession and I get to drive through red lights on the way to the cemetery, but Jim's crowd was too small. I was disappointed. At the cemetery, we stood in silence and watched them lower the coffin into the ground. It was a gray, rainy morning; at least the weather fit the occasion.

Norris Feely caught up to me and Rose as we walked back toward the cemetery gate. I'd have ducked him, but I don't move that fast.

"Very nice of you to speak today," he said. But his eyes were squeezed half-shut in a way that didn't look like he thought I was very nice at all.

"Jim and I went back some years," I replied, ignoring the subtext. "Sorry, again, for your loss."

"Emily is still pretty broken up about her dad."

"So sad to hear that," said Rose. "Is there anything we can do?"

"I just want to see to Jim's interests for her."

"Mighty decent of you," I said. "We'll let you go, so you can get busy on that."

"That's part of why I wanted to talk to you. I figure Emily is entitled to a share of all that gold."

"I don't know what you're talking about, Feely," I said.

"Oh, stop bullshitting me," he said. "I know all about the treasure."

"Hey, I object to you using that sort of language in front of my wife. And I haven't got any gold. You seem to have some very mistaken ideas about Jewish people."

"You're not the only one Jim shared his secrets with, and I know he set you after Ziegler. If you're hunting him, I want in."

One thing a cop learns real fast is that people who talk like they think they're in movies are useless or worse. "If you want some of Ziegler's gold, I suppose you'd better take it up with Ziegler," I told him.

"I don't know how to find him," Norris sputtered.

"That's the problem you need to solve, then," I said. "Let me know how it works out." I was sort of curious about how one might thread that needle myself.

"Jim told me that when you found out Ziegler was alive, you'd hunt him to the gates of hell."

Jim Wallace had no particular reason to hold me in such esteem, but people seemed to like me despite my best efforts to make them go away and leave me alone. It must have had something to do with my rugged good looks and effervescent charm. But after coming up with a big goose egg at the police station, I didn't deserve the accolades.

"Jim was confused toward the end. I don't know if you noticed, but I am very old. I don't think I'm still the man Jim was remembering when he said that. In fact, it's not even safe for me to be standing here in the rain talking to you. Do you understand? It's mortally dangerous for me to catch the sniffles. What do you expect me to do?"

"I expect you to do what Jim wanted you to do. What he wanted the both of us to do."

"I'm not real sure I owe anything to Jim." I'd already missed a great deal of quality news analysis and commentary because of Wallace, and I was a little offended that Norris had not recognized the magnitude of my sacrifice.

"Well, I owe him," Norris said. "I lost my dad when I was young, and Jim has played a pretty important role in my life since Emily and I got together. I feel like this is . . . I don't know . . . his legacy. And I feel like you're squeezing me out of it. You and that slick little preacher."

I said, "I just met Dr. Kind today, and I didn't like him that much."

Norris balled his hairy sausage fingers into puffy little fists. "Don't lie to me." His voice was high and strained, like a fiddle with its strings pulled too tight. "Y'all are already fast friends. My wife had the generosity to drive you home less than an hour after her father died, and you barely thanked her. We invited you to join us for dinner, and you turned us down. But within five minutes of meeting you, smooth Reverend Larry is giving you a big ol' hug. I'm sure he's already got designs on my share of the money, and you seem inclined to let him have it."

"What makes you think Kind even knows about the treasure?"

"He visited the hospital just before Jim died, and the two of them spoke, alone. I'm pretty sure Jim told the story, and it's the sort of thing the reverend would find very interesting. Kind always makes time in his busy schedule to visit the dying, and he's gotten real good at wringing bequests out of them."

There was no point in bothering to pretend this was interesting. I didn't give a damn about church politics. "Well, if Kind is looking for the treasure, he's doing it without my help. I've got no idea if there's any gold, or how to find it if it exists."

"I'm supposed to believe the great detective is sitting out the treasure hunt?"

"Norris, I worked homicide, and I retired thirty-five years ago. I was a mediocre detective in a department that was more concerned with spraying fire hoses at colored folks than it was with solving murders. Being a homicide detective isn't a hard job if you don't care a whole lot about being good at it. I'd find a dead girl, so I'd lock up her boyfriend. If the case was any more complicated than that, most of the time there was no arrest. I have no idea how to track a man down, with nothing to work from other than the fact that somebody saw him sixty years ago halfway around the world."

Feely didn't say anything, but he had finally managed an expression that looked to me like genuine sadness. Or maybe he just had gas. It was hard to tell.

"Come on, Norris, Jim didn't exactly provide us with a treasure map. The trail is cold. Maybe there's no trail at all."

He let out a little moan. "For whatever it's worth, it's not just about the money," he said. "I cared a lot for the old man. Miss him."

The fact that he felt that point needed clarification meant that it mostly was about money to him, which I knew anyway. But at least he was decent enough to lie about it.

I lit a cigarette. "Forget about the gold," I told him. "Take care of your wife."

He lowered his head, muttered something that indicated capitulation, and walked away, toward the sound of Emily's sobs. But I knew that guy was too pigheaded and too greedy to be rebuffed for long by an appeal to common sense and human decency.

6

As soon as we pulled out of the cemetery parking lot, Rose shot me a look that let me know I was in for an earful.

"Buck, what was that man talking about?"

"I don't know." I made a dismissive gesture. "Probably just crazy. Don't worry about it."

She kept that stare fixed on me. The only sound in the car was the rhythmic scraping of the wipers across the windshield.

"Buck, do you think I am going to believe you when you talk about how it's not hard to be a mediocre detective?"

"That one was one hundred percent true. My problem was that I never got the hang of not caring."

She frowned at me. "What are you getting yourself mixed up in?"

There was no use in lying to Rose. She'd had far too long to learn my habits.

"I'm not mixed up in anything. Jim Wallace told me before he died that Heinrich Ziegler, the Nazi, escaped Germany. I kind of want to find him, you know, so I can take his gold."

Rose drummed her knuckles on the inside of the window. That meant she was annoyed. "Nazis don't have gold, Buck. You're thinking of leprechauns."

She had a point. Every time I said it out loud, the idea of chasing Nazi gold seemed ridiculous. In my mind, it made sense; it felt like something I had to do.

"So, what are you going to do?" Rose asked. "You're going to catch this man, after all these years, when nobody else has?"

"Reckon so. I've got nothing better to do."

"You can't run off to Europe or South America or Egypt chasing after a phantom. How are we going to keep track of your medications?"

"I don't know. I doubt I'll even find enough clues to lead me out of Memphis. The trail is cold."

"But, even if you don't find anything, once you start hunting Nazis and treasure, you're going to run afoul of some dangerous folks."

I laughed. "Like who? Feely?"

"Buck, you always find somebody dangerous to get on the wrong side of."

"Well, I like to keep things interesting. And anyway, I've always been good at handling dangerous people."

"Maybe you're not as good anymore as you used to be," she said.

The thought had already occurred to me. "Best thing about dying, sweetheart, is that you only have to go to one more funeral."

She didn't seem to think that was cute. "Buck, you've got to ask yourself: is this about what you're chasing after, or what you're running away from?"

I didn't have an answer for her.

Rose and I buried our only son six years ago. He was fifty-two, and he's gone. We're still here. Dragging that reality around gets exhausting. I was a hard man, once. Immovable, like the face of a mountain. But wind and rain can erode even granite if they have enough years to do it. No matter how tough you think you are, if you live long enough, eventually you get all squishy.

The rain kept beating on the roof of the car, and we rode the rest of the way home without saying anything.

Something I don't want to forget:

Heinrich Ziegler grew up in a little village in the Bavarian countryside, in a cottage with a thatched straw roof and stone walls and a view of the Alpine foothills. It was probably kind of charming, but when I went there after the war, I wasn't in a mood to be charmed.

I banged on the door so hard that it rattled in its frame, and a middle-aged woman opened it. She squinted at my fatigues and at the American insignia sewn on them, and then she started wailing and threw herself at me, thrashing her thin arms and beating at my chest with her tiny fists. I grabbed her wrist, wrenched it behind her back, and threw her to the ground.

She bared her teeth and hissed at me like an alley cat.

"English?" I asked.

"Too late," she said. "Gone. All dead."

"Heinrich Ziegler?"

She started crying, so I decided to search the house. Inside, it was dark. Dishes were piled in the sink, and roaches scuttled across the kitchen floor. On the side table in the bedroom, I found four hand-delivered letters, notifying Greta Ziegler of the deaths of her sons Gustav, Albert, and Heinrich, and of her husband, Karl.

I picked up the papers and took them outside, where Ziegler's mother was still crying in the dirt.

"Where is he buried?" I asked, pointing at Heinrich's name on the paper. I shouted it at her a couple more times before she pointed toward a church steeple just visible over a rise in the distance. I threw the letters on the ground and stepped on them as I stalked back toward my motorcycle.

She'd lost everyone she cared about, but I didn't have sympathy for any Germans. As far as I was concerned, the whole damn lot of them richly deserved whatever *tsuris* they got.

The churchyard was full of fresh graves, and the three Ziegler brothers were buried there, along with their father. I looked at Heinrich's grave marker for a while. The dates matched the letters, and the letters matched the records I'd seen in Berlin. I smoked a cigarette, and when I was finished, I ground it out on the stone, leaving a black smudge.

A lot of people have lied to me over the years, enough that I can usually spot the giveaways. If Greta Ziegler showed any sign of falsehood, I don't remember it. She really thought her son was dead. I don't think Heinrich tipped his mother off to his con; he abandoned her to her grief, and he ran. Maybe he couldn't face her, couldn't go home after the things he'd seen and the things he'd done. Or maybe he just didn't care.

7

Billy called the house the next morning to let me know he was a much better detective than I was. When the phone rang, I was moving my oatmeal around a bowl and giving Rose trouble about how it wasn't hot enough.

"How's it going, Pop?"

"I'm still here," I said.

"I shared your story with a girl I know who volunteers for the Anti-Defamation League."

"Yeah, so?"

"We figured that your friend Jim Wallace couldn't have been the only person to see Ziegler and recognize him, so we thought that we might get some more information from people who keep track of fugitive war criminals. She told me I should check with an organization called the Simon Wiesenthal Center. They do advocacy for human rights, they fight anti-Semitism, and they used to spend a lot of time hunting down Nazis."

"I've heard of that."

"Yeah," said Tequila. "So I called them up. They gave me all kinds of fascinating information about your friend."

"Enlighten me," I said. I was stuck someplace between being intrigued and being annoyed.

"Ziegler first came to the attention of Nazi hunters in 1969 when the Israeli Mossad intelligence agency got a lead that he was still alive. Another fugitive they'd caught confessed to helping Ziegler procure false papers. Following the aliases this source provided, the Israelis tracked your Nazi to the United States."

"So he's here?" I took a bite out of an apple. My dentist asked me once how I managed to make it to eighty-seven with all my own teeth. I told him my secret was that I always moved my head out of the way when somebody tried to sock me in the mouth.

"In this country, probably," Tequila said. "In 1982, someone within the Israeli government leaked information on Ziegler to the Wiesenthal Center, possibly the name he was using and where he was living. An investigator named Avram Silver started looking into the case. Silver tried several times to convince federal authorities to initiate proceedings to either try Ziegler in federal court for war crimes or extradite him to Israel, but prosecutors never brought charges. In 1990, Silver resigned from the Wiesenthal Center and made aliyah."

"So, did they tell you where to find Ziegler?"

"No. That's the bad news. A lot of things seem to be missing from their files. Silver may have taken some souvenirs when he moved to Israel. But the good news is, if we find Silver, maybe he can lead us to Ziegler."

"How do we find Silver?"

"Oh, that's no problem. We have his name, a former address, and a former employer. With that kind of information, it's pretty easy to look him up using Google."

"Oh, damn it," I said. "All that talk was just the setup to play the stupid Google prank on me? Well, the joke's on you, Wild Turkey, because I heard it already. It's Clint Eastwood. I get it. Ha, ha, ha."

"Grandpa, what the fuck are you talking about?"

"Somebody already showed me the Google. I don't see what's so funny about it."

"Nothing's funny about it. It's a search engine."

"I don't know what that means."

"It means I already did the search. I've got Avram Silver's current home address and telephone number. I thought we'd talk to him together."

"What? Seriously?" If he'd asked, I'd have had to tell him I was impressed. Thank God he didn't ask.

"Yeah. I bought an international calling card that I can use to dial Israel," he said. "We can ring him now and have a conference call."

"Oh." None of that made much sense to me. "Well, then, that's useful, sort of, I guess."

Jerusalem time was eight hours ahead, so it was around half-past four there, but we caught Avram Silver at home. When we told him why we were calling, he got agitated.

"That's a problem you don't want to mess with," he said. "Don't waste your time. Nobody there cares about old Nazis."

"We care," Tequila told him. "We want to bring him to justice. Have you got the file?"

"Of course I've got it. Nobody cares about it but me."

Tequila was too young to know when someone was trying to snow him. "Mr. Silver, we're calling because we care," he said.

"You shouldn't bother to care," Silver said. "Nobody else does."

"Regardless, we'd appreciate it if you'd send us a copy of whatever information you have, or fax it to us."

"The United States has some ass-backwards priorities on crime. I'll tell you that. Let me warn you, as a fellow Jew, you don't want to waste your time with this."

Slowly, we coaxed the story out of him. According to Silver, the Wiesenthal Center had not supported his efforts to get Ziegler arrested, and the federal authorities had been reluctant to open a case. The U.S. Attorney's Office claimed that the evidence in the substantial dossier Silver had prepared was insufficient to justify further action.

"Can we please see a copy of this dossier?" Tequila asked him.

"You won't find anybody willing to look at it."

Tequila sighed.

Silver continued his tale of woe: frustrated by the reluctance of everyone else to move against a war criminal hiding in the United States, after years of phone messages and letters, he decided to go to St. Louis himself and see if he could get his hands on some proof the feds couldn't ignore.

"St. Louis?" I interrupted him. "Ziegler was living in St. Louis?"

"Yeah," said Silver. "Perfect place for him. I think they hate Jews there more than anywhere in America."

Silver's clever plan to find evidence: he broke into Ziegler's house, tripped an alarm, and got himself arrested. The same people who had ignored all the evidence that Ziegler was a blood-thirsty war criminal were eager to book Silver for burglary.

"Anti-Semites." This was punctuated with a loud thump, maybe Silver slamming his fist up against something. "Fifteen years working to end bigotry, and those Jew haters tried to lock me up."

Of course, our boy was too clever for that. He posted bail and promptly fled, exercising his right to return to his people's eternal homeland.

"Thank God there's one place left in the world where Jews can find sanctuary from persecution."

What an asshole. "That's clearly His intended use for it," I said.

"Now I have a good job with the Israeli government. In a Jewish country, where there's no bigotry, my kind of talent gets a proper measure of appreciation."

"What kind of talent?" I asked. "What do you do for the Israeli government?"

Silence on the line. I lit one of my Lucky Strikes.

"We'd really like to see your file on Ziegler," said Tequila.

"It's a waste of time."

And we were back to that again. I'd heard about enough of it.

"Oh, stow it, the both of you," I growled into the phone.

They stopped talking. I took a bite out of my apple and kept the receiver in front of my mouth so they could hear me chewing.

"Riesling, if you're ever going to be much of a lawyer, you're going to have to learn how to talk to someone who doesn't want to give you information."

"My name is Tequila," said Tequila. "And why wouldn't he want to give us information? Don't we all want the same thing here?"

"Of course we want the same thing," I said. "And this goof figures if we get it, then he can't steal it."

"You're talking about Ziegler's supposed stolen Nazi treasure," said Silver.

I made a phlegmy, vaguely sarcastic sound. "Well, I'm glad somebody finally mentioned it, not that I don't enjoy sitting around yanking on my *putz* as much as the next guy."

"I didn't want to say anything about that, because I thought we were playing it close to the vest. I wasn't sure if he knew about it," said Tequila. It was downright unseemly for a grown man to go around whimpering like a kicked dog. The sound of his voice was like a razor blade scraping against the grain of my skin, and I hated him a little bit right then.

"Don't be a damn fool," I said. "Money is never a secret. Everybody always knows about it. This jackass has known about that gold at least as long as he's known about Heinrich Ziegler."

"What do you mean?" Tequila asked.

"He never pushed for action on Ziegler when he was at the Wiesenthal Center. In fact, I'd bet he stole the file from their offices when he left, to make sure nobody there ever did anything with that information he doesn't want to give us. Most likely, he spiked the investigation so he could chase after the gold. Why do you think he really broke into that house?"

"I was seeking evidence," Silver said, proud and defiant and so full of shit that his eyes were probably brown.

"You thought you could bust in there and steal all that loot, and Ziegler wouldn't be able to call the authorities for help, because he was a fugitive." I paused to take a drag on my cigarette. "But you got pinched anyway, because despite all your supposed talent, you're just about the worst thief I've ever heard of."

"Now, I resent that. I won't have you make me a villain in this. I went after a perpetrator of atrocities, and as thanks for the trouble, I was treated like a criminal myself. I am, if anything, a victim. A victim of hate crimes."

I cut him off. "Didn't I already tell you to shut up? I don't like repeating myself over and over again. And if I have to hear you whine about anti-Semitism one more time, I am hopping on the next plane to Jerusalem, and do you know what I am going to do when I get there?"

He didn't say anything, so I went ahead and told him:

"I am going to stick a prayer in the Wailing Wall asking God for peace and good health, and then I will go to your house and punch your teeth down your throat. Let me tell you, you're the reason there's anti-Semitism."

"Mr. Schatz, I don't think I have to listen to this anymore," said Avram Silver.

"Then don't. I had my morning coffee about an hour ago, and I'm looking forward to a nice bowel movement pretty soon. I don't want you spoiling it."

"To hell with you, Mr. Schatz."

"I'd take even money that you get there first," I told him.

I heard a click as he hung up.

"Why did you do that, Grandpa?" Tequila shouted at me. "Now he'll never give us that dossier."

"We don't need him."

"Of course we do. He's got the name Ziegler's using, and he was the only lead we had on that. How are we going to find your Nazi now?"

"We don't need that silly crook. We don't need his information. We don't need his damn dossier."

Tequila was quiet for a moment. "Why not?"

I took a bite out of my apple.

"Silver told us he got arrested for breaking into Ziegler's house in St. Louis. So we pull the police report, we get the address, the victim's name."

"We get Ziegler," Tequila said. "We don't need his damn dossier." He didn't say anything for a moment. And then: "I can come home to visit for a few days. I've got a frequent-flier ticket to use. If you're going to St. Louis, I can drive you there."

"My heart leaps with joy," I said. "I'm going to have myself a crap."

"You have a good time, Grandpa."

"I intend to. Best part of my morning."

8

Since the funeral, Emily Feely had been calling the house, talking about wanting to have dinner with us, and Rose decided to accept the invitation.

While they were talking on the phone, I was complaining that it was too far for us to drive, apparently loud enough for Emily to hear on the other end of the line. She offered to bring everything to our house. Rose said that sounded lovely. More or less, I was cornered like an animal. Norris had trapped me somehow.

"I don't like those people," I protested as I sprinkled Sweet'N Low over a bowl of raisin bran. "Did you see how Norris talked to us?"

"You fight with everybody, Buck. That's why we don't have any friends left."

"That suits me fine."

"Well, it doesn't suit me. I'm bored and lonely. And Emily seems like such a nice person, and she wants to be close with people who were close to her father."

"Her father was a schmuck," I said.

"We're the only people who showed up at the funeral."

I pounded my fist on the breakfast table. "But I didn't want to go," I told her. "And I can't stand that bloated louse of a husband she has."

"I'm sure that you and Norris can patch things up and get along."

"You said yourself, he's a dangerous character."

She crossed her arms. "And you laughed and said you could handle him."

"False bravado. I'm terrified of that guy."

"Then it's a good idea to make nice with him," Rose said.

"I'm putting my foot down on this."

She smiled, and her eyes were filled with genuine pity. She knew I would never win. "You can spend all day putting your foot down if you'd like," she said. "But they'll be here at six sharp, and you need to wear something nice."

I growled at her through a mouthful of cereal.

"Oh, by the way, Emily is going to invite that preacher from their church. You two seemed to get on well, so I thought you would enjoy seeing him again."

"Oh, goddamn it," I said.

Tequila landed at Memphis International Airport later that afternoon and came over to the house in his mother's little Japanese car, just ahead of the other guests.

"Hey, Grandma. Hey, Pop," he said as he tromped into the house, letting the screen door slam behind him.

Billy was a little on the short side, with thick, sandy hair he wore in that messy style the young people like. Not a bad-looking kid, but it wouldn't hurt for him to lose ten or twenty pounds and stand up straight once in a while. He resembled his father, and he maybe looked a little like I used to look once upon a time, except I was in better shape at his age. He usually dressed sloppy, in blue jeans and T-shirts and zip-up hooded sweatshirts. Despite his deficiencies, I was glad he was there. Maybe because he was family, I disliked him less than most other people.

Norris and Emily showed up a bit later with a bunch of food in Tupperware containers and covered casserole trays. I would never eat anything they gave me under any circumstances.

"Buck, it's so good to see you," said Emily. And she hugged me. She didn't have any visible mucus on her, but I tried not to breathe until she'd backed away to a safe distance. "I can't thank you enough for being such a comfort to me and Dad."

"Uh, yeah," I said. "This is my grandson, William."

Tequila stuck out his hand, and Feely shook it. "Call me Tequila. Everyone does."

"Oy," I muttered.

Lawrence Kind arrived late. Tequila and I met him at the door.

"I brought you this," he said, and he handed me an ashtray.

I allowed myself a chuckle, and I barely even flinched when he touched my shoulder with his hand; barely even recoiled when his lips peeled back off of his slimy gums. I had not expected the spiritual doctor to have a sense of humor.

"Larry, this is my grandson, Mojito. Mojito lives in New York City, where he spends the money he inherited from my late son."

"Good to know you, uh, Mojito," said the preacher.

"It's Tequila," said Tequila. "It's a fraternity nickname that kind of stuck."

"Of course," said Kind.

"Dr. Kind delivered the soul of my dear friend Jim Wallace unto the bosom of the Good Lord Jesus Christ," I told Tequila.

"I'm sure he appreciated that," Tequila said.

Kind gave one of his bounteous smiles to Tequila and then fixed his eyes on a point somewhere behind me.

"Good to see you again, Norris," he said.

I turned around and was surprised to find Feely standing there. Used to be, I was tough to sneak up on, but I'd been having some trouble with my hearing. For some reason, the outside parts of my ears had grown bigger and fleshier, while the inner workings had dramatically scaled back operations. A tangle of bristly hairs had grown in the ear canals, like weeds sprouting in the ruin of an abandoned building.

"Eat shit and die," Feely told Kind. His eyes were narrowed to little slits, and he was baring his teeth like an angry Chihuahua. I supposed he was trying to be menacing, but since he was basically just a marshmallow covered in hair, he only managed to look a little constipated.

Tequila cocked a questioning eyebrow at me. I shrugged back at him. I had no idea what that was about.

"Buck, I think I'm going to go see how Emily is doing," Kind said, and he turned his back on Feely and walked toward the sound of Rose and Emily chatting in the kitchen.

I started to follow him, but Feely grabbed my arm. I wondered what they taught in that church that made these people think it was okay to touch me.

"Can we talk in front of him?" he asked, jerking his head in my grandson's direction. There were little beads of sweat on his forehead and on his upper lip.

I squeezed the bridge of my nose. "Norris, you and I don't share any secrets."

"All right. All right," he said, his eyes flicking toward Tequila, who was chewing the insides of his face, trying not to laugh.

"You know why that rat-bastard preacher is here, right?" Feely asked me, lowering his voice to a rough whisper.

"Probably because your wife invited him," I said.

"He's after our treasure, just like I told you. This proves it."

"Norris, there's no treasure, and there's no us."

But Norris didn't seem to hear me. His shiny pink cheeks were quivering with rage. "Emily inherited Jim's share, fair and square. We're going to have to do something about Lawrence Kind."

"Jim doesn't have a share," Tequila interjected. "He took a bribe and let a war criminal escape."

"You told him?" Feely slapped a hand against his forehead, which made a sound like creamed corn splattering on a linoleum floor. Then his face screwed up again to show how angry he was, and he jabbed a fat finger into my chest. "Whatever he gets comes out of your cut, Buck."

I mustered the best snarl I could twist my own sagging jowls into and poked a finger right back at him.

"Norris, I expect you to go apologize to the reverend, and behave yourself in a way that doesn't ruin this evening for Rose," I told him. "You and Kind can settle up how to divide Jim's piece of nothing on your own time, but don't waste any more of mine. I don't want any part of your delusional fantasies."

"Well, if that's the way it is, I damn well intend to settle things with that son of a bitch, and with you as well, if you're throwing in with him." Feely turned and stomped off toward the kitchen.

"Grandpa, you've got some weird-ass friends," said Tequila.

"And you don't know when to keep your stupid mouth shut," I told him.

Rose remained unaware of the tension between Kind and Feely as best I could tell, and the dinner was civil, although the conversation was strained and a little awkward.

Norris and Emily had brought over some kind of meat roast with gravy. I found a hair on my portion, and I didn't eat any.

I got rid of everyone a little before nine, explaining that old people had to go to bed early. After the guests left, I made an Oscar Mayer bologna sandwich, on rye bread with mustard and some iceberg lettuce. I enjoyed it thoroughly.

9

The next morning, I woke up feeling kind of unsettled. The malaise was familiar. It was my cop early-warning system, the low rumbling growl my watchdog instinct sent reverberating through my brain stem to let me know somebody nasty was looking for me and planning to make trouble. Rose read some kind of psychology book once and told me that this was my subconscious mind perceiving associations between things I hadn't consciously connected yet. I never paid much attention to that stuff, but it sounded like the kind of thing that might be true.

I hadn't had that feeling in thirty years, though, and it scared me. I wasn't concerned particularly about Norris Feely or Lawrence Kind or Avram Silver; I was mostly just scared about the implications of the tingling at the base of my skull. Paranoia was one of the early symptoms of senile dementia.

I figured a walk on the treadmill would clear my head. But somewhere between the house and the Jewish Community Center, I started getting real suspicious of a red Honda trailing four car lengths behind me.

Sunlight was reflecting off my shadow's windshield, so I couldn't see the driver.

I turned left. So did he.

I changed lanes, and he did as well.

I swallowed hard, wondering what I had stirred up by calling that Israeli. Probably nothing; this probably meant nothing.

It was all in my head.

A couple of weeks previous, I'd had an unpleasant talk with my doctor. He was clutching a folder full of test results and giving me that thin-lipped, scrunched-eyebrow look medical folks get when they're giving you the bad news. He was just a kid, in his early forties, but he'd been taking care of us for about five years, since our old doctor retired to Boca Raton and dropped dead on a golf course from some kind of massive embolism. I guessed the new guy was doing a good enough job; Rose and I were still breathing.

"Buck, I can put you on a medication to try and improve these memory problems you've been having, but I don't necessarily think that's a good idea."

I tugged at my shirt. "You think I have Alzheimer's, don't you."

His lips curled downward in his best compassionate frown. "No. Many older patients have some confusion, some memory loss. There are a number of factors that can contribute to these difficulties."

"How long have I got before I turn into one of those zombies, staggering around a nursing home with no pants on?"

I'd gone for a consultation with a neurologist after an embarrassing episode; I'd been driving in my car, and I realized I didn't know where I was and couldn't remember where I was going. I pulled into a parking lot and called Rose from a pay phone. She had asked me why I didn't call on my cellular. I'd forgotten I had one.

"Your neurological tests don't show sufficient impairment to meet a clinical diagnosis of Alzheimer's-type dementia. You may have what we refer to as mild cognitive impairment, but it's difficult to make that kind of distinction in some patients."

"So you're telling me you don't know whether it's Alzheimer's?"

He avoided looking at me, kept his eyes fixed on the chart. "I've conferred with the neurologist. Your MRI shows no visible lesions on your brain, and my assessment is that you're still pretty sharp for a man your age. Nonetheless, your test results may indicate a pre-Alzheimer's state that we would ordinarily combat with an aggressive drug regimen in a younger patient."

Over the years, I had dealt with my share of doctors and lawyers and car mechanics. They always started talking technical when they were trying to put something by me.

"Younger than what?"

"Buck, my goal as a provider of medical care to the elderly is to try to provide the maximum number of quality life years to my patients. Do you understand what that means?"

It sounded like a pile to me. "Suppose I don't?"

The doctor put down the chart and leaned against his desk. "It means nobody lives forever. Life is a degenerative, terminal condition."

I made a phlegmy noise that expressed my contempt. "You missed your calling. You should have been a writer for Hallmark cards."

The doctor shuffled the papers on his desk. I pulled out my pack of Luckys. "Mind if I smoke?"

"Of course you can't smoke here. This is a hospital."

"Come on, Doc. You're telling me I'm dying. I could use a cigarette to take the edge off that."

He closed his eyes and rubbed his temples. "I did not say you are dying. It's hard to tell the difference between the pre-clinical stages of Alzheimer's and a normally functioning brain in an eighty-seven-year-old patient. Medications commonly prescribed for dementia can cause bruising of the skin and bleeding of the lining of your stomach, which could be problematic when combined with the anticoagulants you're using."

I looked at the expanding purple mark on my arm, from where the nurse had pricked me to take a blood sample.

"You're telling me I have Alzheimer's and you're not going to do anything about it."

"I'm not saying that at all. Your recent episode may have been caused by dehydration. Remember, the pills you take also function as diuretics. But even if you are suffering from the early stages of dementia, it will take six to eight years for the disease to progress to a point of causing significant impairment. Patients in your age group face more immediate hazards such as complications from cold or flu, heart attacks, stroke, and injuries from household mishaps. Frail patients on complicated medications are extremely vulnerable to harmful drug interactions, so I don't want to give you more pills."

So that was it. I was too old to be worth treating. I was so brittle, I might topple over like a rotten tree in a stiff wind.

"Look," said the doctor. "Many studies show that simple exercises to improve mental acuity can be very effective in staving off the progression of mild dementia."

I crossed my arms. "I'm getting a little old for calisthenics."

"No. I want you to try to make an effort to do puzzles, like the crossword or Sudoku."

"Sudoku?" I asked. "Sounds Japanese."

"Uh, it's, like, a grid. With numbers on it."

"Tell you what: I'll look at the crossword."

"Good, good. And you should also try to keep a notebook with you and write down things you don't want to forget. A lot of experts say that making a conscious effort at recall slows the deterioration of the memory."

I was not happy with his suggestions. "This seems an awful lot like doing nothing," I told him. "Placebo effect, or what have you."

"Keep the notebook, Buck. The way I see it, you have two choices here; you can decide to trust me or not." He smiled. "And let me tell you something about paranoia—"

I looked in the rearview as the Honda pulled under a shade tree, breaking the glare on the windshield for a moment. In the driver's seat, I saw a lumpy shape that could have been Norris Feely.

I made another left turn, and so did the Honda. If I kept turning corners trying to shake him, I was likely to get myself lost again. I turned on my hazard lights and pulled off the road, and my shadow cruised past. The driver was a heavyset woman.

No tail, or at least that car wasn't tailing me. Used to be, I could trust my instincts. I pulled my notebook out of my right chest pocket and wrote down the red car's license tag number.

Then I flipped back to the first page, on which I'd written:

"Something I don't want to forget: Doctor says paranoia is an early symptom of dementia."

I thought about it for a minute, and I scratched out the note about the Honda.

Something I don't want to forget:

As worked up as folks seemed to be getting over the Nazi gold, after sixty years, I had to wonder where somebody like Ziegler could have got his hands on such a treasure. As it turns out, when the Jews of Europe were evacuated to ghettos and death camps, Hitler's regime confiscated all their assets. Genocide, it seems, isn't a charitable enterprise; liquidity is the best reason for liquidating people.

The Nazis converted the wealth they plundered into gold bullion, and it was a damn lucrative business. The take from this racket added up to billions, and that's in 1945 dollars. They stashed a lot of the gold in official buildings in Berlin, and after the war, the fleeing Nazi brass stole as much as they could carry with them. That's how they financed their false identities and fraudulent official documents. That's how they bought protection from Arab and South American regimes. That's how the most wanted men on earth escaped capture for decades.

And if Ziegler had looted one of Hitler's caches, he could have got away with a staggering amount of treasure. Jim Wallace told me that Ziegler came through his checkpoint in a big Mercedes-Benz and that the car was weighed down by the heavy gold in the trunk.

According to Tequila's Internet, there was very little civilian industrial production in Germany after 1938, because all the factories were converted to war production. Hitler seized and scrapped most private cars to fuel his war effort. So the only sort of Mercedes-Benz automobile Ziegler might have been driving in 1946 would have been built for war, meant to carry lots of men or heavy guns and shells.

The few civilian luxury cars made for Nazi officials during those years, like the big Mercedes 770 Grosser limousine, were built on chassis that could support heavy armor plates designed to withstand machine-gun fire. A car like that would have to be carrying at least eight hundred pounds in the trunk to be riding visibly low on the rear shocks.

That's pretty impressive, in my estimation. Rose recently made me give a family friend, a heavyset lady who doesn't drive anymore, a ride to her doctor's office. When this woman climbed into my Buick, the whole passenger's side of the car sank toward the pavement. Which is probably why GM went into Chapter 11.

Goes to show that even the Nazis took pride in craftsmanship, which is more than can be said for folks these days.

10

At one in the morning, Dr. Lawrence Kind decided to stop by again and ring the doorbell ten or fifteen times. I wouldn't have been particularly pleased to see him even under normal circumstances, and I was not happy at all that he woke me in the middle of the night.

I didn't tear into him as much as I might have, though, because he looked pretty torn up already. He was ashen-faced and disheveled; certainly less confident and self-assured than he had been the previous evening.

The whites of his eyes were pink, to match that unsettling reptile mouth of his. There was a rust-colored spot on his shirt-sleeve. Could have been blood. Could have been some kind of food stain, maybe tomato sauce. His hair was lank and tangled; not his normal shampooed, Christian coiffure. He stank of stale cigarette smoke, cheap whiskey, and desperation.

"Reverend, do you have any idea what time it is?" I asked

"I'm sorry," he said. "I have to talk to you about Jim Wallace's gold."

Well, obviously. I let out a distended, theatrical groan, to make sure he was aware of my annoyance.

"Jim Wallace was flat broke," I told him. "You were at the funeral. You buried the guy in a cardboard refrigerator box."

"Emily came to speak to me after he died. She told me about Heinrich Ziegler, and about you. She says her husband is obsessed with the gold, and he thinks you're going to find it and split it with him. You can't let Norris Feely get his hands on that treasure. He's not a nice man, Buck. He treats her quite poorly."

"Funny, he had so many nice things to say about you," I said. And when he didn't respond: "I guess you think the money should go to you?"

"To the church," he said. "To further Christ's divine mission."

Kind's concern clearly had little to do with giving effect to Jim's wishes. I could hear need around the edges of his voice and see it in the quivering corners of that lascivious pink mouth. He was hurting for cash.

"I don't know if there is any gold, or where it is," I told the minister. "Norris Feely doesn't know, and neither did Jim Wallace. What do you need that money for, anyway? Your church is enormous."

He looked at me, eyes brimming, and what he told me sounded like the truth. "Churches are built by the tithing of the flock and the grace of God, but they're also built on credit. God has to make the mortgage payment like everyone else, or I do, rather, and God has led me to you, Buck Schatz."

I recognized the tone; recognized the look on his face. In Kind's glassy pink eyes, I saw the sort of weary resignation that had crossed the faces of dozens, maybe hundreds, of suspects I'd stared down across an interrogation table. He was about to confess something to me. People had always liked to confess to me.

I always told them I couldn't help them. I was never dishonest about that. But they spilled their guts anyway.

Kind could keep his mouth shut as far as I was concerned. Whatever his problems were, I didn't see why I should care about them. "Dr. Kind, I appreciate the work you're doing and the hospitality of the church when we went to the funeral, but there's nothing I can do for you."

"Please, Mr. Schatz, I've fallen to temptation. I owe too much at the casinos in Mississippi, and some of the money I threw down that hole belonged to the church." Kind choked back a sob. "I'm underwater. You have to help me."

He pressed the back of his hand to his forehead, striking a mournful pose he must have thought exhibited his boundless oceans of regret. In their minds, people's boring, puerile problems always take on Shakespearean proportions. This degenerate had no self-control; oldest story in the world. I didn't need to hear it again.

Desperate people always thought I had to help them. I didn't have to help them. I was retired from hearing confessions, and even when I had been in that business, I was an instrument of punishment, not a vessel for absolution. But guilty people would get some vague notion that beneath my gruff exterior, I was some kind of softy. Every drunk who beat his girlfriend to death, every junkie who did a murder to get a fix, every arrogant asshole who thought he could make some problem disappear into the Mississippi River; each believed his situation was surrounded by mitigating circumstances. Surely I would weep to know such pain. So, hanging over the abyss, they all confessed unto Buck and threw themselves upon my mercy.

They thought I'd understand. And maybe they were right. Maybe I did understand. But I didn't forgive.

"Tell me what to do, Mr. Schatz," said Lawrence Kind.

I laid a friendly hand on his shoulder. "Maybe you should pray." Then I shut the door in his face and went back to bed.

"What was that all about?" Rose asked, half-asleep.

"Next time you decide to make some new friends, you can leave me out of it," I told her.

About seven hours later, while I was sipping coffee and looking at the paper, the biggest Russian I ever saw showed up at my house and said he wanted to get to know me.

He didn't need to ring the bell, like Kind had. He just pounded with his meaty fist, and the sound rolled like a thunderclap through the house.

"Mr. Buckshot," he said when I opened the door. "My name is Yitzchak Steinblatt."

He was fully six and a half feet and maybe three hundred twenty pounds of thick, rubbery features, dense muscle, and bristly black hair, topped with a yarmulke. He smiled at me the way a grizzly bear might smile at a salmon.

Interesting.

"Pleasure to meet you, Yid's Cock," I said.

"I am from Israeli Ministry for Diaspora Affairs. I work to maintain the special bond between the Jews of America and the state of Israel. I have come to spend time with Jews of the

American South, and I am told, in Memphis, I must speak to Mr.
Buckshot. They say you know everyone."

This was true. "When you've been around, you get around."

He enveloped my hand with a monstrous paw and shook it
with ursine enthusiasm.

"Careful there, big guy," I said. "I'm on a blood thinner, you
know. I bruise pretty easily."

"I am very sorry."

"Why don't you come on in, and have a cup of coffee." No
reason to be inhospitable, I figured.

"Rose," I called out. "We have a visitor from the Israeli government."

She came in from the kitchen and sized up the Russian for a
moment.

"I'll put on a fresh pot."

We sat at the kitchen table. Steinblatt took his coffee with lots
of milk and three packets of Sweet'n Low. I drank mine black
and bitter. We didn't speak for a moment. The kitchen was nice
in the morning. The window by the table opened out onto Rose's
garden, and we got a lot of sunlight through it.

I was glad for the quiet; I needed to decide how to treat this
guy. The Israeli Diaspora Ministry seemed like a public relations
department, but I figured its operatives probably carried diplo-
matic credentials. "Diaspora" was the term Israelis used to describe all the Jews who didn't live in Israel, and there were Jews
everywhere—all over the United States, in every country in Europe, even in China. An affiliation like that would really let a guy
travel.

I looked at the way those big, sinewy hands folded around the
coffee mug, and I considered all possible implications of Avram
Silver's good job with the Israeli government. Forty-eight hours

had elapsed since the former Nazi hunter hung up his phone on me and Tequila. Had he set this behemoth loose on us?

"So when did you make aliyah?" I asked.

"I immigrated to the Jewish homeland in 1992," Steinblatt said.

"Right after the Soviet Union collapsed."

"Yes. It was tumultuous time. I feared for the safety of my family."

"Because you were Jews?"

He paused a tick before answering, and I saw feral intelligence flickering in his dark, deep-set eyes.

"Yes."

He had to be ex-Russian military or former KGB. An undercover Mossad assassin, right there at my damned kitchen table. Or maybe he was a simple flack for the state of Israel who just happened to be unusually large. My doctor had warned me to report any paranoid feelings; they were an early sign of dementia among the elderly.

I cleared my throat. "So, who was it again who told you to come by and talk to me?"

"I spoke to someone with the Memphis Jewish Federation," he said.

"You didn't talk to Avram Silver?"

His face hung slack and expressionless. "I don't know who that is."

I took a long sip from my coffee.

"Let me tell you a story," I said, wagging a finger at him. "I used to be a police detective, back in the prehistoric days, before I got old. Did you know that?"

"I did not."

"A rookie cop recently asked me how I could tell when an investigation was heading in the right direction. It's an interesting question, one I have been thinking about. Part of it is intuition, and part of it is instinct. I also know I am making progress when facts that don't seem to relate to anything start fitting together into a logical story."

He nodded. "Makes sense."

"But mostly, I know I am on the right track when some kind of heavy shows up to try to intimidate me."

"Heavy?"

"Yeah. An enforcer. A goon. Muscle. Meat on the hoof. You follow?"

His expression was unchanged, as far as I could tell. I squinted to make sure, since his face was so hairy.

"I think I understand," he said.

"Sometimes they make overt threats," I continued, keeping an even, conversational tone. "Sometimes they behave in a friendly or at least polite manner, while still managing to convey that unmistakable menacing subtext. Sometimes they don't even talk to me; they just show up and give me the stink-eye."

The Russian set the coffee cup carefully on his saucer.

"I remember this one case. Somebody had strangled a girl in a cheap apartment in a run-down part of midtown, and I liked a highly placed aide to the mayor as the killer."

"This sounds like story out of detective novel," said Steinblatt. His voice was flat and calm and toneless. He was a hard guy to get a read on.

"I know, right? But these powerful guys always had mistresses, and the mistresses always threatened to tell the wives, and these guys always killed the mistresses. Whenever we showed up at an apartment or a hotel room with a dead girl inside it, somebody would have to check to see if the mayor had an alibi."

"So what did you do about this politician?"

"Well, you know, I am a man of class and subtlety, so I kicked in the door of his house at five in the morning, threw the cuffs on him in front of his kids, and frog-walked him into the police station in his bathrobe, so all the press I'd tipped off could take his picture."

Yitzchak flashed his grizzly bear grin. "I imagine he didn't like that."

"I suppose not," I said. "But, since I didn't have any evidence, I had to cut him loose after twenty-four hours, and the same afternoon, a heavy showed up outside the police station, a guy about your size, actually. He didn't say anything to me, but when he saw me notice him, he just nodded and cracked his knuckles."

I glanced at the Russian's big hands, resting on my kitchen table.

"The next morning, I stopped at the coffee shop for a cup and a short stack, and there was the same guy, standing across the street. And he nodded, and cracked his knuckles. And when I left work, there he was again, nodding and cracking. I went bowling with some of my buddies, and this guy was outside the bowling alley, with his goddamn knuckles."

"Did that frighten you?"

"It was a little disconcerting. This guy kept showing up everywhere I went for a couple of days, and when I tried to take my family out to dinner, and he was waiting for me at the restaurant, where my wife and son could see him, I decided I'd had enough."

"What did you do?"

"I shot him."

I finished the coffee and slammed the mug down on the table.

The big Jew didn't flinch at the noise, he just stroked his beard. "That is a good story. Thank you for sharing it."

"You sure you never heard of Avram Silver?"

"I don't believe so."

"Okay," I said. "Why don't you meet me at the Jewish Community Center at around four this afternoon, and I will introduce you to some people."

"I would like that very much."

I was there, on time, waiting. He didn't show up, though.

12

Later that night, I found myself in the enormous auditorium of Lawrence Kind's shopping mall church, thinking about Yitzchak Steinblatt and those dangerous hands of his.

Kind wasn't being very conversational. I didn't hold it against him, since somebody had hacked off his lower jaw and flung it against the wall, leaving a red splotch on the white stucco.

"That happened while he was still alive," said Detective Randall Jennings, pointing at the stain.

"I guess he was not at peace in his final moments," I said.

"Guess not," Jennings agreed.

I lit a cigarette, and nobody told me to put it out.

Less than twenty-four hours after Kind had spilled his guts to me as he begged for redemption, someone else had spilled them all over the stage of the church. They were uncoiled on the floor in a grayish-pink tangle next to the emptied-out torso, as if Kind had exploded while giving a sermon. The carpet around the body was soaked black with congealed blood and bile.

Jennings and I were sitting in a couple of those cushy movie-theater chairs, where so many worshippers had watched Kind preach. Technicians combed the stage, taking photos and collecting samples.

Had the big Jew done this? I would imagine the Mossad killed cleaner.

"As much of a mess as he made, it doesn't look like the killer left any physical evidence for us," Jennings told me. "There doesn't appear to be any of the attacker's tissue under Kind's fingernails. No defensive wounds on the arms. It don't look like the preacher got a chance to draw blood, so we won't be finding any DNA. We're still searching for a lead of some kind, but I'd be surprised to find anything. A lot of care went into this murder."

"A careful scumbag is still just a scumbag," I said.

"Well, I've always been an admirer of proficiency and attention to detail. It's something we could use more of in this town, even among our criminal elements."

"Why'd you call me out here to look at this?" I asked.

"Thought you might be interested."

"I retired from being interested in this kind of thing thirty-five years ago."

"Yeah, but this one was a friend of yours."

I paused for a second, trying to figure out how much the detective might know. It could be that he was making a guess and trying to get me to confirm it for him. I couldn't think of any reason why Jennings would be aware of my conversations with Kind, so I decided to lie to him.

"I met this man once, at a funeral here last week."

Jennings tilted his head. "Now, that's not quite the truth, is it, Buck?"

Maybe Max Heller's protégé wasn't quite as dumb as I had him figured.

"I know he came to your house, twice in the last few days. I know he came to visit you at one o'clock this morning. As far as I know, you were the last one to see him alive. Other than the guy that did this to him, I mean. So, like I said, I thought you might be interested."

I yawned. "Not really."

"Well, I am interested in why he was visiting you at home."

Had Jennings been staking me out? Why would he do that? I was not going to admit anything.

"What makes you think he was at my house?"

"There is a GPS navigation computer in his car. It has a record of every place he's driven in the last week."

I didn't know what a GPS navigation computer was, but it sounded like it could be a real thing, so I ceded the point. God-damn DNAs and DVDs. "My friend Jim Wallace, who died recently, said something to Kind about leaving money to the church. Kind was concerned that Jim's son-in-law, Norris Feely, might be trying to keep the money for himself. He came to my house to ask if I knew anything about it."

I didn't see any reason to tell Jennings about Ziegler and the treasure.

Jennings nodded. "What did you say to him?"

"That I didn't know anything about any money."

He squinted at me. "If that's the truth, why would you lie to me about it?"

"Because sometimes, old men forget about things," I said. "My doctor tells me I might have the dementia."

He peered at me. "You're old; I'll give you that. But I think you're forgetting things on purpose."

He leaned in toward me, so close that I could smell the coffee on his breath. I suppose he thought it was kind of an intimidating thing to do. I belched loudly in his face.

"Also, you're an ass, and I don't like you," I said.

That seemed to conform better to his worldview; he leaned away and wiped at the bulbous tip of his nose with a handkerchief. "Fair enough," he said. "Do you think Feely did this?"

The possibility was worth thinking about. I considered telling Jennings to get his forensics team to search the scene for knuckle hair, but then Tequila walked into the auditorium.

"What's going on in here, Grandpa?" he asked. Then he saw the inside-out mess that used to be Lawrence Kind. "Oh, holy shit, that's fucked up."

"You were supposed to wait in the car," I shouted at him.

"Who the hell is that?" Jennings asked me, pointing at Tequila.

"Detective Jennings, this is my grandson, Jameson."

"People call me Tequila," explained Tequila. "It's a fraternity thing."

"What is he doing here?"

"Somebody had to give me a ride," I told him. "It isn't safe for a man my age to drive at night."

"How did he get into my crime scene?"

"I was wondering that myself. You should run a tighter ship."

His mustache seemed to bristle a little. "The crooks down at City Hall keep cutting the budget. There's never enough overtime, so I've never got enough men. Without resources, without guys to bang on doors and chase leads, without rush jobs on lab work, the only way we catch a killer like this one is dumb luck. But if the homicide clearance rate falls, it's my ass hanging out." He refocused his annoyance with the situation on Tequila. "Does he know anything about this?" he asked, pointing a stubby finger in my grandson's direction.

I shook my head. "He's a student at NYU. He's here on vacation."

"Anything I can help with?" Tequila shouted to us. He was still standing at the back of the room, and he looked terrified that he might have to go near the stage.

"Go back and sit in the car like I told you to."

Tequila left without complaint.

"Every year, they give us less and expect us to do more," Jennings said. "And every year Memphis becomes a more savage place. We pour blood and sweat into locking up the scum, and the system gives them two days' credit against their sentences for every day in prison they don't stab somebody. We put these shitheads away, and they just let them walk right back out the door to pile more corpses in the streets and more open files on my desk."

"That's what they pay you for."

"Not nearly enough. The health insurance just kills me, and the kitchen needs to be redone, and the kid needs private school, and my old man is in one of those nursing places for four grand a month. His Social Security ain't enough to cover that. And when they don't pay you a decent wage to do a clean day's work, it's damn hard to turn away when somebody tries to slip you something under the table."

"I didn't come out tonight to hear about your homosexual activities, Detective."

He chuckled a little bit. "I must have forgot who I was talking to."

"I been forgetting stuff lately myself," I said.

"Yeah, you told me that already."

"Sorry. I forgot."

"You're so full of shit," he said. And when I didn't respond, he asked, "So, what do you think about Feely?"

"He seems a little too delicate to be a slasher, but I don't know him that well," I said. "I heard Kind had a gambling problem."

"From who?"

"Kind told me, last night. He was hurting for money. That was why he was so concerned about anything Wallace might have left to the church."

Jennings cocked his eyebrow at me. "You know more than you're telling me."

"Nothing I can remember," I said. "Seems to me like this might have been done over gambling debts or unpaid loans."

"We've already got guys snooping around the casinos in Tunica County," Jennings told me. "Believe it or not, the world didn't grind to a halt when you retired. We can still do police work without Buck Schatz."

"Then why did you drag me out to this crime scene?"

"Shits and giggles, old-timer."

"Have I mentioned that I don't like you?"

He laughed. "Yeah, but I didn't think you meant it." He handed me a business card. "That's got my cell number on it, and I'll answer it anytime. Do me a favor and give me a call if your memory improves, or if you start feeling guilty about impeding a murder investigation."

13

From the church, Tequila drove me to the Blue Plate Cafe, down on Poplar Avenue in East Memphis. It was a cozy little place, built in what used to be a house. They served breakfast all day, and everything on the menu was soaked in grease. I wasn't allowed to smoke in the restaurant, but I liked the buttery biscuits with cream gravy, and Rose never let me get near food like that.

"When I was a kid, Dad used to take me to work with him sometimes, in the summer, when I wasn't in school. We'd always stop here for pancakes on the way downtown," Tequila said. "It's strange coming home, since he's been gone. You know, we never talk about Dad."

I ran my fingers around the edges of the memory notebook. "I got nothing to say to you about that."

"Last night, I sat in the living room, looking at his clock on the wall above the fireplace. I remember, every night he used to climb up on the ottoman, and wind that clock with a little key. Mom doesn't know how to do it, so it's stopped. It just hangs there now."

I took a long sip from a cup of black coffee and dunked a biscuit into the bowl of gravy.

Tequila crossed his arms. "It's not right. He shouldn't be dead."

"Lots of people shouldn't be dead, and they're dead anyway," I said. "That preacher back there, far as I know, did nothing to deserve what happened to him."

"Deserve's got nothing to do with it," Tequila said.

"What?"

"Never mind. It's from a movie." He paused for a moment. "Horrible, what happened, though."

"At least you managed to keep from vomiting."

I'd seen the way plenty of soldiers and rookie cops reacted to that first eyeful of a ripped-up human body, and Tequila had handled it pretty well. Of course, kids these days see lots of that kind of stuff at the movies and in those computer games.

"Who do you think killed him, Grandpa?"

"I don't really know." I had some ideas, though.

The most likely scenario was that Kind, up to his eyeballs in gambling debt, had fallen behind on payments to some bad people, and one of them had made an example of him. But I'd met some hard gangsters and vicious killers in my assorted travels, and it took a special sort of mean to butcher a minister in a church over money. There was no strain of violence too rare or exotic for Memphis, but we were deep in Jesus country, and the local crooks had been raised to fear the wrath of God.

Yitzchak Steinblatt seemed like a pretty good suspect. I had first met him only that morning, but he could easily have been watching the house the night before, when the preacher came by. If the Israelis were after the treasure, then Kind's interference would have been unwelcome. But I couldn't figure out how the big spy would have known that the visit from Kind was connected to Ziegler and the gold. Maybe he was listening with some kind of high-powered microphone.

Norris Feely also deserved some consideration; he seemed like he had a capacity for viciousness, and there was plenty of animosity between Feely and Kind. But I thought I had convinced Feely that I wouldn't be fetching any riches for him, and it seemed unlikely that he would disassemble a man in a dispute over money neither of them could lay hands on.

Of course, there was always the possibility some unknown, unrelated enemy I didn't know about had brought the preacher to his messy end. I was only casually acquainted with the man, and as much as I prided my instinct, I had no way of knowing what he might have been mixed up in.

"What do you think?" I asked Tequila.

He poured syrup over his pancakes. "I dunno," he said. "I guess Jesus didn't save him after all."

"That's not funny," I told him. "I didn't like Lawrence Kind much, but as far as I know, he was a decent enough sort. Facile, maybe, and kind of crooked, and not as smart as he thought he was. But whatever else he did, Kind seemed to believe in the product he was selling, and I think he really cared about people."

"I never thought I would hear you expound the virtues of caring about people."

I frowned. "I care about people. I just don't like them."

"Well, it doesn't matter what he was anymore," Tequila said. "Now he's nothing but dead."

He stared at me for a long moment, and I stared back at him. I wasn't sure if we were talking about Kind or about Brian. But we were done talking anyway.

With two quick strokes, Tequila carved a wedge out of his short stack. He stabbed it decisively with his fork and popped it into his mouth.

Something I don't want to forget:

On one of the end tables in the sitting room, there's a photo of me with Brian and Billy, all dressed in Boy Scout uniforms, at scout camp, the weekend Billy got into the Order of the Arrow.

The order is sort of an elite group of scouts and adult scout leaders, elected by their troops and inducted through a ritual hazing process called the Ordeal, where the candidates spent a weekend in Hardy, Arkansas, eating very little food and taking apart the summer camp at the Kia Kima Scout Reservation free of charge, all while under a vow of total silence. The event concluded with a campfire ceremony where the youth Arrow leaders dressed up like Indians and solemnly welcomed the new members.

Arrowmen get to wear a white sash with a red arrow on it over their scout uniforms, and they get to wear an Order of the Arrow lodge-flap patch on their shirt pockets. The lodge patches are the most colorful scouting patches available, so membership in the order is coveted.

Brian and I went through together in 1964, when he was a scout and I was a scout leader. I was seventy-six when Billy got tapped for the order, and a little past the point in my life where I was participating in camping trips with the Boy Scouts, but I made a trip to Kia Kima to see my grandson do the Ordeal.

At some point, when the candidates were out tearing down a campsite, somebody had knocked over a hornet nest, and a whole angry swarm of the buggers went after the kids.

Billy showed up at the ceremony with half his face purple and distended and his left eye swollen shut. One of the youth leaders told me later that Billy didn't cry out when he got stung. He treated his oath of silence as a very serious matter; he was a serious boy, and damn tough as well.

The photo caught him in that moment, proud of himself, but

grimacing in pain, trying to hide the messed-up side of his head from the camera.

Billy quit the Boy Scouts after he found his first girlfriend, around the time he turned fourteen. He earned the Eagle rank before he left, though. He was a bright little kid.

I showed him the photo from his Ordeal last year, and he told me he thought the Boy Scouts was a homophobic paramilitary organization of white supremacists and religious fanatics and that the Indian-dress Arrow ceremonies were a sort of racist minstrel show.

It meant a lot to him when he was twelve, though. And I think it meant a lot to Brian.

At three in the morning, the phone rang.

Nobody calls me at three in the morning. I don't call anyone at three in the morning. It's just not something people should ever do. I don't care what the problem is. If someone is having a medical emergency, they should call an ambulance and leave me alone. If someone is dead, they'll still be dead at a decent hour.

So I let the machine get it. The caller hung up without leaving a message, and then the phone started ringing again. I continued ignoring it, so whoever it was kept calling.

Rose stirred and wiped at her eyes. "Are you going to get that?"

"Wasn't planning on it."

We listened to the ringing for twenty minutes, until I finally got out of bed and pulled all the phone cords out of the wall.

Then my cell phone started ringing. That was odd. Nobody had that number except family. It was unlisted.

The little screen on the front of the phone showed a number I didn't recognize. Area code was 662. Mississippi. I stuck the cell phone under one of the sofa cushions to muffle the noise and went back to the bedroom.

"Who was it?" Rose asked.

"I don't care," I told her.

Forty-five minutes later, Tequila buzzed the doorbell.

"We got a call from a stranger saying that we should check up on you, and your phone was off the hook, so Mom thought I should come over," he said.

I made a noise that let him know I was not pleased to see him.

Tequila crossed his arms. "Sorry, but we worry about you."

"Mississippi area code?" I asked him.

"Yeah."

I stomped into the living room and pulled the cell phone out of the couch. It was still ringing. I answered it.

"What?"

"Uh, is this Buck Schatz?" said the voice on the other end. He sounded startled, but after sitting there punching his redial button for over an hour, I supposed he wasn't expecting an answer.

"Who's asking?"

"My name is T. Addleford Pratt," said the voice, recovering a little bit of composure.

"Whatever you're peddling, we don't want any."

"I am the director of collections for Silver Gulch Saloon and Casino, down here in Tunica County, and I am looking to recover on a li'l ol' debt."

The redneck shtick covered the menace in his voice about as much as a squirt of Pine-Sol covers the stink coming off a week-old corpse.

"I don't go to Tunica," I told him. "You're talking to the wrong man."

"Well, see, I don't reckon I am. I'm owed money by a feller named Larry Kind. He told me he's got a share of some kind of

Nazi gold that'll clear the books for him, and that you know about it."

"I don't give a good goddamn about what Kind owes. You'll have to take that up with him."

"You know as well as I do that ol' Larry done got himself cut up."

"Are you telling me you had something to do with that?"

"I ain't sayin' shit, old man. But what goes around gets around, and we got this problem of his outstanding debt."

"We don't have a problem," I said. "You've got a problem."

"It's your problem now, Buck, because I'm your new partner in this little treasure-huntin' enterprise."

I sighed. "Let's meet up face-to-face in your office tomorrow, and we can talk this over."

I hung up the phone and went over to the coat closet by the front door. I pulled a shoebox off of a high shelf and carried it to the kitchen table. Inside: my old Smith & Wesson .357 Magnum revolver, wrapped in cheesecloth. I examined it. Several times each year for the last three decades, I had disassembled the weapon; cleaned and oiled every part. It was in perfect condition.

What Eisenhower told me was, when you have nothing else to hang on to, you hang on to your gun.

I held it at arm's length and peered down the sights. My arm shook a little from the weight of it. I had no reason to believe the gun had gotten any heavier, so I figured my arm had gotten weaker since the last time I'd aimed it. That was the bad news. On the bright side, though, my eyesight had gotten much worse since the last time I'd had to shoot somebody.

15

The Armani-suited downtown Memphis business types from the Baker Donnelson law firm or the Morgan Keegan bank might have been toasting one another in the Diamond Lounge over at the Harrah's, but they didn't come around the Silver Gulch. Somebody like Lawrence Kind would have stayed away as well, unless he'd run out his credit everywhere else. But for the right kind of clientele, Silver Gulch was the best place in Mississippi to stuff a welfare check into a slot machine.

Conveniently located an hour's drive from Memphis, the Gulch catered not only to the kinds of rednecks who would only throw a wrinkled flannel over their stained wife-beater undershirts for dressy occasions, but also to mean-looking colored guys from Orange Mound who wore oversize basketball jerseys and baggy pants and carried fat rolls of bills wrapped in rubber bands.

Walking in, Tequila gave me a nudge and pointed at a white whale who must have easily weighed five hundred pounds, sitting on two stools and playing three slot machines. He was wearing a sleeveless T-shirt big enough to cover a small car. His naked upper arms were each as big around as a woman's torso.

"Leave him alone," I said. "He's just trying to get comped to the buffet, same as everyone else."

Endless mountains of soggy fried chicken, overcooked pork ribs, and crusty macaroni and cheese. To a certain kind of person, Tunica probably looked like heaven.

We walked past rows of machines and the glassy-eyed gamblers yanking at the greasy levers and asked the pockmarked attendant at the players' desk if Pratt was around. The kid whispered into a handheld radio for a moment and then led us through a door that he unlocked with a key card, down a yellow-painted hallway with a cement floor, to the dingy office of the DIRECTOR OF COLLECTIONS.

Pratt stood as we entered.

"Howdy," he said. "I reckon you don't mind if I call you Buck?"

I looked him over. Deep-set, piggy eyes; greasy hair. Brown teeth piled on top of each other. I'd have suspected methamphetamine use if he weren't forty pounds overweight. I made him for a two-bit shakedown artist. With the heater strapped against my ribs, I felt like myself again, more than I had in years. If I went at Pratt hard, I could cow the son of a bitch.

"Sit your ass down," I told him, and he did.

I leaned over his desk, narrowed my eyes, and curled my lip to show him my own teeth, which were nicotine stained but still looked much better than his.

"Thirty-five years ago, I'd have put a bullet through your head, told folks you had it coming, and nobody would have said any different," I told him.

Pratt didn't flinch. "This ain't thirty-five years ago, partner," he said. "Your friends up and died on you, and Tunica is my town."

I glared at him, and he glared right back.

"So, how's about you take a seat there, Buck, and stop breathin' old-man stink on me."

Used to be, I'd have had a quick retort for him, but when I started to cuss at him some more, it was like my throat was stuffed with cotton balls. Side effect, damn it, of all the pills I take.

I opened my mouth, and closed it, and opened my mouth again, like a fish flopping in the bottom of a boat, but the only words that sprang to mind were some things my doctor had said about signs of cognitive impairment among the elderly.

I reached, reflexively, for my memory notebook, but I felt, instead, the weight of the gat, snug against my side, underneath my jacket, and I had a sudden and powerful urge to let it do the talking for me; to just cave in Pratt's whole damn face around those tangled teeth and those mean, beady eyes; to empty his skull onto the cinder-block wall. I knew, though, that wasn't a good play. It would create more problems than it solved.

So I chose the path of restraint and just punched him in the nose. It wasn't much of a punch. My shoulder didn't seem to rotate like it was supposed to. My back didn't twist right to put my weight behind the follow-through. The bicep couldn't snap the arm out.

He took the punch like he was leaning into a warm spring breeze, and then he smirked at me. I stared, dumbstruck, at my fist. My fingers and knuckles were already blue black, and the whole back of my hand was turning purple.

"You got that out of your system now, Mr. Buck?" Pratt asked.

I didn't have anything to say, but Tequila filled the silence.

"Pratt, you haven't got a claim against us. We've made no agreement to assume Mr. Kind's obligations, and Mr. Kind had no interest in any property we possess. Your only recourse as a creditor is against Mr. Kind's estate, which is no concern of ours."

Tequila always spoke with a kind of precise, uninflected diction. He didn't sound like Memphis, but he didn't sound like New

York either. His speech sounded kind of haughty, like he thought he was too good to have come from any particular place. Directed at Pratt, though, Tequila's manner lent him an air of authority, like he was a psychologist talking to a disturbed child.

Pratt broke eye contact with me and smirked at Tequila. "Now, is that a fact?"

"I can tell you, if you try to go into court, you won't be able to obtain relief against us. We're not responsible for anyone else's gambling debt."

"Oh." Pratt nodded. "Well, let me tell you something, Mister New York City. This ain't got nothin' to do with no court. You find yourself, at this moment, in Mississippi, and around these parts, whatever claim I say I have, folks take serious, and whatever responsibilities I say folks have, they find they are responsible. And if and when we do go to court, all the judges 'round these parts know who butters their biscuits, and it sure as shit ain't y'all. I am going to collect my money, and that's just that."

I sat and shushed Tequila just as he was starting to say something else. Talking law to this Mississippi swamp beast was like preaching the gospel to the back end of a horse, but my grandson had bought me the precious seconds I needed to shake off my senility and come up with a plan of some sort.

"Fine," I said, holding my throbbing hand. "I'm too old to futz around with you. When they find the treasure, you can have whatever my share would have been."

This surprised him. "When who finds it?"

"The Israelis."

"What Israelis?"

"Didn't you know? All those Nazi assets were stolen from Jews in the war, so they go back to Israel when they're recovered. If you find it, the Israelis just pay you a small commission."

His face slackened. "Huh?"

"Turns out they pay you the same if you just tip them off as they do for actually hauling in the damn gold, ain't that right?"

"Uh, yeah. International Convention for the Recovery of Stolen Assets," Tequila lied. "Codified in federal statute. Your lawyers can look it up."

"So we just called up the Israeli embassy. They sent a man over to take care of it," I told him. "An Israeli government agent by the name of Yitzchak Steinblatt. Can't miss him, he's real big, with a big beard. That's who is hunting the treasure."

"No," said Pratt. "No, Kind said you were the one going after that."

"You've never been lied to by someone who owed you money?" Tequila asked.

Pratt thought on that for a second.

"Shit."

He didn't have much else to say, so I maneuvered out the door as quickly as I could. I wanted to open up some distance between myself and Mississippi, but Tequila insisted on putting twenty bucks in a slot machine.

"As long as we're down here, we might as well try our luck," he said.

I crossed my arms. "I want to leave now."

He stared at me with eyes full of contempt. "I'm your ride, and we'll go when I say we go."

So he spent fifteen minutes tugging a lever. The guy at the next machine was two hundred and seventy-five pounds of mean, wrapped in black leather and prison tattoos, and my grandson didn't even seem to notice. I watched both our backs with my hand stuffed inside my jacket, clutching the butt of the .357.

Tequila kept a blank expression as he watched the reels spin. I wondered if his sheltered upbringing had retarded his ability to comprehend danger in this place, in this situation.

He pulled the lever again, and the game took his money. He punched it, annoyed.

The guy with the prison ink glanced away from his own machine to eyeball Tequila.

"Hope you have better luck," Tequila told him.

As we walked out into the parking lot, I explained for my grandson's benefit that Pratt had undoubtedly been watching us the whole time we'd been in there on the casino's security feed.

"Don't you think I know that?" Tequila growled at me. He stopped walking and crossed his arms. "How does it help us if he looks at that monitor and sees us bolting for the door like frightened rabbits?"

"It ain't safe here. Under the circumstances, we're better off getting far away from this place," I told him, flicking my lighter. "You let me do the thinking for us. I have the experience."

"I don't trust your thinking, Grandpa," he said, furrowing his eyebrows and leaning forward, forcing himself into my space. "Your thinking brought us out here, because your thinking was that you could tell this guy how things work in his own house. But your tough-guy bullshit was obsolete even when you could put some torque behind a punch."

"Listen to me," I began.

But he cut me off.

"I'm through listening to you. You're not an educated man, and you're not in control of this situation. Five minutes of lawyer talk over the phone would have convinced that guy we were a kind of trouble he didn't want. Instead, we've shown him there's blood in the water here. Maybe we've thrown him off the scent, for the moment, with the Steinblatt thing, but he'll be damn hard to get rid of. And on top of that, you want to let him see us run away. What the hell kind of a plan is that?"

I recoiled a little from his outburst. "I may not know law

books, but I know people," I stammered. "You don't understand the kind of man you're dealing with."

"I know what kind of man I'm dealing with. An ornery, senile, half-crazy old fuck."

Neither of us said much after that. On the way back to Memphis, I looked out at the soybean fields surrounding the casinos and wondered how many folks were buried under them.

Something I don't want to forget:

On the night Billy was born, Brian brought the baby, wrapped in a blue blanket, out of the delivery room for Rose and me to see.

The baby was small and very pink, with just a little tuft of light-colored fuzz on his head. When I leaned down to look at him, Billy peered back at me with big, bright eyes, green and wet.

"Hi, kid," I said. "I'm your grandpa. I'm going to help look out for you."

"I love him so much, Dad," Brian told me, and his eyes were wet as well.

"If you ever felt before that your life lacked an animating purpose, I reckon you're realizing right about now that you'll never feel that way again," I said, squeezing his shoulder. "This is the thing that gets you out of bed in the morning. This is why you try to force a cruel and arbitrary world to take on a shape that makes sense. This is what you are for: to protect this boy. To keep him safe and make sure he knows he's never alone."

"Yeah, Dad. I think that's just about right."

I found my whiskey flask in my jacket pocket. I took a long belt and handed it to my son. "Well, I know the feeling," I said.

16

There was an ass in every one of the two thousand cushy movie-theater seats in the stucco-and-glass auditorium. The church had its sheriff's deputies trying to untangle the jammed-up traffic in the parking lot. Judging from the attendance at his memorial service, it seemed that despite his unsettling appearance and his gambling problem, dead Larry had been a pretty solid hand at the pastor racket. A lot of people were crying.

I found a nice perch on the end of an aisle, at the back lip of the room, where I could see the crowd. Tequila slid into the seat next to me. We hadn't talked about yesterday's blowout in Tunica, and I suspected we wouldn't. That wasn't how things worked in our family.

He had showed up at the house earlier that morning with fresh bagels and coffee from Starbuck's. A peace offering.

I accepted it and let him drive me to the funeral. So now we would pretend it had never happened, although the things he'd said had got under my skin.

I'd been to the church three times now in the span of a week.

This was the life of an old person—going to the same places all the time, over and over, and attending a lot of funerals.

Somebody had already replaced the carpet on the stage where Kind had bled out. Somebody had repainted the splattered walls. Somebody had mopped up Kind's various bits and scraped them into a heavy-looking oak casket with brass rails for the pallbearers to grab on to. The box was closed, of course, and it was so completely covered with cascading flowers that I could barely see how expensive it was.

"Maybe if the reverend had given that fancy coffin to those guys in Tunica, they wouldn't have ripped his face off," Tequila said.

A heavyset, middle-aged woman in front of us turned around to give us an ugly look.

Tequila winced a bit and tried to look contrite. "We all have different ways of expressing our grief," he told her.

"What makes you think the casino people did him?" I asked.

"Nothing in particular," he said. "My theory is actually that you did it."

I fiddled with the pack of cigarettes and considered lighting one. I decided against it. "Nobody says you're innocent either," I told Tequila.

"Well, if anyone starts snooping around and wants to know where I was that night, you can tell them you were with me, and if anyone asks about you, I'll say the same."

That was reassuring.

Lots of classy folks in the crowd. No Mexican day laborers would need to be conscripted to carry the late reverend; a judge, a councilman, and the mayor were on deck to help bear the departed to his resting place. I wondered idly if those three had alibis for the night of the murder.

The luminaries would be sharing the load with Kind's former

assistant and interim successor, a straight-backed, severe-looking fellow called Gregory Cutter. He'd got himself a promotion out of Kind's death, and that was a motive. I added him to my mental list of suspects.

"Hey, there's somebody we know," Tequila said, gesturing toward T. Addleford Pratt, who was sitting nearby, dressed for the occasion in a red leather coat with a white fur collar.

"We got friends all kinds of places," I said, jamming an elbow into Tequila's ribs and jerking my head to the left and forward, toward Yitzchak Steinblatt, who was examining a Baptist hymnal with a sort of intense Hasidic zeal.

"Shit," said Tequila. "That is, like, the Dikembe Mutombo of Orthodox Jews."

I didn't know what he was talking about.

Detective Randall Jennings had shown up as well; he was sitting near the front, in the same seat he'd occupied the night of the murder.

"I don't see Feely," Tequila said. "Do you think that means he's the killer?"

I looked around and didn't see him either. What I suspected it meant was, when Norris Feely didn't want to go someplace, his wife couldn't force him to go anyway. I would have to find out how such a feat could be accomplished.

"Nothing means anything," I told him. "Bad guys sometimes return to the scene of the crime, and sometimes they put rubber to pavement and never look back. I'm not their psychologist. I just lock the bastards up."

He smirked. "You used to lock the bastards up."

"That's what I said." My elbow was starting to throb; sticking Tequila had been a bad idea. I was sure I had bruised it.

"So, how come we're not in St. Louis?" he asked. "I have to go back to New York pretty soon."

"A man's murdered, and that may be related to our treasure hunt," I told him. "Wherever the gold is, it's been there a long time, and it can wait a little longer. We need to make sure we're safe before we do anything."

Kind's parents and brother sat in the front row. The father was crying. I avoided looking at them, but Tequila was staring in their direction.

"Who's the pretty girl sitting with the family?" he asked the lady in front of us.

"That's the pastor's wife," she said. "Poor Felicia. This must be so hard on her."

Felicia Kind was younger than her husband, maybe twenty-four or twenty-five. She wore a wide-brimmed black hat, with a black veil on it, and a tight-fitting black cocktail dress with a plunging neckline that put piety's earthly rewards on full exhibition.

"Hard-on indeed," Tequila said in his best, most sympathetic tone. "That's a hell of a dress for a funeral."

The big woman clucked like a mournful hen. "She must have been so dazed with grief, she didn't even realize."

I watched a tall man with carefully mowed hair lean in toward Felicia to whisper in her ear. She laughed at whatever he said.

"She knows exactly what she's doing," Tequila said. He leaned back toward me. "What do you think, Grandpa?"

"I can imagine a chain of events starting with that woman and ending with that box."

"You think she did it?"

"Everyone's a suspect," I said. "But when I look at that shiny coffin, I've got to suspect the life of the departed reverend was heavily insured."

"So you think she killed him for money?"

I thought about it for a moment. "You have to understand, a

filly like that don't want to be kept in the paddock. She wants to nibble at the sweet new grass and get some sweat on those shapely flanks."

"Does that mean you think she's sleeping with somebody?"

I shrugged. No way of knowing. "It'd be kind of a shame if she wasn't," I said.

Gregory Cutter, Kind's replacement, patted Felicia's hand, hugged the weeping father, and then stepped up onto the stage in front of the coffin. The crowd fell silent as the preacher grasped his microphone.

"Lawrence would be pleased to see you all here today, I'm sure," he said. "He was a friend and a counselor and a listener and a guide, and he touched many lives throughout our community with his wisdom and his compassion."

Kind's father sobbed.

"The way I see it," Tequila said, shifting in his seat, "if this has something to do with her, it's got nothing to do with us."

I turned that over in my mind as I half listened to Cutter orating on the stage.

"We've all wondered over the last few days what sort of monster could have done this to someone like Larry. And the police are still hunting for the killer. But I know who was behind this crime. I know who wanted to destroy Lawrence Kind and who wants to destroy this church."

"That makes things a whole lot easier," Tequila whispered to me.

"Each of us has an Enemy," Cutter shouted from the stage, pointing his finger into the audience. "Each of us has a foe, savage and cruel. And that Enemy is fearsome enough to lay low the best among us, even men as pure and strong as our pastor."

I'd followed General Eisenhower's advice and hung on to my gun, and that had kept me alive for eighty-seven years. But poor

Lawrence Kind was never the sort of man who could operate that way. I wondered whether I'd had a chance to save him when he showed up begging on my doorstep. I suspected that by then the trap was already sprung, but even if I could have helped him out, Kind had only himself to blame for his ending.

"The Enemy clouds our judgment. The Enemy tempts us to ruin. The Enemy demoralizes us," boomed Cutter.

T. Addleford Pratt was looking at us, smirking.

Tequila scowled back at him.

"That guy is a fucking clown," he whispered. "The wife seems more dangerous to me."

"But even when that Devil lays the best of us low, we have to stand strong in the face of torment, like Jesus did and like Larry did. And, in the end, we know we will each come face-to-face with that Enemy, when we are totally alone, in the dark, when we are weak and afraid," Cutter shouted. "But I look at all our friends here today, and I say, we are unyielding in our faith, and we will prevail over evil, and all of us who are strong in our love will walk with Jesus and Pastor Kind in the promised land."

I rubbed gingerly at my bruised elbow. "Even a silly-ass sumbitch is capable of being dangerous."

"Capable or not, he doesn't have the stones to get rough with a retired Memphis cop in Memphis," Tequila said.

"Wouldn't have thought he'd get rough with a minister," I told him. "But somebody put Larry in that coffin."

In the front row, Felicia Kind crossed and uncrossed her legs. I squinted at her. Her mascara wasn't running. Her lipstick wasn't smudged. She was a very poised young lady; unusually so, considering the circumstances. If I'd looked at the Kinds in 1965, when I was at the peak of my career, I'd have immediately suspected— hell, I'd have been near to certain—that the death of the lumpy, reptilian pastor was somehow related to his bombshell wife. Kind wasn't rich, but maybe Felicia bumped him off to get out of marriage to a hopeless gambler or to free herself to run off with somebody else. That certainly seemed more plausible than the goofy spy stories Tequila and I had been telling each other. It was unlikely that Avram Silver was capable of deploying an assassin halfway around the world. But it seemed awful risky to turn my back on a man like Yitzchak Steinblatt.

Onstage, Gregory Cutter was chopping emphatically at the air with his raised right hand.

"Here in this church, I say we will not give the Devil his due. We will stand up to the evil that threatens us. And those of us who have worshipped here will not forget Dr. Lawrence Kind, our pastor, our shepherd, our friend."

The police didn't just escort the funeral procession, they closed off the streets between the church and the cemetery. But a shiny box and a thousand mourners didn't change the fact that Kind was buried forty feet from the fresh mound of dirt they'd piled onto Jim Wallace.

17

As the crowd around Kind's grave dispersed, I tapped the Dikembe Mutombo of Orthodox Jews on the arm.

"Shalom, Yid's Cock," I said to him.

Tequila giggled into his shirtsleeve.

"You haven't met my grandson, Manischewitz," I said to the Russian. "He's a real mensch. So proud of this one. I got buttons bursting off my shirt, and *nachas* oozing out of every orifice."

Steinblatt's bushy eyebrows knit together with confusion. "Manischewitz? Like the kosher wine?" he asked.

"People call me Tequila," said Tequila. "It's a fraternity thing. My name is Will."

"Ah, I understand," said Steinblatt. He couldn't fully hide his disapproval; growing up in Soviet austerity and fighting for survival on a tiny strip of Middle Eastern turf were probably not experiences that instilled much appreciation for the American college fraternity lifestyle. But poor Yitzchak had to pretend to like Diaspora Jews as part of his job.

Tequila stuck out his hand, and Steinblatt's swallowed it.

"So," I said. "How did you know Dr. Kind?"

"I didn't know him. Not personally. But he was well-known to my agency. I am here mostly to be speaking to Jews of American South, but also, I am involved in representing Israel among our other friends."

"Lawrence Kind was Israel's friend?" Tequila asked.

"Oh, very much. The Evangelical Christians have been unwavering allies to state of Israel. They believe our presence there hastens the return of their Christ. Many people here think the political influence of American Jews preserves the special relationship between Israel and the United States, but Evangelicals are at least as important. Christian tourism is also bright area in our economy."

Most of the mourners had left, so I loosened my necktie and unbuttoned my collar. "Then taking care of Kind fell under your job description?" I asked.

"Absolutely," said Steinblatt. "I never met him myself, but he was quite close with several of my colleagues, and all are deeply saddened to learn of his passing. He led tourist groups from his church to Israel several times, and the Ministry for Diaspora Affairs helped him organize those. Since I am here in Memphis, I come to share regrets."

"Nice of you to do," I said.

Steinblatt tugged at his beard. "He was such a young and vibrant man, and he died such a horrible way. It saddens me greatly. I find that, although I can never get far away from such violence, I can never get used to it, either. Mr. Buckshot, you have also seen a great deal of suffering. How does a man become accustomed to such horror?"

"Some men seem to learn to like it."

His big, fleshy lips turned downward. "Perhaps you are right," he said. "Are you one of those who relishes this violence?"

I shrugged. "There are worse feelings than putting a couple of holes into a man who's got it coming to him. What about you? Do you like killing?"

"I have seen too much of it, too many wars. Violence is a self-perpetuating monster, and it feeds on the blood of the guilty and innocent alike. I was in Afghanistan, you know, in the war there. Then, I leave Soviet Union for Israel, and we have this Palestinian intifada. The lust for violence among the Arabs is barbaric. I cannot fathom the mind of a man who would blow himself up to kill civilians, and yet these people celebrate such atrocities. One moment, children are sitting in café. Next, boom. In pieces." He bowed his huge, woolly head. "Even here in America, where there is plenty for all, the violence is unceasing. Things like this happen to people like Dr. Kind. Did you know that the rate of violent death per capita here in Memphis exceeds that of Jerusalem at the height of Palestinian resistance?"

"Probably better off here than in Gaza, though, isn't it?" sniffed Tequila.

"What we do there is self-defense," Steinblatt insisted. "It is our right to raise our children in cities free from terrorism."

Tequila frowned at him. "God knows, bombing their homes to rubble will curb their militancy."

I hit my grandson in the ribs, hard, with my bruised elbow and winced a little at the pain that shot up my arm.

Steinblatt turned to me. "Tell me, Mr. Buckshot, how did you know Dr. Kind?"

"That's actually a funny story," I said. "I'm sleeping with his wife."

The big Jew was quiet for a moment, and then his bushy eyebrows arched. "You speak to me with contempt. Have I angered you?"

"You said you were going to meet me at the Jewish Community Center, and then you didn't show up. When a fellow gets older, he starts to feel like time is precious, so I don't like people wasting mine."

"I am sorry," he said. "I was unavoidably detained. I hope someday I can make it up to you."

"It must take something mighty powerful to detain a fellow your size," I said. "What was it, exactly, that kept you?"

He frowned. "I'm afraid that is a matter I have no liberties to discuss."

"I was just wondering, because around the same time you were standing me up at the center, somebody was murdering Lawrence Kind."

His big hands clenched into fists. "Are you accusing me of this?"

I lit a cigarette. "I'm just observing things."

"I do not appreciate the implication, sir."

I narrowed my eyes. "Yid's Cock, do you know a guy named Avram Silver?"

"I do not," he said, and his voice had turned hard. "Now, if you will excuse, I must get to another appointment."

"With who?" Tequila asked.

Stony silence from Steinblatt.

"Don't let me hold you up. I know you have important things to do. Whoever you're seeing, send them my best wishes. I do know everyone Jewish in Memphis."

The big Russian gave a curt nod and stalked away from us.

"What a nice guy," I said to Tequila. "I wonder if your grandmother would like to have him over to the house for supper sometime."

18

Tequila was sitting in my spot on the sofa and getting damn smug about his Internet. He'd turned on his computer after the funeral, and by dinnertime he had uncovered information that would have required a proper detective to burn a lot of shoe leather and cigarettes, waste a lot of time in the records room and the newspaper morgue, and probably bust a few heads as well.

I turned up the volume on the television to drown out the self-satisfied little purring noises he was making as he tapped on his keys. Some academic types were talking about old war movies on the History Channel. I liked old war movies, and I wanted to write what they were saying into my memory notebook.

"I think the continuing significance of Nazis as mass culture villains is connected to the fact that this is an unambiguous evil that has been essentially defanged," said a bearded, bespectacled man on the screen. It took me a second to recognize him as the same NYU film professor who had been popping up on every channel the last few weeks, talking about the end of the tough-guy era.

"We can hate them," the professor continued, "but we don't need to fear them, because they are vanquished. They are buried. They are an anachronism."

"How are you getting on the Internet?" I asked Tequila. "I don't have any Internet in here, and your computer isn't even plugged in."

"I'm piggybacking on your neighbor's WiFi network."

"Oh. That makes sense," I said, even though it made no sense at all.

"If they're buried, though, then why do we persist in digging them up?" asked the red-faced, heavyset television host. "Why preserve, as you say, an anachronism as the most prominent incarnation of absolute evil in our symbolic vernacular?"

Tequila glanced up from his screen to look at mine. "Why do you watch this?" he asked.

"Why does anybody do anything?"

For six bucks on his credit card, Tequila had obtained the St. Louis police file on Avram Silver, which included the address of the house Silver had been arrested breaking into. Heinrich Ziegler's house. The report listed the home owner as being one Henry Winters, so we knew Ziegler's alias. And a search of real estate transaction records, a few keystrokes on Tequila's keyboard, told us he sold the house in 1996. He had listed a place called the Meadowcrest Manor as his forwarding address.

"Meadowcrest Manor?" I asked Tequila. "Do you think he cashed in his gold bars and bought some kind of mansion?"

"No," said Tequila. "Look at this."

The computer screen explained that Meadowcrest Manor was a full-service community for active seniors. In other words, a rest home. I shuddered.

"The Nazis are universally recognizable, even by audiences poorly acquainted with history," said the bearded professor.

"Jackboots and swastikas and German accents form an easy short-hand for wickedness. But we can hate the Nazis without fearing them, because they are alien to our experience. Because they are gone."

"I ran a LexisNexis search on the St. Louis papers for Henry Winters, and didn't find any obituaries, so as best I can tell, he's still there, at Meadowcrest," Tequila said.

Ziegler had been shut in the rest home for more than a decade. Served him right to be locked up, but he was the most formidable enemy I ever confronted, the only one ever to push me to the precipice. How could he have decayed so much?

"So, we can vilify them without finding reflections of ourselves in them because they are foreign and because they are relics of an era that has limited modern relevance," said the television host.

The computer also had a contact number for the Israeli Ministry for Diaspora Affairs, and it had an office in New York. Tequila had called them with a new kind of cellular phone that was itself a tiny Internet. I couldn't understand how he dialed the thing; it had no buttons.

The Israeli agency confirmed that Yitzchak Steinblatt was its employee, that he was in Memphis, and that he matched the description of the man I'd spoken to. So his story checked out. But then again, a secret assassin would be able to manufacture a passable cover.

Older sorts of networks supplied helpful information as well. While Tequila busied himself with the Googles, I'd spent an hour kibitzing with the resident gossips and all-purpose oracles ensconced in the lobby of the Jewish Community Center, and they confirmed for me that the big Russian hadn't met with any rabbis or scheduled speeches at any synagogues or arranged to do much of anything else.

"So does that mean he has nothing to do with anything?" Tequila asked.

"Does he look like someone who has nothing to do with anything?"

"He's really big."

I scowled at him.

"Well, if Steinblatt killed Kind, I don't see how the wife could also have been involved," Tequila said. "We're suspicious of everyone, but they can't all have done the murder."

"What I learned from being a cop is that nobody's innocent," I said. But he was right. We were long on paranoia and had no evidence of anything. My doctor had told me paranoia was an early symptom of dementia in the elderly.

"Precisely," said the bearded professor on the television as an ugly little smirk crawled across his face. "We don't fear them the way we might fear modern foreign enemies, or illness, or the unhinged and dangerous people who might be living in our neighborhoods, who might have insinuated themselves into our communities, into our lives."

"We don't fear them, in other words, the way we fear the things that are actually going to kill us," said the host.

I sucked a lungful of smoke out of a Lucky Strike. Cigarettes are the best treatment, in my opinion, for existential panic.

"Honey, could you make a pot of coffee?" I shouted in the general direction of where I thought Rose might be.

"She's already turned in for the night. I'll get it," said Tequila, and he started to stand up.

Rose shuffled out of the bedroom. "Don't you dare," she scolded him. "I've been fixing coffee for longer than you've been alive."

"It's no trouble," Tequila said as he rose to his feet. "Why don't you go back to bed?"

"Shut up and leave it alone," I told him.

"Okay," said Tequila. He paused for a moment as Rose made her way to the kitchen, and then he slid back down onto the couch. "Uh, so, let's assume Steinblatt is a Mossad assassin working with Avram Silver, to get Heinrich Ziegler's gold. Why is he hanging around here? Why doesn't he go straight to St. Louis?"

"I don't know," I said. "Maybe he doesn't know where it is."

"Okay," said Tequila. "What's here that he needs?"

"Maybe something to do with Wallace? Maybe Norris Feely has a clue we don't know about." I wondered if I was the first person ever to suspect Feely of having a clue.

Tequila scratched his chin. "Wallace told you he hadn't seen Ziegler since 1946, right?"

"Maybe there's more to the story that he didn't tell me."

"No," Tequila said. "It's not Wallace. It's got to be you. He showed up after you called Silver. He came to your house."

I lit another cigarette. "But I don't know anything. The only real clue we found is the one Silver gave us. It's been nearly twenty years since Silver fled the country with that dossier, and as far as we know, he's never done anything about it. Now, we make a phone call and ask a few questions, and he's got an angry Jewish giant sniffing around after us?"

"Fe-Fi-Oy-Vey," said Tequila.

"How do you take yours, Billy?" Rose called.

"Cream and sugar?" he yelled back to her.

From the kitchen, the sound of cupboards opening and closing. "I've got half-and-half and some Sweet'N Low."

"Black is fine."

I lit another cigarette. "Silver had some plan to get the gold, and he's worried that we might get to it first," I said. "Maybe he's been waiting for Ziegler to die, and now we've startled him. Maybe he's getting rid of other people who might be chasing the treasure."

"So if you think Steinblatt killed Kind, how do Pratt and Felicia fit into the story?"

"I learned a few things in thirty years on the streets of this town, and let me tell you, nobody's innocent."

"Yeah, Grandpa. You already said—"

He was interrupted by a loud clattering noise.

"Rose, be a little more careful," I shouted.

No wisecrack. No insult. No retort.

"Rose?"

Tequila jumped up off the couch and ran into the kitchen.

"Pop," he yelled to me. "You need to call an ambulance. Right now."

On the television, the bearded professor said, "It's no mystery why we enjoy our Nazi-fighting fantasies. We get enough mundane tragedy in our everyday lives."

19

I sat in an antiseptic white room, on the same floor where Jim Wallace had died. Same sliding glass door that sealed itself. Same filtered air.

I listened to the rhythmic beeping of the machines and held Rose's hand. It was cold. Poor circulation. The gun, which I had been toting around all the time since my trip to Mississippi, was snug in its holster beneath my jacket, pressed against my right side. It wasn't much of a comfort. My pack of Luckys was sitting on a tray next to the bed, and I wanted one, awfully. But I couldn't leave her.

I pulled the memory notebook out of my left jacket pocket. I didn't read it, and I didn't feel like writing in it. I just clutched it tightly.

Rose was awake when the paramedics arrived, but she had been sedated since then. A doctor had offered me drugs a little while before, to help me sleep. I didn't take them. Somebody had to keep the vigil.

When I woke up in the hospital in November 1944, Rose was waiting for me. That's something I don't want to forget. I was surprised to see her there, in France. I was surprised to be alive at all, really. As it turned out, she'd been sitting there every day for the five weeks I'd been unconscious.

The war was over, so there were no U-boats patrolling the Atlantic anymore and it had been safe for her to make the sea voyage. I figured she must've had nothing better to do.

She handed me a bottle of bourbon. She'd been running a whiskey distributor while I was gone. But she came to France as soon as she heard I was laid up. She said she'd never forgive herself if she missed her only chance to watch me die.

I hadn't eaten anything in over a month, and my mouth was dry and cottony. I looked around to make sure the nurse wasn't watching, and then I took a long gulp of the whiskey. It burned going down.

I remember the way she smiled at me. She wasn't wearing any makeup, and her hair was tangled, but I thought I'd never seen anything more beautiful. I told her so.

She said to me, "Buck, you look like shit."

In her bed in the geriatric intensive care unit, she looked very small, and I didn't feel too big myself. I felt fat tears welling up in my eyes. It was late, and I was so tired. But I knew I wouldn't be able to sleep.

I touched Rose's hair. I guess it's funny; she had seemed like she was at her most beautiful during those months when I was recovering after the war, even though that was a period in our life when I wasn't able to do much about it. That was the point we'd come back to.

It had been a long time since I could pick her up and carry her to the bedroom. I'd gotten so weak, I could barely carry in the groceries. I had to switch from the big brown paper sacks to those little plastic bags with the handles, and I needed a couple of trips out to the car to haul everything in.

Not that it mattered. The last time I had a proper hard-on, Ronald Reagan was president. They've got pills nowadays to get the old dog barking again, but there's a risk of dangerous interactions with the other stuff I have to take, and I've got the bruising problem, and she has brittle bones.

We were something once, though, back when her hair was like black silk and her skin was soft, and I was straight-backed and hard-jawed. When I was strong enough to lift guns and fists against any threat; when I was strong enough to protect her and strong enough to love her in ways that weren't gentle.

I didn't have that need anymore, but I still needed her. I couldn't handle being alone in the house with nobody but the television. After sixty-four years of her constant presence, the idea of silence and emptiness terrified me. And she counted my pills. She fed me. She remembered everyone's birthdays, and everyone's funerals. Remembered phone numbers and shopping lists, things that floated in my mind like tiny boats in an ocean of fog. She kept all the things I didn't care to remember, and the things I didn't want to forget but forgot anyway. I knew I didn't work alone, without her. Couldn't function. Couldn't survive.

I didn't even know how to work the coffee machine.

The doctor, our doctor, came in through the sliding door, and it clicked shut behind him. His eyes were red with sleeplessness, and I knew he'd come to the hospital just for us. I looked up at the muted television screen, and it said it was 2:43 A.M.

I nodded at him. "Thanks for coming in, Doc."

"Listen," he said, "I don't want to upset you too much. I think she's out of immediate danger."

I let out a lungful of air and wiped at my eyes with my sleeve. No need for him to see tears.

"She's cracked several ribs," he said. "There's nothing we can do about that. It's going to be painful for a couple of weeks. I can give her some pills to take the edge off. She'll want to avoid moving around too much."

"Okay," I said.

"I think she may have bumped her head. Possibly a mild concussion. She could experience some disorientation over the next few days or so. Ordinarily, I'd want to keep her around for observation, but I am pretty concerned that the hospital is not a safe place for the two of you."

"Yeah," I said. "If Steinblatt showed up, we'd be cornered here."

The doctor frowned at me and fidgeted with his clipboard. "Actually, I was concerned that the two of you might be susceptible to infections or communicable diseases you might be exposed to here in the hospital. It's very common among elderly patients, because the immune system weakens with age. So I don't want to keep you here if I can avoid it."

"Right."

"When she wakes up in the morning, she'll be in some pain, but she should be lucid, and if everything looks okay, we can send her home. She'll want to stay in bed for a while, though."

I let go of her hand and laid it gently by her side.

The doctor set down his clipboard. "What I need to talk to you about, Buck, is the significance of a fall event. This is a source of extreme concern when treating a geriatric patient."

"She slipped in the kitchen," I said, squaring my shoulders and raising my defenses against him. "It could happen to anyone. You said yourself, you want to send her home tomorrow."

"Even minor injuries can lead to reduced or painful mobility, and that often sets off a series of cascading health problems. And the first fall dramatically increases the likelihood of a subsequent, more severe fall event within twelve months."

"She's going to be all right, though?" I asked.

"Like John Maynard Keynes said, in the long run, we are all dead."

I rubbed at my eyes again. "Our run is a lot longer than regular people's. We ain't even broke a sweat."

The doctor sighed. "Try to look at this the way I see it. Rose is having difficulties with equilibrium, problems getting around. You're having episodes of confusion. What happened tonight could have been much worse. If Rose had landed hard on her hip, she would have been permanently relegated to a wheelchair. If she had hit her head harder, she could have died."

I snorted. "Lots of bad stuff could have happened to us over the last nine decades."

"I haven't suggested disturbing your self-sufficiency before, because you seem to be very good at managing your pills. But neither you nor Rose could safely function alone, and even together, you have to ask yourself, how much longer can the two of you go on living in that house?"

"We outlived our last three doctors there."

"Jousting with me isn't going to change your situation," he said, staring at me over his wire-rimmed glasses. "There are a number of excellent assisted living facilities that provide quality care and a perfectly tolerable environment."

"I'd rather just cut out the bullshit and move straight into a cemetery plot."

"That is a possible outcome here, a fact we should both be mindful of," said the doctor.

"Fuck you," I told him.

His bottom lip quivered a little. "I want to make sure you heard me, and understood," he said, his voice low and shaky.

"No, I want to make sure you understood me," I said.

"There are certain realities—"

"Fuck you," I repeated.

"No. There are certain realities that you can't shout down, that you can't bully, that you can't beat into submission. I've been putting off discussing this with you, because I knew you would get very upset. But cursing at me won't protect you from having to face your limitations, and the next time there is an event like this, you need to be somewhere with emergency care available. I'm only trying to do what's best for you, Buck. And what's best for Rose."

I stared at him.

"Yeah, I know," he said. "Fuck me. Fuck me." He turned his back on me and left. The glass door slid shut behind him and clicked, softly.

I looked at the last thing I'd written in my notebook. It was something the replacement preacher, Cutter, had said at Kind's memorial service.

"In darkness and solitude, when we are most afraid, we have to face our Enemy."

I woke up the next morning on the vinyl couch in Rose's hospital room. She was awake, sipping orange juice and reading the *Commercial Appeal*.

Tequila and his mother, Fran, were waiting as well.

"I'm ready to get out of here, but I didn't want to interrupt your beauty rest," Rose said to me.

I wiped at my eyes with the bruised backs of my hands.

"If you weren't so damn clumsy, we wouldn't be here in the first place," I told her.

An hour later, we were out of the hospital. Fran had agreed to put Rose up in her house for the next few days, since I wasn't strong enough to help lift my wife in and out of the bed. Tequila would stay with me so I wouldn't be alone. Rose had already told him how to count out my pills and what foods he should not allow me to eat.

We carefully put Rose in the front seat of Fran's little Japanese car, and we folded up the wheelchair the hospital had given her to move around in while she recuperated. Tequila put it in the trunk. I didn't even want to look at it.

Rose and I had not spent a night apart in a couple of decades, and I found the plan a little upsetting, but if she wasn't going to mention that, neither would I. I fastened the seat belt in the backseat. I trusted Fran's driving, sort of, but I would have preferred to be in control.

"If Rose is going to be with you anyway, I think maybe I'll take Billy on that little road trip we've been discussing," I announced.

Fran's expression told me she hadn't heard anything about this, and I was surprised that Tequila had the good sense to refrain from telling her everything.

"Where are you going?" she asked.

"Just up to St. Louis, for a night or two," Tequila said.

"Why?"

"Feh," said Rose. "These two idiots are chasing after leprechauns."

"We think someone Grandpa knows from the war is in a retirement home up there," Tequila explained. "We're going to pay him a little visit."

"Oh, that will be nice," said Fran. "They can catch up on old times." She peered at me in the rearview mirror. "I hope you won't be driving, Buck."

"No, I'll be taking care of that," said Tequila. "But I thought we had some things to do here first, though. We have to visit Grandpa's friend Norris Feely and pay a condolence call on Reverend Kind's widow."

"No, we don't," I said. "Pack a bag. We're going to Missouri after lunch."

I didn't need to explain myself to him. Buttoning up Lawrence Kind's murder wasn't my job. I'd been retired for thirty-five years,

and like Randall Jennings said, they could do police work without me. Tequila had shown me that my methods were antiquated
anyway. These newer folks could do anything I knew how to do,
faster and easier. They could catch the killer on their own, and I
could let them.

If Kind had been killed because of the treasure, if the Enemy
was circling around Heinrich Ziegler, I no longer saw the point
of caution. Death was close, and it smelled like hospital. Like
nursing home. No point in buttressing the walls. No point in bar-
ricading the door. It was coming in anyway.

I lit a cigarette.

Might as well ride out to meet it.

Something I don't want to forget:

Five hours is a long time to spend alone in a car with somebody you don't have much in common with. Eventually they try to talk to you, and that never ends well.

"The last time I was in town before he died, Dad wanted me to ride with him up to Nashville for some business thing he was doing."

I looked out the window at some cows grazing along the side of the highway and avoided Tequila's gaze. He kept talking.

"I asked him if there would be anything for me to do there. He said, not really. He just wanted some company for the trip. I told him to fuck off. I was on spring break."

I turned to look at him. "Why are you telling me this?"

"I just don't know how to forgive myself for that. It's been a few years, and it hasn't gotten easier. I feel stuck, you know?"

"So what do you want? For me to forgive you?"

"No." He paused, drummed his fingers on the steering wheel. "I mean, maybe. I think this is a big part of why I came down here—to find some kind of catharsis, or something. I don't actually care that much about Heinrich Ziegler."

"Yeah, you don't care about anything. And that's what you end up regretting." They always confessed to me, and always thought I'd understand.

Tequila looked wounded for a second. "That's observant of you," he said. "Uncharacteristic, for you to be so on the point."

And then his face went blank and he plugged his Internet telephone into the car radio. He blasted loud music for the rest of the trip. It was weird noise and hard to listen to. But it was a relief not to have to talk anymore.

21

I checked us into an Embassy Suites. I'd stayed in plenty of motels—low-slung, concrete buildings, off the side of the highway, with dingy bathrooms, threadbare sheets, and the smell of road tar filling my nostrils as I fell asleep to the rumbling of passing trucks. I didn't have a problem with squalor. I wallowed in it throughout my professional life. But I didn't go out hunting Nazis every day, so it seemed like an occasion to travel in style.

I thought the Embassy Suites was a swell establishment. Happy hour with snacks every evening at five. Full breakfast in the morning; they'd cook up some eggs the way I liked them, not too hard, not too runny. And the rooms were built around a lovely atrium, overlooking an indoor garden, little ponds with ducks in them and footbridges over them, all inside the hotel. They even had a palm tree.

We arrived around nine at night, too late to visit Meadowcrest Manor. The inmates would have already taken their tranquilizers. So we went to the hotel, dropped our bags in the room, and headed down to the restaurant off the lobby for a late supper.

The place was nearly empty; the only other diner was a dark-haired young woman with glossy pink lips and olive skin, who was listening to music through tiny white earphones and tapping at the keyboard of a portable computer. I noticed her with idle, fleeting interest. Tequila's gaze hung on her a little longer, but we followed the bored-looking waiter to our table and ordered a couple of sodas.

"God, this place is such a middlebrow cliché," Tequila said. "Did you see that ridiculous fucking palm tree?"

I decided not to respond to that. "Your mother said you've been having some romantic troubles."

His eyes shifted, for a moment, in the direction of the woman at the other table.

"She exaggerates," he said. "I was dating a girl for a while, and now we're not dating anymore. These things happen."

"She thinks these things happen to you a lot. And you're alone up there in New York. Your grandmother is concerned about you, too."

He threw me an icy glare. "What do you think, Pop?"

I tugged at my shirt collar. "I don't care one way or the other."

"Then quit giving me shit about it," he said, rising to his feet and leaning toward me.

The pretty girl glanced up from her computer screen at us. Tequila saw her looking and turned very red. He slumped back into his chair.

I looked at the menu. "I think I am going to get me a well-done hamburger," I said.

"Mmm-hmm," he said.

"Look," I said. "I'm sorry about what happened at the casino the other night."

"It's fine," he said.

"I'm glad you've been here," I said. My mouth had that dry,

cottony feeling again. "I wouldn't have found any kind of lead on this thing if you hadn't helped me."

"I'm sick of all this bullshit. I ace college, I blow the LSATs out of the water, I get into a top law school, and it doesn't even matter. I got an internship, a job for the summer, with a big corporate firm. It pays three thousand a week. That's dollars, American. Did you ever make three grand a week?"

"I don't think I ever took home that much in a month."

"Yeah, but I do all that, and what the hell is it worth?"

I set the menu on the table. "About three thousand dollars a week, I reckon. But I haven't had as much schooling as you, so my math could be a little off."

"See, that's just it. Whatever I do, I'm a big damn disappointment."

"Oh, come on. You know that isn't true."

"What do you mean it isn't true?" he said, pounding his fist on the table. "You can't shut up about how much money I'm spending up in New York. I've been listening to your shit about it since I moved there."

I leaned back a little in my seat. "I'm joking because you're so successful. We brag about you to everyone. You know your grandmother and I are always proud of you, no matter what you do. And your mother, too."

"Dad never was."

"You don't really believe that."

"I don't know, Grandpa. I don't know. If you're so damn proud of me, why do you always treat me so coldly?"

I didn't say anything for a long moment while he stared at me, and then finally, quietly, I told him something true.

"You remind me of him."

Tequila opened his mouth to speak and then changed his mind and closed it. I recognized the reaction; when it happened to me, I always blamed my meds, though. He wiped his eyes with his shirtsleeve, sniffed loudly, and then made a show of looking around the restaurant.

"Where is that shit-bird waiter with our sodas?" he growled. "How long does that take? He's got two goddamn tables."

I lit a cigarette, and that brought the waiter scurrying from whatever hole he'd been hiding in.

"I'm glad you came back," I told him. "Somebody forgot to leave an ashtray over here. Can you bring me one when you fetch our drinks?"

He gave me a thin-lipped frown. "We haven't got any ashtrays, sir, because people don't smoke in our restaurant."

I took a long drag on my Lucky Strike, disproving his contention. "That's okay," I said. "I'm easy to please. If you just bring a glass about half-full of water that I can ash in, I'm fine with that."

"You must be having a little trouble following," said the waiter. "This is a smoke-free establishment. You have to put that out."

Tequila jumped to his feet so fast, the chair he'd been sitting in fell over backward. The dark-haired girl took out her white earphones and looked up from her computer screen.

He pointed at me. "Do you know who this man is?" he asked the waiter. His voice was low, from between clenched teeth; unmistakably a challenge.

"It doesn't matter," said the waiter.

"Oh, I think it matters a hell of a lot," Tequila told him. "This man fought in a world war. This man was wounded serving his country. And you're going to tell him he can't have a cigarette, while he waits for you to do whatever it is you were doing instead of getting our fucking sodas?"

"He can have a cigarette if he goes outside," sniffed the waiter.

"I think maybe you and I had better go outside," Tequila told him.

The waiter shrank back, away from Tequila. "Look, this policy is a courtesy to our other customers."

"It doesn't bother me," said the dark-haired girl, who had taken off her headphones. She had a foreign accent that was familiar, but I couldn't quite place it. "I wouldn't mind a cigarette myself."

"Be my guest," I said, holding out my pack of Luckys toward her.

"Neither of you can smoke," the waiter said, mustering as much authority as he could manage with Tequila six inches from his face. "This is a nonsmoking restaurant. That's the rule. I didn't make it."

Tequila and the dark-haired girl were looking at each other, and I knew my grandson was hankering for something other than a hamburger. I decided to remove myself from the situation.

"It doesn't matter," I said. "I'm not that hungry, anyway. I'll head back to the room and forage in the minibar."

"That's fine," said Tequila as he righted the chair he'd knocked over.

The waiter took the opportunity to melt into the scenery. I suspected the sodas would not be forthcoming.

"You should go ahead and stay," I said. "Get whatever you want, and bill it to the room."

He hesitated a moment. "Okay, Grandpa. Thanks."

I looked back once as I shuffled toward the glass elevator. Tequila had moved to the dark-haired girl's table. She was laughing at something he'd said.

22

When I got up to the room, I called Rose from my cell phone.

"What do you want?" she asked.

"Just calling to let you know we made it to St. Louis safely. How is my stumbling sweetheart?"

"I'm doing as well as can be expected, considering I am an injured old woman who has been disgracefully abandoned by her capricious husband. Did you take your pills?"

"Yeah," I assured her.

"Did Billy count them out for you?"

"Yes. He followed your instructions to the letter."

"He's a good boy."

"He's okay. How are things in Memphis?"

"Fran has an age-defying skin cream. I tried it out. It is supposed to make my face ten years younger, so now I have the sumptuous perfumed flesh of a coquettish seventy-five-year-old."

"Well, you know, you always look lovely, even if you are prone to pratfalls."

"Thanks, Buck."

We were quiet on the line for a few moments, and then I cleared my throat to break the silence.

"What are you really doing up there, Buck?" she asked.

"When I spoke to the doctor last night, he wanted us to move to a place where they will take care of us. I don't want to give up the house," I told her.

"What does that have to do with chasing phantom Nazis in St. Louis?"

"He's not a phantom. I think he's here. Tequila does, too."

"But even if he is, what does it matter? How does it change anything?"

I sighed. "I don't know."

If there really was gold, we could maybe afford to hire a full-time nurse to move into the spare bedroom. That would at least let us stay where we were, instead of moving into some facility. But I knew there was no amount of money that could slow or stop the escalating health problems that threatened our independence in the first place.

"Buck, you can't fix everything by dashing off to do something heroic."

"Maybe I can sometimes."

"Maybe sometimes, sweetheart," she conceded. "Oh, and Buck?"

"Yeah."

"Happy birthday."

I grunted. "I don't have birthdays anymore."

I'd known too many guys who lived to make it to their birthday milestones. Seventy-five, eighty, whatever. They'd throw a big party to celebrate their longevity. The whole extended family would come into town. Everyone would toast and sing, and the guest of honor would bask in the attention. And of course, they'd always have an enormous cake with dozens of candles. And three weeks later, they'd all have to schlep back for the funeral. When somebody celebrates like that, he's just begging for the other shoe to drop. I can't tell you how many times Rose has dragged me to the home of some grieving family on a *shiva* call, and all the visitors were standing around eating the dead guy's leftover birthday cake.

"Whether you believe it or not, Buck, you're eighty-eight today. Find a candle and make a wish."

"Nothing doing," I told her.

"You're irascible," she said.

"Yeah. I love you too."

"Sweet dreams, birthday boy."

"Watch your step, precious."

I heard her laugh, and then the phone clicked.

The last birthday party I had was for my eightieth, seven, I guess, eight years ago. Brian and Fran flew in a few out-of-town relatives. Billy was there, of course. He was still in high school. Table for nine. Private room at the back of a restaurant. Cake and ice cream and the birthday song. I didn't know about it in advance, or it wouldn't have happened. I'd like five minutes alone with whoever invented the surprise birthday party.

That night, I got my gun out of its box on the high shelf, loaded it, and put it on the nightstand before I went to bed.

"What are you doing with that, Buck?" Rose had asked me.

"It's for just in case," I told her.

She stared at me over her reading glasses. "What, exactly, do you think is coming for you?"

"I don't know," I told her. "But I'm going to sleep with one eye open, and when I see the bastard, I'm going to blast him full of holes."

"Great," she said. "I've got that to worry about if I get up in the night to use the bathroom."

"You know I'm always careful."

"You have got to accept that there are some things a gun can't protect you from."

And I knew she was right. But I felt more in control when the piece was nearby, so I kept it next to the bed for about six weeks before I removed the cartridges from the cylinder and put the weapon back up in the closet.

It was half-past twelve, and Tequila still hadn't come back to the room.

I pulled out my memory notebook so I could put that story in it, and I put my handgun on the night table, because I still didn't trust birthdays. I also lit a cigarette; one of those was worth at least eighty-eight candles. I took a long drag and made a wish for good health.

23

I was wondering whether to get worried about my grandson sometime after breakfast the next morning, when he came into the suite looking very content and somewhat pleased with himself. I was happy for him, and happy for me as well. I'd had about as much of his pouting and rage as I could handle. He'd needed something to cheer him up, and I was glad he'd found it.

"She's great, Grandpa. I think you'll like her."

"Shut up," I told him. As thrilled as I was by his happiness, this was the day we were slated to get face-to-face with Ziegler, and I was nervous.

I tossed him the keys. "Do you know where we are going?"

"Yeah," he said. "I ran the directions off of MapQuest."

I didn't know what that meant, but I decided to trust him. We got to Ziegler's retirement home at high noon, which seemed appropriate.

The parking lot at Meadowcrest Manor was about the right size to accommodate visitors and staff, but there was no parking for the residents. The part of their lives that involved going places was apparently over.

The home was, more or less, a medium-rise apartment building; someone driving by might have mistaken it for a hotel. Not a nice hotel like the Embassy Suites, but a hotel nonetheless.

There was a big button next to the outside entrance that visitors could press to unlock the front door. From the inside, that door wouldn't open for anyone unless the heavyset colored girl sitting at the front desk buzzed them out. Everyone insisted these places weren't prisons, but, whatever they called it in the brochure, the old folks were locked up. The lobby looked innocuous enough. Area rugs and shapeless residents dozing on shapeless couches or in their wheelchairs.

"Hi there," said the girl behind the desk, a little too cheerily. She was pretty shapeless herself, an impassive mass in a green golf shirt emblazoned with a Meadowcrest monogram. "You thinking about coming to stay with us, sir?"

"Hell, no," I said. "I'm here on a visit. Do I look like one of these people?"

"No," she said. "You older than most of them."

"Yeah, and you could stand to lose some weight," I told her.

Tequila stuffed his hands deep into the pockets of his jeans. "Uh, we're in from out of town, hoping to drop in on someone my grandfather knows from the war," he said. "We think he's a resident here. His name is Henry Winters."

The girl knit her eyebrows. "Never heard of him."

"He's been living here for about fifteen years," Tequila said.

"I been here a while, and I know nearly all of them, but I don't know Henry Winters," she said. "You sure he ain't dead?"

"Is there any way you can check?" Tequila asked.

She punched the name into a computer console on her desk and raised one eyebrow at whatever it told her.

"Oh," she said. "He in dementia. Don't see those folks much. He don't leave, and nobody visits."

"What do you mean, he's in dementia?" I asked.

As it turned out, the Meadowcrest Manor, being a full-service residential community for active seniors, had a special ward, behind another set of locked doors, for the active sort of seniors who couldn't feed themselves, couldn't clean themselves, and couldn't be trusted not to wander out into traffic.

The girl from the desk led us away from the lobby and the main dining room toward a set of plain-looking, locked double doors and punched a code into a numeric keypad on the door frame.

"We can give the code to family members, so they can get in and out when they want," she explained. "It's good for the residents to see the guests coming and going."

"What happens if the inmates learn the code?" I asked.

"Don't matter," she said. "They can't remember it. Can't remember what to do with it."

The lock clicked, and Tequila pushed on the door.

The dementia ward was a smaller, more acute circle of rest home hell nested within Meadowcrest Manor, and it came complete with its own sad little lobby.

Someone had gone to great effort to try to keep this place from looking like a hospital. The walls were festooned with brightly colored paintings, and end tables with potted plants on them were scattered about the public areas. Big windows let in lots of sunlight. But there was no carpeting on the floors, there were wheelchair bumpers running along the walls, and the couches were upholstered with a plastic-looking fabric; easy to wipe clean. The dementia residents managed to look even more pathetic than the people outside. Most of them were wearing baggy sweats or tracksuits, and many were also wearing stains I decided to assume were from food. The girl from the front door handed us off to a nurse in hospital scrubs who supervised the dementia residents, then returned to her station.

"Welcome to our home," said the nurse, aiming a warm smile in my direction. Everyone was happy at Meadowcrest Manor, and it was really irritating. "Are you thinking about coming to stay with us?"

"I'd eat my gun before I'd come to live in a place like this," I said.

"I want to eat something," said a man in a grubby-looking blue sweatshirt, who was sitting on one of the sofas. "When's lunch?"

"You just had lunch twenty minutes ago," the nurse told him.

"No, I didn't," he protested. "I'd remember if I ate."

"Why don't you burp a little bit and see if you don't taste egg salad," she told him.

He let out an exploratory belch and then settled, satisfied, back into his seat.

"So," said the nurse. "You're here to see Mr. Winters?"

"Yeah," I said. "Henry Winters."

"So you're about the same age?" she asked, sizing me up.

I nodded.

"The oldest-old, those around ninety, are one of our fastest-growing demographic segments here at Meadowcrest, and we're experts in meeting your special needs," the nurse told me. Always a sales pitch at these places. "You know, about a third of men your age suffer from significant dementia, but for those who survive an additional five years, that percentage will double. If you're in good health and you anticipate continued longevity, you should make your long-term care plans while you are still able."

"I'm just here for Henry Winters," I told her, through my clenched teeth.

"Well, you know, with Mr. Winters, a judge had to decide

where to put him when he couldn't take care of himself anymore. You don't want to end up like that. Nobody ever comes to visit the poor man. It's so hard to get him out of his room most days. I'm glad you're here. This will be good for him."

"A visit from my grandpa brightens anyone's day," Tequila assured her.

"Okay. Before you see him, though, I have to give you the warnings, since you are first-time visitors to our facility," she said. She looked at me. "I'm sure you've heard most of this before. You probably know quite a few folks who enjoy the kind of lifestyle places like Meadowcrest offer."

I did. Had some friends in assisted living and a few in the locked wards. I knew a fair number of other people who had moved on from such places to smaller, danker quarters. But I usually couldn't stand to visit these hellholes, so when people went away, I didn't see them much after that, unless they had family who would bring them out to the Jewish Community Center. I'd never actually been on a dementia floor before.

"He's not going to recognize you," the nurse explained. "I see him every day, and he can't recognize me. It doesn't mean he's being rude, or that you aren't important to him, but he has a disease in his brain that affects his ability to recall things. Do you understand?"

I nodded.

"Okay, that's good. He's likely to lose track of the conversation, because he can't hang on to new memories, not even stuff that is still happening. It doesn't mean that he's bored with you. He can't follow a television program or read a newspaper article either. This is a terrible disease he is living with, so try not to get frustrated with him. When you upset one of the residents, they forget what happened, but they still know they're upset. When they feel that way, and they don't know why, they get scared."

"We certainly wouldn't want to ruin his afternoon," I said.

She walked us down a hallway, off the main lobby, and stopped in front of a door with a nameplate that said the resident was Henry Winters. Taped on the door, below the knocker, there was a picture of a Thanksgiving turkey made of construction paper. It was the kind of art project a child might make by tracing the outline of his hand and cutting it out with blunt scissors.

"His grandkids?" I asked, gesturing toward it.

The nurse shook her head. "Regular stimulation slows the progress of the disease, so we do arts and crafts on Tuesdays and Thursdays."

Tequila stifled a laugh.

The nurse glared at him over her eyeglasses. She didn't seem to think anything was funny about former SS officers making construction paper hand-turkeys. "Before you go in, let me make sure he's up to receiving visitors," she said.

She knocked, waited a minute, and knocked again.

"Mr. Winters?"

No answer.

"Mr. Winters?"

"Fuck off," said a voice from the room. No trace of a German accent, but I thought I could detect the faintest hint of the sort of strained precision I'd heard before in the voices of Europeans who had almost mastered the American accent. Or maybe it was just my imagination. I glanced at Tequila, and his worried expression told me I wasn't the only one thinking that Heinrich Ziegler couldn't possibly have ended up in Missouri, doing arts and crafts while wearing a stained sweatshirt.

"Our patients can be a little belligerent sometimes," the nurse said.

"Oh, so can this one," said Tequila, playfully pointing a finger at me.

I scowled at him.

"That's why I have a key," said the nurse, and she unlocked the door and threw it open. The ammonia stink of stale piss was so overpowering that I recoiled. Tequila actually took a step back. The nurse didn't react at all; no surprise registered on her face. Dealing with such stenches was evidently part of her job.

The room was dark and the miniblinds on the window were shut, but I could make out the shape of a man curled up on a plastic-covered mattress.

"Uh, incontinence is a major problem in the dementia ward," said the nurse. "These poor folks forget they've got to go until it's too late to get to the toilet. We put disposable absorbent adult undergarments on them, but when the residents are alone in their rooms, a lot of them will strip those off, so we find little surprises in the beds sometimes."

Tequila couldn't quite manage not to laugh at that, but I didn't think it was funny. I was, myself, a slip in the shower away from sporting disposable absorbent adult undergarments while making arts and crafts in a full-service residential community for active seniors.

"Why don't you two wait in the lobby, and I will bring him out when I get him cleaned up and dressed?"

"I'd prefer to speak to him in private," I said. "There are some personal matters I'd like to try to discuss."

She frowned. "Let me clean him up and then I'll come get you," she said.

The door closed behind her and we went back to the lobby.

"Excuse me, gentlemen," said the man on the sofa in the grubby blue sweatshirt. "Do either of you know when they serve lunch here?"

24

As we waited for the nurse to hose the piss off Heinrich Ziegler, I tried to prepare myself to stare into the face of the man who almost killed me. There are things that blur together, rough edges that smooth out, and hard feelings that mellow as I age. The night in September 1944 when Heinrich Ziegler beat me into a coma is not one of them.

We already knew by then that the Germans were in retreat from France. But we'd been hearing it for a while, and we were still waiting to get sprung. Rumor was that we'd retaken Paris in August. But days and then weeks passed, and nobody came to rescue us. Our hopes flagged. If the Germans were really getting beat out there in the world, it just made the ones guarding the prison camp meaner. And Heinrich Ziegler was mean enough to begin with.

Ziegler was not Wehrmacht, regular German army; he was SS, one of Hitler's elite paramilitary storm troopers and a sincere devotee of the ideology of racial superiority. The very idea of a Jewish army lieutenant offended him.

A man called Baruch Schatz couldn't hide his enthnoreligious persuasion behind a Tennessee accent. My father had wanted to name me Grant, but my mother thought that would cause problems for me in the schoolyard, what with so many folks in Memphis still sore about the North's aggression. So instead, I got saddled with a moniker that was perfectly good for my maternal grandfather, who spent his whole life in a nineteenth-century Polish shtetl, but it wasn't what a fellow wanted stamped on his dog tag when he was captured by the Nazis.

There were five Jewish guys in the camp when I arrived, but they weren't too durable, and pretty soon they were out on the compost heap, incubating maggots. My situation was slightly better, but still fairly unpleasant. Whenever Ziegler and his guards needed to vent some anger, they would haul me into their offices for what they called an interrogation. They never asked any questions, but after they finished, Wallace and some of the other guys would have to carry me back to my rack.

When Ziegler called everyone to the parade ground that night, the Nazi brass had just denied his last request for ground support to defend the camp and ordered him to take his men and retreat. I didn't know anything about it. But Ziegler's jaw was clenched, his eyes were red, and a fat, throbbing vein stood out on his forehead.

Rain was falling in sheets from the slate gray sky, plastering his yellow hair to his scalp. He peeled off his wool uniform jacket, with the SS lightning bolts pinned to the collar, and stood barechested in front of the prisoners.

"Do you men want to leave?" he shouted at us in English.

None of us answered. He shouted something in German to his guards, and one of them opened the front gate. The prison was an evacuated village of low-slung houses, which the Germans had surrounded with several rings of barbed-wire fence. The fences weren't what kept us in; they were just an obstacle to slow down any would-be escapees while one of the snipers stationed on the camp's three wooden guard towers lined up a clean rifle shot.

The gate blocked the only clear route out of the prison. It was still covered by one of the towers, but a man running zigzags on foot had about even odds at getting out of rifle range alive, while a guy caught up in a barbed-wire fence was a very easy target. Ziegler usually kept two armed guards on the gate.

Nobody had seriously tried to break out of the camp since we'd arrived. We were unarmed, and the camp was in territory occupied by the enemy. Even if we got out, we had no very good idea where to go. A lot of us had fully embraced the belief that we'd soon be freed, and all of us suspected the guards had some informants among the prisoners, so plotting an escape seemed unnecessary, and unnecessarily dangerous.

But that open gate looked damn tempting.

"If the Jew can get through me, every one of you may go through this gate."

Ziegler wasn't looking for a real fight. He was angry, and he wanted to take it out on somebody. He'd already done plenty to make sure I was in no shape to make much of a contest of it.

Two broken fingers on my right hand were taped with torn strips of bedsheet, but there was no good way to splint up my crushed toes. There were no bandages, either, for the wounds on my back where Ziegler had lashed me, and no antibiotics. My rain-soaked T-shirt was striped with blood and yellow-green pus.

I was so delirious, I barely heard him shouting for me. I was burning with fever, and Wallace was propping me up so I wouldn't fall out of line.

The guards had recently decided they liked strangling me, and the rope burns they'd left on my neck stung when the rain ran over them or when I tried to breathe too deeply. My chest and ribs were mostly purple with bruises.

"How about it, Buuuuuuuck," Ziegler called in some kind of singsong Kraut version of a cowboy-movie accent. "You got any fight left in you?"

Somebody tousled my hair, and somebody else squeezed my arm. It hurt.

"I reckon I got 'nuff," I said.

The tendons in his neck stretched taut beneath his flesh as he sneered at me. "Enough for what?"

"I got . . ." I paused as I stumbled in the mud. "I got 'nuff to fuck you up pretty good."

He was about to kill me, and my vision was swimming. But I figured I was damn well going to take a swing at the bastard. I folded the broken fingers into my fist. My whole arm screamed with pain, but at least it woke me up a little.

The crowd of prisoners parted, and I stepped into the middle of the parade ground. The storm had turned everything to mud, and each time I lifted a foot to take a step, the ground pulled back against my boot.

Ziegler was a real big sumbitch; he had at least six inches on me, and he must have been close to two hundred and forty pounds of hard, sculpted muscle. He looked like the classical god of Jew bashing. I was greenish pale with illness and gaunt from months of near starvation.

I coughed, long and rattling, and then I spat a mouthful of bloody phlegm into the mud. I rested for a moment with my hands on my knees, and then I lifted myself as erect as I could manage.

"I ain't had a smoke in five weeks, and I sure as shit ain't dying without one," I told him. I'd have clawed through a brick wall with my fingernails if there was a pack of Lucky Strikes on the other side.

A few of the men cheered, but Ziegler pounced at me, throwing all of his considerable bulk behind a hard right hook.

"You'll die when I tell you to die," he hissed.

My head was just clear enough and my reflexes were just quick enough that I was able to shift somewhat out of the way, and his hand glanced off the side of my head instead of hitting me full in the face.

While he was off balance from the punch, I threw an arm around his neck. He seemed to know how to box, and he thought that was the same as knowing how to fight. I gouged the thumb of my good hand hard into his eye and showed him the difference.

I heard him yelp, but hanging on to my powerful, writhing foe was almost unbearably painful. I could feel the crust of scabs and hardened goo over my wounds cracking as my flesh twisted with the effort. I ignored my body's protests and tightened my grip on Ziegler's throat, trying to close his windpipe and strangle him unconscious. With one of my arms around his neck and my other hand in his eye, his fists were free to pummel at my belly; but his flailing legs gave him no leverage against the slick, muddy ground, and I held him too close to give him room to throw a proper punch, so there was little force behind the blows. I could have ended it there if he hadn't raked his fingers across my back, ripping everything open from my neck to the crack of my ass.

I howled in agony and dropped him. He scrambled quickly to his feet and hit me twice. One of his punches landed solid, and my head snapped backward. I lunged at him, and we both tumbled to the ground. I managed to yank a boot out of the sucking mud and planted it in the middle of his chest. He flopped back to the ground while I hauled myself upright.

Ziegler shouted in German. I heard a single shot from one of the guard towers, and then I felt an eruption of pain in my right shoulder.

I tried to raise the damaged arm, but it wouldn't respond. It was dead meat, hanging at my side. Blood poured out of me in a hot torrent, and my strength went with it. I collapsed to my knees.

He scrambled to his feet and pivoted around to my defenseless right side.

"Well, shit," I said.

His fist hit my head, and there was nothing I could do about it, so he hit me again. My vision swam, and the ground rushed up to kiss me good night. After that, I don't remember anything until I woke up in the hospital, and by then it was November.

25

What happens to criminals and villains who escape justice and avoid capture is the same thing that happens to everyone else. They get old.

Josef Mengele, the mad doctor of Auschwitz, enjoyed injecting chemicals into children's eyes and killing and dissecting sets of identical twins. American soldiers actually caught him in 1945, but he got some phony release papers and escaped to South America. He stayed ahead of the people chasing him until 1979. Then he went swimming in the ocean one day, something popped in his brain, and he passed out and drowned.

Alois Brunner was Sancho Panza to Adolf Eichmann's Don Quixote. He was personally responsible for sending one hundred and forty thousand people to the gas chambers. Brunner escaped Germany using a bogus Red Cross passport and fled to Syria, where he was hired as a "government adviser" to teach the Arabs how to torture people. The Mossad sent Brunner some letter bombs in 1961 and in 1980, and they blew off a couple of his fingers. Nobody ever caught him, and nobody knows if he's still alive; the last credible sighting of him was in 1992. Probably he's dead, but if he's not, he's a hundred years old, which is pretty much the same thing.

Old age had found Henry Winters as well. The nurse had washed him, dressed him in clean clothes, and propped him in a plastic-covered recliner wedged next to his freshly made bed, but there was little she could have done to conceal his infirmity.

His mouth hung slack on the left side, and his left eye didn't seem to focus on what he was looking at. I'd been around enough to know a stroke victim when I saw one.

But despite the years and the wrinkles and the loose skin, despite the sagging eyelid and the drooling mouth, I recognized Heinrich Ziegler. He had the same cold in those eyes that he had when he clocked me in the skull. The half of his mouth that was still hooked up to his brain curled in the same contemptuous half sneer.

"Is it him?" Tequila asked.

"I think so," I said. I turned to Winters. "Do you know me?" I asked him.

"Never seen you before," he said. "Never seen either of you. Are you the men who took away my house?"

"It's been over sixty years," Tequila said. "How sure are you?"

"If you check his left arm, on the bicep, below the armpit, you should find his blood type tattooed there. The SS guys did that, in case they were brought into the medics unconscious and needed transfusions. We used the tattoos to identify the criminals after the war, when they tried to hide among the civilians."

Winters's left arm hung limp at his side, disabled by the stroke. Tequila grabbed it, roughly, and yanked on the neck hole of Winters's sweatshirt to check for the mark.

"Type A," he said.

That was enough to eliminate all doubt. Henry Winters was

Heinrich Ziegler. I leaned forward and showed him my teeth in a way I thought might be menacing. "Hello, Heinrich."

"My name is Henry," said Ziegler. He seemed more confused than afraid. "Who are you?"

Tequila dropped the arm, and it fell to Ziegler's side. I remembered not being able to lift my own arm after he'd shot me.

"Nice ink you've got. I've got marks from the war, too." I pulled my shirt aside and let him see the concave, fist-sized circle of waxy scar tissue on my shoulder where the bullet that had gone in through my back had blown a cone-shaped exit hole through my shoulder. The gesture pinched the strap of my holster tight against my body, reminding me of what I was carrying.

"I know you from the war?" He squinted his good eye. "No, that can't be right. The men I know from the war are young." He pointed at Tequila. "Maybe I've seen that one."

"The war was sixty-five years ago," I growled at him. "This here is my grandson, Jägermeister."

"Give me a fucking break, Grandpa," Tequila said.

"Sixty-five years?" Ziegler asked. He thought about it, then he looked at his dead arm and registered surprise that it didn't work. He caught himself and reflexively tried to hide his confusion. "So, uh, I know you from the war, then?"

I narrowed my eyes but didn't say anything.

"*Sprechen Sie Deutsch?*" he asked, dropping his voice to a conspiratorial whisper.

I didn't know what I had been expecting to find here, but it wasn't this. "No, I was on the other side," I told him.

"Oh," he said. Then he looked at me again, and for a moment, comprehension seemed to flicker across his face. "So, you've come to kill me, then?" he asked, almost like he wanted it.

It was a good question; there was a time I would have killed him. I became very conscious of the weight of the handgun tucked in my armpit and, for some reason, acutely aware of a corner of my memory notebook that was jabbing into my side.

I had told myself the objective here was to defy death or face it down, to rain justice on a villain even though people like my doctor thought I was feeble and fragile; even though my own grandson thought I had lost my marbles. I wanted to carry a gun and hunt a dangerous fugitive, to put my boot against the throat of something evil one last time. I wanted to prove that Buck Schatz wasn't the kind of person who could be leveled by a "fall event" or "cognitive impairment."

But seeing hard, cruel Heinrich Ziegler crushed by age stripped away that pretense; I was a coward. I'd used my pursuit of this man as an excuse to flee from the things I couldn't handle: Rose's injury and my own mortality. And what a cruel irony that my escape attempt had brought me here, where the Enemy I was afraid to face was wrapped all around, crawling on the walls, oozing from the electrical sockets, waving the wasted shell that used to be Ziegler at me like a rag doll.

"Get something," I said quietly, to myself, as I reached into my jacket to touch the butt of the gun. "Get something persuasive between myself and whatever means to do me harm."

"Grandpa?" Tequila looked at me, his expression blank and questioning; he didn't seem to know what our trip was about. I wasn't sure he knew what he wanted me to do. Even with the tension between us, he trusted implicitly that whatever I chose was the right thing.

Had I come here to kill him? How could I? Looking at him was like staring into a damn mirror.

"How's about it, Heinrich?" I asked. "You got any fight left in you?"

His good eye was aimed at me, but there wasn't any sign of comprehension there. The three of us spent a long, silent moment looking at each other.

"No," I said finally. "No, Heinrich, I'm not going to kill you."

Ziegler wiped drool from his face with the back of his hand. "Who are you people?" he asked, and his right brow knit with confusion. "Can you help me get back to my house?"

"Yeah, uh, so we saw him. I guess we've done what we came here to do," I told Tequila.

He crossed his arms impatiently. "The gold, Grandpa."

"Shit." The gold. That was what I wanted. That was still out there to chase. I wondered how I could have let it slip my mind.

"Tell me about the gold, Ziegler," I growled.

"I want to go home," Ziegler said. He pouted and stuck out his wet chin.

Disgusted, I slapped him hard across the face. "What happened to the gold you swiped in Berlin?"

"Make new friends, but keep the old," said the Nazi. "One is silver, the other's gold."

"Maybe he's talking about Avram Silver," Tequila suggested. "Or the Silver Gulch Casino."

"I don't think so," I said. "It's nonsense. His mind has turned to mush. We won't get anything more out of him."

I looked around. Ziegler's little apartment was maybe two hundred square feet. He had a kitchenette area set off from the sleeping space, with a few cupboards, a steel sink, a small refrigerator, and a microwave oven. He had his plastic-covered bed, his plastic-covered chair, and a chest of drawers. Small closet.

He sure wasn't stashing any treasure here. Was he spending it to live in this place? Had he buried it in some secret spot and forgotten about it? If he had, it was lost. We needed to get some kind of clue here, or this was the end of the trail.

Ziegler rubbed his cheek where I'd slapped him. "Who are you people?" he asked. "Why does my face hurt?"

"Toss the room," I told Tequila.

He scratched his head. "Toss?"

"Search the place, goddamn it. And hurry up; get it done before that nurse comes back."

26

On a high shelf in Ziegler's closet, we found a promising lead: a box containing his financial and health records, assorted correspondence, and an old-looking key in a small brown paper envelope, secreted away among his bank statements.

"What do you think this unlocks?" Tequila asked.

"From the look of it, maybe a safe deposit box," I told him. I turned to the much-diminished god of Jew bashing. "Hey, Ziegler, have you got a safe deposit box?"

"Who are you?"

"If he has any treasures, I'll bet they're in that box," Tequila suggested, ignoring the drooling wreck in the plastic-covered armchair.

"But if he has the gold, what is he doing here?" I asked. "Why wouldn't he be someplace, you know, better?"

"As nursing facilities go, this one is actually fairly upscale," Tequila said. "It seems like that nurse is dedicated to a pretty small cluster of folks. And the residents get private rooms, and the furniture is nice. Some of the places they put people look like army barracks."

If a man needed a half ton of gold to buy care like this, I was in trouble. All I needed at my age was to be sent back to an army barracks.

"There are documents here that look like they convey his house to the Meadowcrest Manor," Tequila said. "If a court had declared him incompetent after his stroke, this place might have been appointed as his guardian, and it would have taken his assets to pay for his care."

"And Meadowcrest got the treasure too?"

"Nope." Tequila grinned and ran his tongue over his teeth. "How would they know about it? Even if Ziegler was cogent enough at some point to remember he had it, telling anyone about it would put him in a pretty bad situation, you know, with the war crimes tribunals. He's been in no condition to retrieve it for over a decade."

Ziegler probably got stuck here after his stroke. He was vulnerable and immobilized, and he couldn't go anywhere on his own, but there would have been nobody he could trust with a secret like that. With no way to get into the box, and no way to find a fence who could convert the gold to cash, the treasure had been left to sit in the bank vault until Ziegler's dementia progressed far enough that he forgot it altogether.

"What are you doing?" Ziegler asked, suddenly upset that Tequila was stuffing papers into his backpack. "I think those things are mine."

I opened a cupboard above the microwave and found a package of Oreo cookies. I gave a couple to the Nazi and he quieted down. Tequila slid the rest of the papers into his backpack and the key into his pocket. He put the empty box back in its place on the top shelf of the closet and closed the door.

The nurse came by a few minutes later and peeked into the room.

"Did you have a nice visit?" she asked, smiling at us. For a moment, my breath caught in my throat, but Ziegler seemed to have already forgotten that we'd searched his home and swiped his stuff.

"It was an experience," I told her.

I left the dementia ward, and Ziegler was still locked away, stuck in a web of dull and disconnected moments. When the girl at the front desk buzzed her button to let us out of the building, I was thrilled to be walking out of that place and not trapped inside like the old Nazi. I told myself that even if we never found any treasure, at least he'd got what he deserved.

27

We returned to the hotel with the pilfered detritus of the life of Heinrich Ziegler and spread it out all over the desk and coffee table in our suite for closer examination. His letters and ledgers mapped out the life he'd led in St. Louis. No wife, no children. In 1954, eight years after he bribed Jim Wallace, he took out a small-business loan to open a jewelry store.

"If he had a fortune in gold, why would he take out a loan?" Tequila asked.

"Can't use crooked money to start a business that needs to look straight," I told him.

I was glad to see he wasn't an expert on everything. I didn't know much about gold or jewelry, but I'd unwound a few money-laundering schemes, and I knew how they worked. A person couldn't buy a house or a luxury car with a suitcase full of cash or a gold brick. Even if the seller accepted that kind of payment, at some point he would try to put that money into a bank and some-body official would start asking questions. Used to be, the IRS would start a federal investigation merely because somebody's lifestyle seemed to exceed his earnings. Fox News said disproportionate consumption now indicated excessive indebtedness more often than secret income, but there were still a fair number of waiters and valets attracting the attention of the federal government for underreporting their gratuities.

Gangsters, of course, famously construct chains of legitimate fronts to filter their illicit funds. But Ziegler had no criminal organization and no support. With a jewelry store he could fence the gold himself, a little at a time, by melting it and recasting it as merchandise.

Necklaces made from mezuzahs and menorahs.

Bracelets made from cherished heirlooms that had been smuggled into concentration camps up somebody's ass.

Diamond engagement rings that used to be a Jew's dental fillings.

He could turn the proceeds of his secret treasure into legitimate income by fixing his books to either overstate expenses or understate revenues. Of course, the amount of gold he could launder this way would necessarily be limited by the amount of jewelry he could sell.

"We figured he must have had eight hundred pounds of gold when he went through Wallace's checkpoint," I said. "How much of that do you think he'd have been able to sell?"

Tequila tapped at his computer keyboard.

"Ingots are nearly pure gold, so their value can be measured by weight," he said, reading from his screen. "But unalloyed gold is soft, much too soft for jewelry. You can scratch the surface of a gold bar with a fingernail. Jewelers use fourteen-karat gold for most commercial purposes. That's about sixty percent pure. For very fine stuff, they might use eighteen-karat, or a seventy-five percent alloy. So we're talking about twelve to fifteen hundred pounds of jewelry he would have had to move through the store over thirty years."

"That sounds like an awful lot," I said.

Tequila's eyes rolled upward as he ran the numbers in his head. "Since he had no supply cost, he could significantly undercut the market price for comparable products if he wanted to move a lot of volume," he said.

I made a dismissive sort of gesture. "I can't imagine he could cook the books enough to hide that much money laundering through a small business. I bet there's a lot of gold left over."

"Our estimates rely on some massive assumptions, though," Tequila said. "We're just guessing about how much gold he had when he met Wallace. And Ziegler probably paid a lot of bribes to get out of Europe. He might have had to abandon some or all of it someplace between Berlin and St. Louis. Gold is very heavy, and he was on the run."

"I think the fact that he opened a jewelry store gives us a good reason to think he had a pretty big treasure left when he settled here."

Tequila nodded. "I hope so."

"So, where do you think he stashed it?" I asked.

"I might have an idea about that," he said, seeming pleased with himself.

Every bank document we had found in Ziegler's room indicated that he had kept all his accounts with the same SunTrust branch bank. Looked like he'd gotten his home mortgage there, too, and he had a couple of certificates of deposits and a small money market account. In other words, he handled all of his financial business out of the same place.

Tequila had spotted an automatic debit that appeared on each January bank statement. He thought this was the fee for a safe deposit box.

"I'm not sure," I said. "If I had some secret treasure, I'd put it somewhere I didn't do my regular banking."

It seemed like odd behavior for a man on the run to have all of his business at one bank. Ziegler must have been either too dumb to cover his tracks or smart enough to figure out that nobody was chasing him.

Tequila shuffled through the papers. "Keeping the box at a different bank would be more suspicious if anyone ever went snooping in his mail and saw the bills." He paused. "Grandpa, if we find this gold, where are we going to hide it? Whether they killed Kind or not, Feely and Pratt are going to be looking for a piece of it, and Steinblatt might be trouble as well."

"Before we figure out what to do with our loot, I suppose we ought to work out how we are going to rob that bank," I told him.

"Rob the bank?" He stood up and ran a hand through his shaggy hair. "We have the key to the box. We just have to go in there and ask them to let us open it."

I smiled at him. It was easy for people who had no idea what they were talking about to be condescending. "Have you ever been in a bank vault?" I asked him. "Have you ever seen a safe deposit box?"

His blank stare answered my question.

"I guess you can't tour a bank vault on the Internet," I said, feeling satisfied.

"You probably can, actually."

"Shut up, Tequila."

He was quiet for a moment. "Okay, then, Pop, what do we need to get into a safe deposit box?"

The appeal of a safe deposit box is discretion, not security. Whether an object is kept in the box or in the home, its protection against loss or destruction is the same: it's covered by a homeowner's insurance policy. Putting valuables in a bank vault merely assures that nobody but the owner is allowed to see them.

"They won't let anyone open a safe deposit box except for the guy who bought the box. Having the key is not good enough. You have to physically present the box holder."

"So you want us to break Ziegler out of Meadowcrest to open this thing up?"

I coughed. "Yeah. That seems like a good idea."

His mouth fell open. "Seriously?"

"No."

He clenched his slack-hanging jaw and rearranged his face into a pensive frown. "So what are we going to do, then?"

I pulled a blue Social Security card and a red-and-white Medicare card out of my pocket, each with the name "Henry Winters" printed on them. I'd swiped them from Ziegler's dresser while Tequila had been going through the closet. As an older guy myself, it felt profoundly wrong to swipe somebody's Medicare card. But Winters was, after all, Heinrich Ziegler, and these identification documents were bogus, or at least they were fraudulently obtained. I wiggled the cards at Tequila.

"I figure I can be Henry Winters," I said.

He didn't look impressed. "How are you going to make that work?"

"One thing I might try is friendly misdirection and gentle persuasion. But if that fails, I'm going to scream like a maniac. That scares the shit out of people. They worry that if I get too worked up, I might have a heart attack."

"This sounds like it will be embarrassing," Tequila said.

"Let's hope it's embarrassing enough. The more awkward the situation is, the less clearly they'll think it through."

Tequila looked at the Social Security card for a minute and then frowned at me. "Do you really think you can pull this off?"

"I spent thirty years tricking people into confessing to murder," I told him. "This can't be much harder."

That made him smile a little. "Want to lay odds on how likely it is we'll find gold in there?"

"Of course there's gold in there," I said. "What else would a Nazi fugitive keep in his safe deposit box?" We were quiet for long enough to ponder the possibility that we were gearing up to do something insane.

When that got too uncomfortable to bear, Tequila said, "Do you want to join me and Yael for dinner tonight?"

I could think of things less appealing than watching my grandson nuzzle some woman he'd just met. But not many.

"That's the dark-haired girl from the restaurant?"

"Yeah. She's here looking at Washington University for her graduate program, but if she gets off the wait list, she might go to Columbia."

"That's nice. What kind of name is Yael?"

"It's Hebrew."

I moved the gunk in my throat around with a long, rattling cough. "That's what I thought," I said. "So she's Israeli?"

"Yeah. Why?"

"Doesn't that throw up a few red flags for you? You know, with Avram Silver and Yitzchak Steinblatt maybe chasing us?"

Tequila's mouth dropped open again. "She's not a spy, Grandpa."

"She liked you, right away. That doesn't make you suspicious? You're not very likable. I've known you since you were born, and I don't like you."

He fiddled with the band on his watch. "She was already here at the hotel when we arrived. We didn't have a reservation or anything."

"Silver has known all along that Ziegler was in St. Louis. It would have been an easy trick for his people to get here ahead of us. And don't underestimate the Mossad."

"She's not Mossad, Grandpa. She's a graduate student. Why

don't you join us for dinner and you'll see there's no reason to be suspicious."

I flipped open the cover of my memory notebook and saw, on that first page, what the doctor had told me.

"Paranoia is an early symptom of dementia in the elderly," I whispered, almost to myself.

"Exactly," Tequila said.

"All right." I conceded the point. Sometimes things were co-incidental. There were lots of Israelis around.

28

Almost every Jew, even the really liberal ones, has at least a little bit of affection for the state of Israel. It symbolizes the resolve of the Jewish people to walk away from the second-class minority status that had stoked the historic crimes like the Holocaust. Israel is also a shelter of last resort in the very plausible event of future persecution. And it represents the Zionist conviction that protection against the forces that conspired to destroy us should be obtained by Jewish sovereignty and force of arms rather than through begging or buying protection from ruling majority regimes.

It is a nation of people, like my great-grandfather Herschel, who are sick of being burned and want to hold the torch.

Where American Jews have become a soft-handed class of dentists and accountants and film professors, the Israelis are battle-hardened, sand-blasted warriors. The country's policy of mandatory conscription, for women as well as for men, meant every sabra, every native-born Israeli, knew how drive a Jeep off-road and fire a rifle.

And to someone like Tequila, a pretty Israeli girl was all that history and all that symbolism wrapped in a tight little package that he could screw. And Yael was exotic: dark and hard and the complete antithesis of the milk-fed little princesses he usually dated, yet entirely kosher.

Under normal circumstances, I'd have been supportive of this kind of pursuit. Romance kept him from sulking all the damn time, Rose wanted to be around to see some great-grandchildren, and, really, I didn't like to see him unhappy. But circumstances weren't normal.

Still, Tequila knew what I knew about Avram Silver and his vaguely described "good job" with the Israeli government. He'd seen Yitzchak Steinblatt dodge our questions about standing me up at the Jewish Community Center.

Tequila was smart, and he'd had lots of schooling. He could rely on his brain to do what it was supposed to and not lose track of the objective or flood his spinal column with paranoid whispers. I had mild cognitive impairment. He trusted his own judgment more than he trusted mine, and I didn't trust either of us. If he thought Yael was safe, there was nothing I could say to change his mind.

The restaurant in the hotel was pretty crummy, so Tequila drove us to an Olive Garden we'd spotted from the highway. There was no-smoking permitted inside; these chain restaurants all seemed to be made out of cardboard, and I guessed they were worried a cigarette might burn the place down. I decided not to make a big deal about it. As we slid into the booth, Yael smiled at me. Her teeth were straight and white, her skin was smooth and brown, and her eyes were ringed by thick, dark lashes. Her hair hung loose in cascading curls. Tequila swooned stupidly every time she looked at him.

"So, I understand you are a soldier?" she asked me.

"I was, a long time ago," I said.

She wrinkled her forehead. "If you are a soldier, you are always a soldier."

That's the kind of thing that young people think is true. Everything seems permanent to people who are firm and strong and don't have to go to funerals all the time.

"No. I used to be a soldier, but I'm not anymore."

Used to be a soldier. Used to be a police detective. Used to be a father.

"What you did is forever," she said. "A distinguished accomplishment. What you did reshaped the world."

And then the world passed me by. Just like my lawn; I took care of it for so many years, and then, one day, I didn't anymore. And the grass kept right on turning green in the springtime.

I considered telling her about the lawn and the Guatamalan, and about the bustling Criminal Justice Center in downtown Memphis, and the business-as-usual cops and techs buzzing around Lawrence Kind's body. I spent thirty years locking up killers. And while I was doing it, I really believed I was the last bulwark against some sort of social breakdown. But then one day, I stopped. And even though all those years had passed, nothing was any different, except, like Jennings had pointed out, the city kept setting new records for violent crime.

I thought about telling Yael what distinguished accomplishment was worth on the day I buried my son; on the day people started telling me to think about not driving anymore; on the day I looked across my breakfast table at an arrogant young man who had my face but didn't understand my values.

I cleared my throat and fiddled with my napkin, and I didn't tell her anything.

"I have seen the numbers on my grandmother's arm, and I have seen her crying in her sleep," Yael said. "We must always be fighters, so we will never again be victims."

"Yael came to the United States for college at the University of Pennsylvania," Tequila told me.

"And then I went back, to serve in the army," Yael said.

"You could have stayed over here, and not gone into the service?" I asked.

"I never would have done such a thing."

I snorted.

"I considered volunteering, after the World Trade Center," Tequila said.

"Why didn't you?" Yael asked.

"Because I told him he was out of his goddamn mind," I said. "Ain't no reason to volunteer so you can go run around in some desert and maybe step on a IUD."

"IED," Tequila said.

I glared at him. "What?"

"Improvised explosive device. IED."

I scratched at my scalp. "What did I say?"

"Something different," Tequila told me. Then we were quiet for a moment, and he turned to Yael. "My father passed away. I needed to be here, for my family."

"Your son?" Yael asked me.

I nodded.

Tequila leaned in close to Yael, and I could tell he had his hand on her thigh under the table.

"These terrorists and insurgents, though, they have no real army," Yael said. "No means to pose a real threat to America. No tanks and no ships. They can destroy a building, maybe, but they cannot create for you the danger we face where I come from. We are surrounded by hostiles. Here, you must stay for your family, but in Israel, it is for our families that we must fight." She looked up at me. "To think this is crazy, you must not know what it means to face a constant existential threat."

"Constant existential threat?" I laughed a little. "Honey, I'm eighty-eight years old. If the guy who makes my sandwich forgets to wash his hands, there's an existential threat."

The waiter showed up, and I ordered the noodles with the red gravy.

Something I saw on television that I don't want to forget:

I found a panel discussion on AMC about depictions of aging in film, to go with a Clint Eastwood marathon they were running. Tequila was off someplace with his suspicious Israeli girl, and I didn't expect to see him again until morning.

"We have a rapidly aging society. Baby boomers are becoming senior citizens," said the television host. "Why don't we see more elderly characters in the movies?"

The camera cut to a bearded NYU film professor, the same guy who had been talking about Nazis the night Rose got hurt. I had been seeing that guy on television a lot lately. Probably had a book out; I reminded myself to remember not to read it.

"There's a very small set of stories to be told about older characters," the professor explained. "They don't begin new romantic relationships. They aren't usually wrapped up in international intrigue. They live lives of routine, and that is not drama. Where you are going to find them as protagonists is in stories about continuity, about passing knowledge on to a younger generation, and about death."

"And that's all that's out there?" the host asked.

"Those are pretty powerful themes. Any movie you are going to see where an older character takes a younger character under his wing is about the younger man coming into his own as the old guy passes off the stage. These characters are going to go on some kind of literal or metaphorical journey together, they'll gain respect for each other along the way, and at the end, the younger character is equipped to continue alone."

The host rubbed at some kind of rash on his neck. As a regular watcher of talking heads on cable, I got to see some ugly, ugly people. "And the older man always dies?" he asked.

The professor nodded. "Everybody dies. Old people are just going to die sooner than the rest of us. The elderly in our cultural narratives signify mortality, either the annihilation of the self, or the preservation of wisdom by passing it on. This character's story arc is a journey toward death, and toward finding his peace with that inevitability."

"Always?" asked the host.

The professor stroked his beard diffidently. "Well, sometimes, at the end of one of these, the old guy learns something that reinvigorates him, and he throws away his walker and starts dancing or does something otherwise implausible, given the character's physical limitations. And that is fine, I guess, in *Willy Wonka*. But, I mean, let's not traffic in denial here."

29

The SunTrust branch where we thought we'd find Ziegler's safe deposit box was in a big old-fashioned bank building, with marble steps and Corinthian columns in front and, most likely, a secure vault dug into the basement. We certainly weren't going to be able to get into that vault by force or any other coercive means, so our plan was to confuse the people in the bank enough that they wouldn't question me when I claimed to be Henry Winters.

The way I figured, getting somebody to let me into a bank vault would be a pretty similar process to getting someone to confess to a crime or inform on a friend. It would just take a little psychology. Confidence men called this play "the Good Samaritan." Police called it "the good-cop, bad-cop." But by whatever name, it was always the same shtick. One belligerent antagonist would unsettle and threaten the subject. A second conspirator would present himself as an ally or rescuer. The idea was to use this staged situation to trick the patsy into trusting the "Good Samaritan" or "good cop."

Tequila and I had gone over the plan the night before, at the hotel, and rehashed it again in our parking space across from the bank as I sipped coffee and tried to steel my nerves.

"Is this going to work?" he asked me.

"It's the best idea I've got," I told him as I climbed out of the passenger side of my Buick. For this little adventure, my .357 would be waiting in the car; I wasn't quite dumb enough to carry a heater into a bank, even though I felt sort of naked without it. I left my coffee cup on the dash to keep it company. The memory notebook and the Lucky Strikes went in with me.

In our scheme, I was the bad cop, so I barreled through the bank's revolving door wearing one of Tequila's ratty sweatshirts, with my eyeballs bugged out of my head, and I filled the place with noise, up to the high-arched ceilings.

"I want my goddamn safe deposit box," I shouted at no one in particular. "Where are you hiding it?"

I paused my tantrum for a moment, to light a cigarette.

A worried-looking teller with short hair and delicate hands scurried up to help me. "Sir, you can't smoke in here."

I glared at him.

"I can't smoke in here?" It was more of a howl than a question.

"You have to take that outside."

I gave that a long moment to make sure everyone in the bank was looking at me, and then I opened up both barrels on the poor kid.

"You'd better get yourself some manners," I bellowed. "I bled on the beaches of goddamn Normandy, and you're going to put me out on the sidewalk like a dog that's fixin' to piss on the rug? Where'd they teach you how to act?"

He swallowed, hard. "Sir, this is a nonsmoking area."

I emptied my sooty lungs, blowing out a cloud of smoke and a fine mist of phlegm right in his face. "Either get me my safe deposit box, or get out of my sight."

Tequila was at my side; he had come in quietly behind me. He had a couple of wheeled duffel bags slung over one shoulder.

"Grandpa, that's not the way we speak to people." He laid a hand on my shoulder and physically interposed himself between me and the teller. "You should apologize to this gentleman."

"I will not."

He stuffed his hands in his pockets and sighed at the teller. "We're really very sorry." He was a good enough liar to seem earnest if he wanted to, and the teller seemed to be buying his shtick.

"We are not sorry. And you've got yourself a lot of balls to be apologizing for me, kid. You are a dirty little thief, and you're here to steal my things."

He seemed flummoxed, but just for a second. "Grandpa," he said sternly, "we can deal with our problems without airing them in public."

"Eat shit," I shouted at him. It's helpful for the subject and the good cop to appear to be similarly aggrieved and abused by the bad cop. I turned to the teller and jabbed my lit cigarette close to his face. "I want my box. These crooks are trying to get at what's in it, and I aim to see it's safe from them."

"Our vault is among the most secure—"

"Stuff it, you little turd. Those are my things, and I'm taking them out of here." I thrust Ziegler's key at him.

"Grandpa, give me a moment, and I promise, we'll let you see your things," Tequila said. He took the teller by the arm, and the two men took a few steps away and began whispering to each other.

I decided to stay quiet; if it looked like Tequila could keep me under control, the bank teller would defer to him. I stuffed my hands in the front pocket of the sweatshirt and tried to listen to their conversation. Normally, my hearing is a little unreliable, but in the marble-floored lobby, I could pick up most of what they were saying pretty well.

"Look, this is a bank," said the teller. "We can't have him behaving like this in here. I'm going to have to get security."

Tequila's expression turned sad and pained. "He's not really like this. He's always been a sweet and generous man. This is the disease making him act out, and I hope you can have some sympathy for our situation."

"Yes, but we have got to do business in here. He's frightening our other customers."

"His brain isn't working the way it's supposed to. He is suffering from senile dementia, and it's just horrible. He's frightened and paranoid all the time, and he can't understand what's happening to him."

"Look, I'm sorry. That must be very difficult for your family."

"What you've got to understand is that, as aggressive as he seems, he's very fragile. If you have your security guys put their hands on him, he could get hurt."

"I mean, I certainly don't want that to happen."

Tequila leaned toward the teller. "All kinds of liability issues for you. Problems you don't need." I smiled a little. My grandson was kind of good at this game. "Look," he said. "I'm sure if we let him see his things, he'll quiet down."

After a moment's hesitation, the teller nodded. "We have no problem at all letting a customer access his safe deposit box."

"Then we're on the same page here," Tequila said.

He walked back over to me. "Grandpa, they will let you look at your box, as long as you don't make a lot of noise."

"I'll need you to sign a signature card, to verify your identity," the teller told me.

I stuck my cigarette in my mouth, took a pen from him, and scrawled an illegible mark on the card.

He looked at the card and then looked back at me. His eyes were wide with fear, and beads of sweat dotted his forehead. "Sir, this signature doesn't look like the one on the original card," he said.

"Are you mocking my Parkinson's, you insensitive little shit?" I pointed an accusing finger at him, making my arm shake more than it might ordinarily.

Tequila grabbed my arm and scolded me. "You need to relax, and watch your language."

I turned to him. "You told your lawyer to make them say my signature was wrong, didn't you? You all want to convince everyone I'm cuckoo, so you can stow me in some facility and take everything. Well, it's not going to work. Whatever is in that box goes with me. I'll have it buried with me before I let you get your dirty mitts on it."

The teller shrank back from me. "Sir, I can't let you into a safe deposit box without proof that you are the owner."

"I'm so sorry," Tequila said to him. "He doesn't really know what he's doing. But when he gets into these moods, he doesn't hear reason. We just want to make sure he's taken care of."

"Taken care of right into the graveyard. I'm on to you," I shouted.

"If you let him into his box, I'm sure he'll calm down," Tequila told the teller.

"I can't do that if the signature card doesn't match."

Tequila sighed. "Look, everyone knows my grandfather. How many ninety-year-old guys have safe deposit boxes here?"

"I don't know him. Does he have some kind of identification?"

Tequila showed the teller Ziegler's Social Security and Medicare cards.

"No driver's license? No passport?"

"Not that I know of," Tequila told him. "He hasn't driven a car or traveled abroad in, like, twenty years."

"How can I let you access this box? You can't match the signature card. You can't even provide photo identification. You can't prove he is who he says he is."

Tequila sighed. "We have the key, and government-issued identification documents. And the signature would match if his hands didn't shake so much."

"Assholes," I shouted at both of them.

"Look," said Tequila. "Nobody has been into this safe deposit box in years. I didn't even know it existed until he started yelling about it a few days ago. But whatever is in there is suddenly very important to him."

"These are the policies," said the teller. "I have to follow the rules here, or I will get in very serious trouble."

"And I understand that. But you say he can't prove who he is, and that's exactly accurate. This man is losing his identity. He's fighting as hard as he can to hang on to his past, to keep his grip on his memories, and that's why he's here today." Tears glistened in his eyes. He snuffled and rubbed at his face with his fingers. "I'm not asking you to do anything shady, or crooked or wrong. But I know you don't really doubt that man right there is Henry Winters. All I'm asking is that you apply your policy with a little common sense and compassion."

The teller hesitated. "I'll have to get an approval from my manager."

"Thank you so much," said Tequila. "We appreciate it."

I spent the next few minutes shouting at my grandson while the teller consulted with his boss. He came back with the manager and two uniformed security guards in tow.

"You gentlemen need to leave the premises," said the manager.

He was short, about Tequila's height, and doughy, with a receded jaw that barely demarcated the boundary between his head and his neck.

"I'm sure we can discuss this reasonably," Tequila said.

"We've discussed it already," said the teller, crossing his arms.

"If we are unsatisfied with the proof you supply to show that you are the owner of a safe deposit box, we cannot provide you with access to it," the manager said. "We have procedures in place to protect people who follow the rules."

This was, of course, false. The procedures protected the bank and the bank's interest in the contents of those boxes.

Nobody ever got a letter from a bank informing them that the bill on a safe deposit box was in arrears, when the box owners died without telling their families about their boxes, the banks waited until the property could be deemed legally abandoned, at which point the banks were entitled to crack open the boxes and sell any valuables at auction.

"You're trying to steal my things," I shouted at him. I meant it, too.

"You need to go, unless you prefer to have these men escort you out," the manager told me.

I sighed sadly. We'd struck out.

30

I thought of the .357, tucked in the glove compartment out in the car, but I knew there was no way we could take the treasure by force. I moved slowly, even when I wasn't carrying bags of gold. And even if I'd been young and fit, the rate of arrest and conviction for bank robbers was damn near a hundred percent; it was the single stupidest crime anyone could commit.

The bank's front door would be the only exit, and the whole place was certainly wired with alarms and cameras. If we got out of the building and made it onto the highway somehow, we couldn't get far before we'd get pulled over or pinned by a roadblock. Force was not an option. If I couldn't convince these people I owned Ziegler's safe deposit box, whatever treasure the Nazi had stashed would stay in the vault.

I would go home and think about moving with Rose into a place like Meadowcrest, for our safety. I couldn't risk her being injured in another "fall event." Eventually, I'd get put into a ward with a locked door and a plastic cover on the mattress, and the nurses there would swaddle me in absorbent disposable adult undergarments, and after that, there wouldn't be much else.

One of the security guards stepped forward and put a hand on my shoulder. Defeated, I started to head back out to the car.

"Take your goddamn hand off him," Tequila said. I guessed he was done being the good cop, not that it mattered anymore.

I turned around to tell him to give it up, and I saw that Tequila was pointing something silver and shiny at the bank manager. For a second, terror flooded my synapses. It looked as though he'd brought the gun in with him. But then the thing in his hand started talking.

"What is going on there?" demanded Tequila's Internet phone. This hadn't been part of the plan. I had no idea what my grandson was doing or who was on the other end of the call.

"These people at the bank won't let us into Grandpa's safe deposit box, and they are trying to throw us out," Tequila told the phone. All the softness had fallen out of his face. His eyes were no longer pleading; they'd gone cold. Almost like Ziegler's.

"Jesus Christ. Am I going to have to come down and sort things out?" the phone asked.

"Well, shit, Counselor," Tequila said, "I sure hope not." He gave an exaggerated shrug for the benefit of the security guards. "My attorney," he explained to them, gesturing at the device.

"Who is in charge over there?" said the phone.

"Uh, I am," stammered the bank manager.

"I have no idea who's talking, so that's no help to me," hissed the voice on the line.

"I, uh . . ." The bank manager paused. "What?"

"Who are you?" asked the voice on the phone, biting off each word as if he were speaking to a very stupid child.

"I'm assistant branch manager Alan Patterson."

"Well, I'll tell you something, assistant branch manager Alan

Patterson. If I have to come down there, your name is going to be Shit. As a matter of fact, I am going to go ahead and just call you Shit, because assistant branch manager Albert whatever-the-fuck-your-name-is requires me to remember way too much about somebody insignificant."

"I don't know who you are, but you can't talk to me like that," said Patterson, trying to find his backbone.

"I'll bet he's bloated, like some kind of bloodsucking insect," said the phone. "A chubby guy with a three-inch penis, on a power trip."

"Yeah, he's kind of bloated," Tequila said. "Chinless, too."

"He sounds chinless," the phone agreed.

One of the security guards giggled a little, which seemed to anger bloated, chinless assistant branch manager Alan Patterson. "Is there a point to this?" he growled at Tequila.

"Here's a point," said the phone. "Have you ever heard of a tort called conversion? That means you took things that don't belong to you and you have to pay for the harm you did. Have you ever heard of a tort called intentional infliction of emotional distress? That means a fragile old man walked into your bank, and you fucked with him, and you have to pay for the harm you did. And if that's not enough, we can probably come up with various age discrimination claims under state and federal law. Those have statutory damages, so you'll really have to pay."

"Look, there's no need for that," stammered the branch manager. Beads of sweat were popping out of his forehead.

"Did that chinless piece of shit just interrupt me?" asked the phone.

"I, uh, I am sorry," said Patterson.

"Nobody cares if you're sorry. Shut up," the phone told him. "Now, your bank has insurance, for the amply foreseeable circumstance in which you are stupid or negligent and injure your customers. For example, if that senile old man you're trying to keep out of his safe deposit box were somehow George-fucking-Clooney, dropping some *Ocean's Eleven* shit on your bank, any liability you have for negligence in allowing him access to a safe deposit box would be covered. But your insurer will not cover intentional torts, such as the aforementioned conversion or intentional infliction of emotional distress. Do you understand what that means?"

The bank manager looked at Tequila, hoping for a way out.

"Don't look at me," Tequila told him. "Answer the question."

"I'm not sure what that means," said Patterson, his voice low and hoarse.

"It means if you don't let that man see his stuff, I will sue you. I will take your house," the phone shrieked. "If you have any money saved to send your chinless kids to college, I will take that. You will be eating cat food when I am done with you. Actually, what you're doing may also have criminal implications. That means you will be eating prison food. I've got a buddy who works for the D.A.'s office. Maybe I'll play nine holes with him this afternoon and we can discuss all the things the law will let us do to a guy who steals from the elderly."

"I don't—," Patterson said. It came out as a strangled wheeze. "I didn't."

"I don't think that will be necessary," Tequila said, his voice soft and soothing. "I think Mr. Patterson will listen to reason."

Patterson looked to the two security guards, who had physically backed away from him. He looked over at the teller, who had retreated back to his position behind the counter. Everyone in the bank was looking at us; the chatter of morning commerce had given way to tomblike silence.

A tear rolled down Patterson's chubby cheek, over the slight protrusion of his jawline, and down his neck to dampen his shirt collar.

"Gentlemen," the branch manager said to his guards, "the signature card looks like a pretty clear match to me. Let's get Mr. Winters his safe deposit box from the vault."

"That's what I thought," said the phone.

31

The two security guards ushered me and Tequila into a small office where we could examine the lockbox.

"It took all three of us to lift this thing," Patterson said. "It's really heavy. What on earth are you keeping here?"

"None of your business," I told him. "Get out."

Patterson used his key on one of the two locks on the safe deposit box and then left us alone with it.

"What are you waiting for?" Tequila asked. "Open it up."

I drummed my fingers on the lid of the box. "What the hell was that with the telephone?" I asked him. "That wasn't part of the plan."

"Deus ex machina," Tequila said, laughing. "God from the machine." He waved the Internet phone at me.

"Don't bullshit me," I growled.

"That was Pete, my roommate. I figured we needed a fallback option."

"We were supposed to run the good-cop, bad-cop," I said. "We had a plan."

"And my backup was for when your plan didn't work," he told me.

I scowled at him. "Does Pete's mother know he has a mouth like that?"

"Open the goddamn box, Grandpa."

"Smartass," I said as I turned my key in the lock. The safe deposit box popped open. It contained eight gold bars, each about eight inches by three inches, stamped with swastikas.

I let out a low whistle. Tequila just stared at it, saucer-eyed.

"I can't believe there's really a treasure," said Tequila. "I wanted to find it, but, deep down, I suspected it was sort of, you know, a MacGuffin."

"You should have gone earlier," I said. "They stop serving breakfast at half-past ten."

"Not a McMuffin, Grandpa. I thought the gold was, like, psychological, or symbolic, or something."

"You think I would schlep halfway across the country for imaginary gold?"

"I mean, I knew you thought there was gold, but I thought that the gold represented your desire for meaning at a point in your life when you're facing infirmity and still trying to make sense of what you saw in the war, and trying to rationalize what happened to Dad."

I cocked one eyebrow. "What?"

"You know, like, you have to go on the quest, because, deep down, you're a romantic. But I thought we'd never find anything, because there isn't ultimately any sense to be made of it."

I snorted. "That's the dumbest thing I've ever heard. Gold is gold, and there it is."

He crossed his arms, and annoyance flickered across his features.

"I guess I felt the same way, kind of," I said. "I didn't think there was any way this was ever going to work out for us."

I picked up a gold brick. It was small, a little bigger than a candy bar, and it fit easily in my hand. It was heavy, though. I guessed it weighed somewhere around twenty-five pounds.

"But it's real, and it's here, and now, it's ours," I said. "So, let's bag it up and see if we can haul it out of here without getting arrested."

32

Gold bars never looked too heavy in the movies; seemed like people on television were always throwing them at each other and stuffing them in jacket pockets.

But carrying the real ones around was a little tougher. Four ingots, half our haul, stacked together, took up about as much space as a hardcover book but weighed as much as a set of encyclopedias. So the rolling bags had been a good idea.

We emptied the box—I grunted with exertion each time I lifted a bar—and gave it back to the teller, locked. He must have noticed it was two hundred pounds lighter, but it was none of his business.

I was relieved but not surprised by his lack of comment; the bank's service to a box renter was to keep other people from ever looking at the box's contents. Whatever went in or out of the box was the owner's affair, not the bank's. They'd accepted me as the owner, so now they would look the other way.

It took Tequila two trips to drag the duffel bags through the lobby, wheels squeaking under the weight of the cargo. In the parking lot, I helped him heave the bags into the trunk of my Buick. Exhausted from the effort, he leaned, gasping for air, against the side of the car.

"How much do you think that weighs?" he asked.

"Maybe two hundred pounds, total," I told him. "Possibly more."

He wiggled his eyebrows at me and then slid with a grunt into the driver's seat. I climbed into the car as well.

As the Buick rumbled out of the parking lot, it looked like we had gotten away clean: no sirens or flashing lights on the horizon, nobody rushing out of the bank behind us.

We'd be prominent players on their security videos for the day, between the scene we'd made getting into the box and dragging the heavy bags through the lobby, but that was a worthwhile risk, considering the reward.

"There's sixteen ounces in a pound," Tequila said. "And gold is trading for around nine hundred and fifty dollars an ounce on commodities markets."

"So that's a pretty decent haul?"

"A little over three million dollars, although it may be less if we have to sell it to some sort of shady fence," he said. "Still, not a bad morning's work."

I glanced in the rearview. "We may not be done working yet," I told him. "I think we've made a friend."

Following a few car lengths back was a black Chevrolet sedan with dark windows. He'd picked us up as we'd pulled away from the bank, and he had been behind us since.

"Are you sure?" Tequila asked.

"I think I saw him yesterday as well." The traffic light up ahead was about to change. "Quick, take the left."

"But I'm using MapQuest directions. I'll get lost."

"Shut up and take the damn turn."

We fishtailed through the intersection, going pretty fast, just as the light changed from yellow to red. My seat belt yanked itself taut across my chest as my weight shifted against the momentum of the car, and I knew I would be bruised later. The sedan ran the red light. Somebody coming across had to slam his brakes to avoid hitting the Chevy, and we heard a chorus of protesting car horns behind us.

"We've got ourselves a tail all right," I said.

Tequila glanced at me nervously. "Should I call the police?"

I snorted. "With three million dollars' worth of stolen gold in the trunk? Yeah, that's a good idea. Let's do that."

"Okay, so what am I supposed to do, then?"

"What do you think?" I asked. "We shake him."

Tequila glanced in the rearview and mashed down on the pedal. "I've never been in a car chase," he told me. "I am not sure how to handle this."

He swerved the Buick through a gap in traffic, narrowly avoiding a beat-up Plymouth hatchback.

"Go as fast as you can," I told him. "And try not to hit anything."

Tequila zipped the car through another yellow light, and our shadow ran through behind him.

"I'm not sure I can lose this guy," he said.

I opened the glove compartment and found my sidearm. I thought I could take out our pursuer's tires or maybe just punch a slug through the windshield and plant it in the driver's face. I started to roll down the window.

"What are you doing, Pop? You're going to get us arrested. Or killed."

He was probably right. I wasn't a cop anymore, and hanging out of a car window shooting into traffic would be considered indiscreet. I holstered the gun and grabbed my memory note-book, to have something to hang on to.

"Let's try to lose him on a corner," I said. "Do you know how to drift with your hand brake?"

"Uh, I think I did that in a video game," Tequila said.

The kid had never learned to drive properly; Brian had let Fran teach him. I tried to keep my voice calm and steady. I didn't want to scare him any more than necessary.

"You're going to enter the turn at speed, then you're going to cut your wheel hard, and pop the hand brake to lock the back wheels up. That should cause them to lose their grip on the road, and the back of the car should spin into the turn. You're going to be cutting the wheel back in the opposite direction, to control the spin, and when you are facing the right way, you release the brake and punch the gas. Understand?"

"I think so," he said with a total lack of conviction. He glanced in the rearview, eyes wide with panic, and almost clipped the side-view mirror off a Range Rover. "Which intersection? When do I do it?"

I looked around. I had known St. Louis pretty well once, but I hadn't been able to maintain my grasp on that information. I had no idea where we were.

"Doesn't matter. Whenever you want to turn. You're not try-ing to go anyplace particular, except away from that Chevy. If you do the drift turn right, he'll go right past as we swing around the corner."

"Okay. I'm going to do this. Fuck me, I'm going to do this."

He gripped the brake. I could see his hand was shaking. His teeth were clenched, and he was sweating. He couldn't drive well enough to shake our tail, and if he tried, he would wreck the car and we would die.

"Don't," I said.

"What?"

"It's too dangerous. It was a bad idea."

His eyes flicked away from the road a moment to look at me. "I can do it, Grandpa."

"Getting into a chase is more dangerous than dealing with anybody who could be tailing us," I told him. "And if we get arrested for traffic violations, we will lose the treasure anyway. Slow down, and drive the speed limit."

He eased off the pedal. "So what do I do, Pop?"

"Pull in someplace up ahead."

Tequila maneuvered the Buick off the road, into the near empty parking lot of an Applebee's restaurant, and swung into a space. I stepped out of the car and so did Tequila.

"Put your hand in your jacket, like you have a gun," I told him.

The dark sedan pulled into the lot behind us and slowed to a stop. The windows were tinted dark like the lenses of sunglasses, even the windshield, so there was no way I could see who was driving.

I unzipped the front of my sweatshirt and let it swing open, to show the driver what was strapped to my side.

For a moment the Chevy sat, idling, its engine growling at us. I moved my hand to the butt of the .357. I didn't want to die in a car crash, but I didn't want to die like Lawrence Kind, either.

Standing there, squinting across a strip-mall parking lot, in a hopeless showdown with a ton of Detroit steel, I felt old and obsolete, like a cowboy whose frontier had turned into outlet stores and golf courses. If the driver hit the gas, he would flatten me. I wasn't fast or agile enough to get out of the way, and standing my turf and drawing down on the son of a bitch would be ineffective and ridiculous.

I was going to die, and there was nothing I could do about it.

So I held my ground, one hand on my last, feeble mode of protest, waiting for him to make a move. And then the driver shifted the black sedan into reverse, backed into the street, and drove away.

"Did you see his license plate?" I asked Tequila.

"No, I never saw the back of the car," he said.

There had been no plate on the front bumper. Missouri required drivers to display a license on the front and back of the car, but Tennessee required one only on the rear.

I wiped sweat from my eyes with the sleeve of Tequila's sweatshirt as I let out a relieved chuckle. "I have to say, for a minute there, I had this crazy thought that the bastard was Death, come to collect me."

Tequila shook his head. "I may not have been the best student in Hebrew school, but I'm pretty sure the Grim Reaper doesn't drive a fucking Chevy Malibu."

33

Tequila wanted to go back to the hotel.

"You must be soft in the head," I told him.

We had spent the last several hours driving around and going nowhere in particular, watching for the black Chevy or any other car that might be following us.

"Our bags are still in the room," he protested.

I didn't care. "We'll leave them."

"My laptop is up there. With all my class notes from school."

"It will be fine. The hotel people will find it. They can ship it back to you."

He looked at me with pleading eyes. "Pop, I want to see Yael again."

I had a feeling this was about her. I sighed. But I guessed he wasn't the first fellow I'd ever met who'd let his brain go soft over a woman.

"Billy, can't you see?" I asked him. "She was in on it all along. If that wasn't her behind the wheel of that Chevy, she was certainly working with the driver."

"That's impossible. I didn't tell her anything about what we were doing here. She didn't know anything about Ziegler or the bank."

Tequila didn't understand. Yael didn't need to get information on Ziegler or the bank from Tequila. She was working for Avram Silver, and he already knew about everything. He was the one who had dropped the clue that had led us to St. Louis in the first place. I'd been arrogant enough to think I'd goaded Silver into inadvertently making a major admission about Ziegler's location, but the crafty bastard had let it slip on purpose; he had been running me the whole time.

Silver had the Wiesenthal Center dossier on Ziegler. He'd conducted the original investigation, and he'd already made one failed play for the gold. I knew when I spoke to him that he had designs on the treasure, and he had almost certainly been keeping track of "Henry Winters."

He must have known about Meadowcrest and the safe deposit box all along. But he had never been able to lay his hands on the box key; he had no pretense to get inside Ziegler's room. And even if he had been able to get the key, he had no way to persuade the bank to let him into the box.

Silver had used me because an innocuous, enfeebled old man could go lots of places other people could not go without arousing suspicion. An elderly man wouldn't look out of place visiting a patient in the locked-down dementia ward. An elderly man could pass himself off as Henry Winters to the bank's employees and get access to the box's contents. And Avram Silver had found the perfect elderly man, one clever enough to get his hands on the gold, but dumb and confused enough not to realize he was being played.

Now the Israelis no longer had to deal with the problem of getting the key; they no longer had to deal with the problem of accessing the secure vault. The gold was in the completely insecure trunk of a Buick, and the only obstacles remaining between Avram Silver and three million dollars' worth of gold were a stupid old man and his lovesick grandson.

The Israelis didn't even need to follow us; they knew where we would be going at every step, even before we knew. They had been here ahead of us, and they had probably been watching us the whole time we were in St. Louis. Maybe Tequila's girlfriend had been our shadow in the black Chevy. Or maybe she was just keeping track of our movements.

But now she was bait. And if we went back to that hotel, they would spring their trap.

"That's a bunch of shit," Tequila insisted. "Yael is not a spy. You don't know her."

I grabbed his shoulder and shook him a little. "For God's sake, Tequila, you met this woman two days ago. Her people will kill us for what we've got in the trunk."

He pushed my arm away. "Don't jostle me while I'm driving."

"You're such a jackass," I said. But it was me who had been the ass the whole time. And the kid had too much of his father—and, really, too much of his grandmother—in him to get anything other than whatever he wanted. He was behind the wheel, and I would go where he drove.

I sighed. "If we're going back there, we need to do this my way," I said.

"What does that entail?"

What it entailed was a reasonable goddamn modicum of caution. We did not want anyone to see our car pulling into the hotel parking lot; our pursuers would certainly be watching for us there. Yael, of course, would be giving them the heads-up anyway, but on the slim chance Tequila was right and she was unaffiliated with Silver, we needed to at least try to slip in and out undetected.

We waited until around dusk to return. It was possible that by that time, anyone staking out the hotel might have decided we weren't coming back, and the low light would make it harder to spot Tequila on foot.

We circled several blocks around the hotel, looking for our pursuer or for anyone sitting in a parked car, maybe staking the place out. Really, we were looking for pretty much anything that felt wrong.

We didn't seem to have a tail, and we had seen only one black Chevy in the last couple of hours, but it had clear windows and a Missouri plate on the front bumper. The coast seemed clear.

But as we rolled past the Embassy Suites, it was hard to miss the three St. Louis police cruisers parked in front with their lights flashing.

"What do you think is going on?" Tequila asked.

"Finding out seems like a bad idea," I said. "Let's get away from this place."

"Give me a break," he said, punching the steering wheel. "It's probably a drug bust or a robbery. Maybe having the cops around will scare the bad guys off."

I didn't like it, but he wasn't going to be convinced. He was going to make his mistake, and I was going to have to try to deal with it.

Since we obviously couldn't leave the car with the gold in the trunk, Tequila parked a few blocks from the hotel. He'd go in, grab the bags, say good-bye to Yael, and check us out. I'd wait with the engine idling and a hand on my .357.

"Don't spend too much time with the girl," I told him. "If we can live long enough to fence this gold and get the money safely into the bank, and you still want her at that point, you can fly her up to New York to visit you. Get in and out of there in a few minutes."

"It will be fine, Grandpa," Tequila said as he climbed out of the car. I didn't really believe him.

I smoked four cigarettes while I waited. As I was lighting a fifth, he came out of the hotel carrying the bags, but he wasn't alone; another man was walking with him.

I squinted, but with my weak vision, it wasn't until they got pretty close that I could recognize the second man as Detective Randall Jennings, the murder cop from Memphis, and it wasn't until the two of them were almost standing next to my window that I realized my grandson was crying.

34

My mind raced, or at least it came as close to racing as it was able. Panic surged through my guts, and that long-dormant cop instinct was coiled around my spine and blaring an alarm inside my skull.

I tried to remember what my doctor told me about paranoia; reached for the notebook to look at it, but my hands were shaking too badly to flip through the pages.

Jennings wouldn't be here looking for us unless somebody had been murdered. While we were here on our wild goose chase, something must have happened back home.

The detective leaned against the hood of my car, smudging his fingers all over my paint job.

"Why is it that whenever I see you, somebody's dead, Buck?" he asked.

An image flashed in my mind: hulking, angry Yitzchak Steinblatt walking up Fran's driveway, carrying a long, serrated knife.

I climbed out of the car and leaned on the door frame, gripping it so hard that my fingers and knuckles turned white. I threw away my cigarette and swallowed hard.

"Tell me what happened," I said quietly, trying to brace myself for the answer.

"The housekeeper in your hotel found a dead girl this morning, in the bed in room 1116," Jennings said.

I let my breath out, relieved, as my body sagged against the door.

"Well, most of the dead girl was in the bed," Jennings clarified. "There was also quite a bit in the sink, though. And some in the toilet."

Tequila sobbed. Based on his reaction, I assumed the corpse must have been his Israeli girlfriend. That was sad; despite her military training, despite her ideology, despite her lean, hard muscle, Yael ended up a victim just like all those other Jews.

"You look happy to be hearing this news," said Jennings.

Not happy at all. My detective's instinct was whispering to me about the cord of Yael's white headphones tangled up in a pool of congealing blood. It told me about long tan legs sticking out of a shredded, hollowed torso.

"I'm relieved, maybe," I told Jennings. "When I saw you, I thought you were coming to tell me that something had happened to my wife."

"Oh, you did?" Jennings asked. "Why's that? Did y'all kill her too?"

That sounded a little accusatory, and it should have been my signal to stop talking to cops and get myself lawyered up. But all the criminal defense lawyers I knew in Memphis were dead. They wouldn't have been much help anyway; none of them had liked me.

Tequila dropped the bags on the backseat of the Buick and

then collapsed against the driver's-side door, making wet, snuffling sounds. He wasn't going to be much use to me right now, but I couldn't blame him. He had sincerely cared about the dead girl.

I remembered all the times I'd watched victims' families getting the bad news, and I thought of how Rose reacted when we heard about Brian, and how Yael's grandmother the Holocaust survivor would respond when she learned what happened at the Embassy Suites.

"What are you doing here, Randall?" I asked.

Jennings spat on the pavement. "I think I asked you first, Buck."

I squinted at him. "Sightseeing. I figured it was about time I got around to takin' a gander at that arch they've got."

"Quit bullshitting me, Buck."

"You're out of your jurisdiction," I growled. "That body up there ain't yours to be asking about."

"Police are better connected than they used to be," Jennings said. "Couple of days back, I posted a Twitter, asking if anybody in law enforcement in the greater region knew anything about y'all, and this morning, I got a message on Facebook from a St. Louis cop I know, telling me you're checked in at a hotel where a murder just happened."

"You used a bunch of words that don't mean anything to me," I told him.

He leaned forward, brushing his fat ass across the side of my Buick. "It means that you two assholes seem to show up around a lot of murders lately, so you're going to have to explain real fast why I shouldn't be very suspicious of you."

He hadn't told me yet that I had the right to remain silent, but that didn't mean I had to say anything.

He took my reticence as an opportunity to tell me my connections to these deaths, counting them on his fingers. Lawrence

Kind paid a late night visit to my house the night before some-body emptied him out. Several hotel employees saw Tequila go-ing upstairs into this girl's room the night before she got turned into some kind of science project. Both killings were done with a knife, both corpses were hollowed out and left to bleed. Any cop would be comfortable with the notion that the murders were con-nected, and Tequila and I were the only common acquaintances between the victims.

"If you were in my shoes, you'd be thinking exactly what I'm thinking, and doing exactly what I'm doing, and you know it," Jennings said.

I frowned. He was probably right.

"You know my reputation," I told him. "You're going to have to trust me when I tell you we didn't kill anyone."

He rubbed at his mustache. "Buck, your reputation is as a gun-slinger. Damn near every story I ever heard about you ends up with you shooting somebody dead. You have killed more people than anyone I've ever met, and I've met a lot of people who killed a lot of people."

"And internal affairs deemed every one of them appropriate," I said. "My record is spotless."

Randall Jennings shot me the familiar and distrustful cop sneer I must have used at one time or another on a thousand dif-ferent suspects. He knew damn well we were withholding infor-mation from him, and he wasn't going to leave us alone until he found out what it was.

"I'd be more inclined to trust you if you'd quit lying to me every time I ask a question," he said.

"Why don't you look it up on your Google," I suggested.

He slapped a hand to his forehead. "Is that what you're angry about? For fuck's sake, this is serious now."

"I was serious then."

"The St. Louis cops are serious too, and you know as well as I do that they're looking for any kind of boyfriend this victim's got. So if you have any information that points another way, this is the time to spill it."

I lit another cigarette with a shaking hand. "Have they got a time of death?"

"The medical examiner carted the body off only a couple of hours ago, and they won't confirm it until the full autopsy report. But probably between eight-thirty and ten this morning."

"It can't have been us, then," I told him. "By eight-thirty, we were all the way across town, robbing a bank."

Tequila's eyes widened, and he choked in mid-burble, but Jennings just shook his head and fingered his sweaty shirt collar. "Stop giving me shit," he said.

Tequila and I had breakfast together downstairs around seven in the morning, and then we left, out the front door. I remembered a security camera behind the check-in desk that looked like it covered the lobby and would have recorded us leaving the hotel well before eight. I asked Jennings about it.

"Nobody's looked at that yet, far as I know," he said. He leaned against the hood of the car, and it creaked downward on its shocks.

"I know you don't believe you can pin this on us, or we'd be having this conversation in an interrogation room," I told him.

He adjusted his weight, and the Buick shifted with him. "Maybe you're right, but until I am satisfied that I know everything you know, you'll be seeing me around. Something stinks here."

He stepped away from the car, cocked his head a little, and took a few more steps backward.

"Buck?" he asked. "Is it just me, or is your car riding a little low in the back?"

"I think it's just you," I said, trying not to let him see a reaction. I looked at Tequila. He was holding his breath.

"You mind popping open your trunk so I can have a look?"

"Can't do that," I said. "It's full of loot from the bank robbery."

Jennings crossed his arms. "Two people are dead, and I'm trying to catch the killer before he makes another mess. This ain't a good time to be a wiseass."

I laughed. "I've been around eighty-eight years, Detective, and I've found that it's always a good time to be a wiseass."

"Why don't you open up the trunk, Buck."

I gestured to Tequila to get back in the car. "I don't think you have any authority to search an automobile in St. Louis, Randall."

He sighed. "I'm asking you to do me a favor. I don't understand why you insist on making it difficult for me to conduct a murder investigation."

"Because you're still an ass," I said. "And I still don't like you."

"This isn't over," he said, pointing an accusing finger at me.

I climbed into the passenger seat and shut the door.

"Let's get on the highway," I said to my grandson. "We've done about as much damage as we can do here."

Jennings stood there, hands on his hips, staring us down as we pulled away.

35

"I'm only going to ask once," I said to Tequila as we drove seventy miles per hour south along I-55, soybean fields whizzing past the windows and vanishing behind us. "Did you kill that girl?"

"No."

My grandson's face was illuminated by a passing truck's headlights, and I took a long look at him. His eyes were still red and watery, lower lip still quivering a little. Unless he was a more devious performer than any I'd seen, he wasn't a psycho killer.

"I think I believe you," I said.

"Great," he said. "What about you? Did you kill her?"

"Don't be stupid," I said. "You know I'm not strong enough to cut somebody up."

"But you would have, if you could have?" His voice was barely a whisper, and hoarse from crying. He always was a sensitive kid.

"No. Of course not," I said.

That was true. I killed four in the war and twelve on the force, but never for pleasure. Well, never just for pleasure. I wasn't some sicko. I'll admit, I was thinking about maybe using a razor blade and taking things slow with Heinrich Ziegler when I went after him in 1946. But I wasn't sure I ever had the appetite for being close and getting stuff sprayed on me.

And I never killed a woman, either.

"I think I believe you," he said to me. He laid on the sarcasm thick enough that I could hear it, even through his rasp.

I punched him on the arm, lightly enough not to hurt myself. "Don't sass me, kid."

"I cared about her," he said. His nose had started running, and he smeared the snot around his face with a shirtsleeve.

"We're going to find out who did this," I said.

"We will?"

I nodded. "We have to."

"After the Kind murder, you said we could mind our own business and let the police do their job."

I checked the rearview for black Chevrolets. I'd been doing that every five minutes since we'd left St. Louis. I didn't know why. Whoever was following didn't need to tail us down the interstate; he could easily pick us up back in Memphis.

"Things are different now. A witness saw you go into that hotel room the night before she died, and the housekeeper found the body the next morning. When a woman gets murdered, the police usually just lock up her boyfriend."

"But what about the security camera that shows us leaving before she was killed?"

"Do you have that tape?"

"No," he said.

"Who has got that tape?"

"The hotel, I guess. And maybe the St. Louis police?"

I nodded. "If you're their only suspect, somebody is going to misplace that piece of evidence, and then everyone will conveniently forget it exists while they nail your miserable ass to the wall. There is no way any homicide detective will take the political heat of leaving the psycho-slashing of a pretty white girl unsolved when the victim had a casual lover who's got no alibi. They will make this thing stick to you."

His eyes flicked off the road for a second to throw an accusing glare my way. "You did that? You lost exculpatory evidence on purpose to close a file you couldn't mop up the honest way?"

"Don't look at me like that," I told him. "I did that job as clean as anyone's ever done it."

He made some noise about how I was being evasive, and I ignored it.

"Anyway, there's probably at least one other way into the hotel, maybe a service entrance or a loading dock," I told him. "We'd be damn lucky if the killer went in the front door, because we could identify him on the security tapes. More likely, though, whoever did it was smart enough not to walk in past the desk."

Tequila grunted.

"And, of course, you could have gone out past the camera, through the front, but reentered the hotel through another door to kill Yael, so the video won't clear you anyway."

"That sounds like a rationalization."

"It's detective work. You piece together the facts you have into the most plausible story you can come up with, and then you try to convict on it. It isn't an exact science."

He scowled at me, and I could tell that, to him, it all sounded like another way of framing a guy. And maybe he was right. But murder wasn't supposed to be a game that people could win by being smart enough and lucky enough to not leave evidence that justified a conviction. Sometimes the evidence needed a little help.

Tequila couldn't understand how frustrating it was to see a killer get off the hook by intimidating a witness into recanting testimony or to lose a conviction because we hadn't been able to dredge the murder weapon out of the river.

Maybe Tequila's moral compass dictated that he ought to let a murderer go free because the rules said he had to. But I could see his white knuckles on the steering wheel, and I could see that his jaw was clenched, and I knew what he would like to do if he could get his hands on whoever killed Yael.

Somewhere deep down, beneath his college-boy diction and his lawyer words, he understood that there were conflicts that couldn't be settled with discussion or process. He knew that a man had to solve certain problems with his hands. But neither of us wanted to discuss that, so I decided to try talking about a less awkward subject.

"Did you have sexual intercourse with that girl last night?"

His jaw dropped open. "What the fuck, Grandpa?"

"Answer the goddamn question," I told him. "They are going to conduct a postmortem examination and autopsy, and they are going to search that crime scene. I need to know what they will find there. So, did you have intercourse with Yael?"

He blinked away tears. "Yeah. We, uh . . . Yeah."

"Did you use a condom?"

His face flushed red. "Yes, always."

"Good," I said. "Your mother will be relieved."

"Jesus Christ, Pop." He wiped at his nose.

"Was the used rubber in the room when you left?"

"What do you mean?"

"Did you leave it on the end table? Throw it in the trash can?"

"I think I flushed it down the toilet."

"You think?"

"I flushed it down the toilet," he said.

"Well, at least you didn't leave your DNA everywhere."

"Does that help?"

"I don't know. We didn't have DNA evidence when I was a cop. But it probably looks awful incriminating to a jury when there was spunk splattered all over a corpse."

He shuddered, either at the word *corpse* or the word *jury*. He sniffled a little.

"The St. Louis people must not even know about you yet, or they would have picked us up while we were driving around the city all day," I told him. "Randall Jennings must not have shared whatever he thinks he knows."

Tequila took a hand off the wheel and ran it distractedly through his hair. "Why wouldn't he?"

"He wants to pin the Lawrence Kind job on you or on me, and he wants to make the bust himself, without sharing the credit with the St. Louis bulls. So much for collaboration among agencies, I guess."

Tequila bit his bottom lip. "Does that buy us time?"

"Not much," I said. "But the good news is I don't expect we'll have to look too hard for the real killer."

"Why's that?" Tequila asked.

"Because he'll come looking for us."

36

Randall Jennings had no authority to look in the trunk of the car in St. Louis, but that fact wouldn't buy us much space to breathe.

To get into a suspect's residence, police must obtain a warrant from a judge that allows them to conduct a search. That's guaranteed by the Fourth Amendment to the Constitution.

It is legal for police to enter a dwelling without that warrant only if there is probable cause; in other words, they must show that a reasonable person would believe a crime was probably occurring on the premises at the time the cops went through the door.

When police search a house without cause or a warrant, the search is illegal, and any evidence, whether it's drugs, stolen property, or a dead body, is considered poisoned and can't be used against the suspect. That means the bad guy goes free.

A vehicle is different, though. The law says it's public in a way a home never is, so there's a greatly reduced right to privacy in a vehicle, even a car's locked trunk. Police get a lot more room to play their hunches with automobile searches.

Maybe the cop thought the driver looked nervous. Maybe the suspect appeared to be holding something that looked like a weapon. Maybe he reacted fearfully or anxiously when he saw the police cruiser. Maybe he changed lanes without signaling. Anything like that is good enough.

Some patrolmen are dumb enough to say out loud, in court, that they pulled a car over just because the driver was black, and when this happens, it forces the frustrated judge to throw out the ten pounds of uncut Afghan smack the cop found in the trunk of the car. That's how criminal defense lawyers get their names enshrined in rap song lyrics.

But as long as the officer is able, after the fact, to articulate a reasonable basis for suspicion, almost any vehicle search will stand up in court.

So we were subject to search at will by law enforcement as long as the gold was in the car. We'd be a little safer once we got the stuff into my house, since Jennings wouldn't be able to muster enough proof to get a search warrant. But we had a lot of highway to cover before we got there. We were vulnerable.

If the cops found the gold, they would confiscate it. Our method of getting into Ziegler's safe deposit box had been extremely illegal. If it didn't meet the technical definition of a bank robbery, it was certainly fraud against a federally insured bank. That was good enough to be a serious felony.

And even if we beat criminal charges, the discovery of the Nazi gold would mean that we wouldn't get to keep it. It would go to Holocaust survivors or charities, and all our effort would have been wasted.

I thought of Jennings giving me that conspiratorial little grin of his and telling me how if I were in his shoes, I'd be thinking the way he was thinking and doing what he was doing. And I knew what I'd do if I were in his place.

I would have an all-points bulletin out on the Buick in Memphis, for starters, and I'd have any friendly folks in nearby departments looking for the car as well. That would ensure that some cop, someplace, would spot us, pull us over, and search us.

I took a long look out the window and puffed on my cigarette. The logic moved inexorably in one direction, and it wasn't a direction I liked. Drastic measures would have to be taken.

"We need to get rid of this car," I told Tequila. "We need some alternative transportation."

"What are you talking about?" he said. "You love this thing."

"Indeed. But sooner or later, you lose what you love."

He wiped at his eyes. "Yeah, reckon so."

Silence between us for longer than a moment. Then he said, "How do we do this? Smash the window of a parked car and hotwire it? Carjack somebody at gunpoint?"

"Yeah, because driving around in a stolen vehicle is going to help us avoid getting pulled over by cops," I said.

He drummed his fingers on the steering wheel, the same way his grandmother did when she was annoyed with me. "Okay. So what is your plan?"

The plan, to the extent it could be described as such, was to stash the Buick someplace out of the way and get a rental car.

That didn't seem like such a bright idea to Tequila. "But you have to provide a driver's license to rent a car, right? I think they usually make a photocopy of it. And can't they track the credit card we use to pay for the rental?"

"The police need a warrant to get that information," I said. "Hopefully, we can get home and stash the gold before Jennings can get in front of a judge."

We got off I-55 in Cape Girardeau, Missouri. It wasn't much of a city, but it had a regional airport. That meant we could rent a car and leave the Buick unattended for a while in the airport's long-term parking lot.

First, we stopped at a Wal-Mart store and got four backpacks to carry the gold in. The hundred-pound duffels were too heavy for Tequila to move around easily. Then, I waited with the treasure and the Buick at the airport while Tequila hiked over to the nearby Enterprise store. He came back driving a purple Volkswagen Jetta. He said it was the only four-door available, but I suspected he'd picked it on purpose, to piss me off.

We drove into Memphis without any blue lights flashing in the rearview. I told Tequila to pass my street and pull around the block.

"We've got to figure the police are watching the front of the house, and we don't want them to see us carrying those bags in. So you need to sneak them in the back, over the fence."

"You want me to jump two fences with fifty pounds on my back?" he said.

"Are you that out of shape?"

He was quiet for a minute. "No, I guess I can do it."

"Okay," I said, handing him the key to the back door. "Don't forget to deactivate the burglar alarm. Stay low to the ground. Sit the bags inside the door, and we'll hide them in the attic after we pull around the front and let the cops see us go into the house empty-handed."

"You're trying to run a lot of misdirection on these people, Grandpa. Are you sure any of this will work? Are you sure there is even anyone watching us?"

I was sure Kind and Yael were dead, and I was sure somebody had chased us after we left the bank.

"If we're in so much danger, why don't we stash the gold in another safe deposit box until the heat dies down?"

"We can't. Not with Jennings on our tail. If a cop sees us carrying those bags into the bank, that would be pretty interesting evidence to show a judge. Along with our circumstantial proximity to the murders, that's good enough to justify a warrant to search the box. If we got here without them seeing us, the gold will be safe in the house, at least from the police, but it's too risky to move it again."

Tequila grumbled about it a little more, but he grabbed one of the backpacks from the trunk, heaved it over the fence, and hauled his ass up after it. The four trips took him ten tense minutes, and he climbed back in the car damp from exertion.

"I've got splinters in my hands from that stupid wooden fence," he told me as he let the Volkswagen roll down my street.

"Exercise is good for you," I told him. "You've been looking kind of doughy."

As he pulled into the driveway, I pointed out a black car parked in front of my house. "Somebody is staking us out." I squinted, but it was too dark to see who was sitting in the driver's seat.

He glanced in the rearview. "Is it that Chevy?"

"Nah," I said. "Toyota."

We flipped on the light over the garage and made sure whoever was watching could see we were only carrying our lightweight overnight bags into the house.

Once we were safe inside, Tequila pulled down the folding ladder that led to my attic and stashed the gold up there.

"Is that car still out front?" he asked when he finished.

I nodded. "I suppose we should show our visitor some southern hospitality," I said.

We went out the front door together. I had my .357 drawn, and Tequila had found my old golf clubs in the closet and was holding up a seven iron like a baseball bat. It was dark out, and the car was parked in shadow. I rapped on the driver's-side window with my gun. The door cracked open, startling me enough that I stepped back into a firing position, planted my feet, raised my right arm to shoulder level, and braced the butt of the .357 with my left hand. I had my finger on the trigger.

A light went on inside the car when the door opened, and we could see that the driver was not armed. It looked like she'd fallen asleep waiting for us and had reflexively reached for the door handle when we'd frightened her awake.

"Good evening, Mr. Schatz," she said as she stepped out of the car. "It's a pleasure to finally meet you."

I lowered my gun. "Hello, Mrs. Kind."

37

Felicia Kind was sitting in my spot on the couch. I was pacing around the room, and Tequila perched on one of my cushy chairs. He stared at her with eyes full of menace. His mouth was a thin, pressed line, and his hands tightly clutched my golf club.

She wasn't as put together as she had been at the funeral; she'd been waiting for us in her car for at least a few hours. But she was beautiful anyway. Looking at her brought to mind the sorts of florid adjectives people ordinarily used to describe violin concertos and Renaissance paintings. She was wearing a zip-front hooded sweatshirt like one of Tequila's, but not baggy; it clung to her body enough that I could tell she wasn't hiding a gun underneath it. Her hair was disheveled from being mashed against the seat cushion, which made her look like she'd just crawled out of bed. She wasn't wearing any makeup, but that suited her just fine because her skin was flawless. And she made me very nervous. Felicia was dangerous the same way water was wet; it wasn't a question of whether she meant to be or not, it was simply intrinsic to her nature.

She looked at me with red-rimmed eyes that almost broke my heart. "You seem angry."

"What tipped you off, bitch? The gun pointed at your head?" Tequila was coiled like a spring; his voice was a hiss through clenched teeth. I could tell he was thinking about going upside Felicia's skull with the toe of the seven iron. Rose would never forgive me if I let him make that kind of mess in her living room.

"You'd better explain double quick why you were staking us out," I told Felicia.

Her eyes widened. "Staking? No, I was only waiting. I need to talk to you, Mr. Schatz."

"Well, talk," I said. "I'm listening."

"I need your help to find out what is going on with the investigation of my husband's murder. Randall Jennings will not return my phone calls, and I am not sure he is taking the case seriously."

"If I were in his shoes, I'd be doing the same thing."

Her eyes were wet now. "But why? Why won't he talk to me? Why is he keeping me in the dark?"

"Ain't good police practice to apprise your suspects of how the investigation is proceeding."

Her jaw hung open, long enough for her to blink a couple of times. "Suspect? Me?"

"Playing stupid has been working pretty well for you, I bet," Tequila said, rising from his chair and leaning toward her. "You put on a dull, surprised look and toss your hair around, and everybody trips over themselves to wipe the drool off your chin."

"I have no idea what you're talking about."

"Cut the act, lady," he said. "I'm way past the point of thinking it's cute. Maybe the reverend fell for that shit. Maybe that's why he got his guts dumped out all over the carpeting."

"That's enough," I told Tequila. "Sit down." He was cracking, seeing Yael's killers everywhere, and it was bad news. If he managed to smother his ability to reason under a blanket of paranoia, we wouldn't have a functioning brain between us.

"I know what she is," he protested. "Black widow. Femme fatale. There's always one like her in these stories."

I grabbed hold of the golf club and gave him a look that made him let go of it. He folded back into his chair. I needed him to help me think, and he'd decided instead to pretend he was Humphrey Bogart.

"There's been another killing," I explained to Felicia. "Looks like the two are connected to each other and somehow connected to us. We're a little jumpy."

"I don't know anything about that," she said, fanning at her face with a hand that still had a wedding ring on it.

I was not persuaded. "You'd better start spilling whatever you do know."

"I'll tell you anything."

I crossed my arms. "Let's start with life insurance."

"Yeah," Tequila growled. "When the good pastor went on to his eternal reward, what was your upside?"

"Not much," she said. "Fifty thousand. I have to pay taxes on it. And we live, used to live, in a house the church owns. They told me I have two weeks to get out. I don't have a job; I've been a full-time minister's wife for three years. I don't know what I am going to do now."

"The funeral you threw for him sure made you look like you were well-to-do."

"The policy provided money for burial expenses, but it was reimbursed based on receipts, so I couldn't get it in cash," she said. "The church also paid for a lot of it. A lot of people in the congregation were embarrassed by the murder, and the deacons felt that an expensive funeral would save face."

What she was saying sounded plausible, but that didn't mean

a word of it was true. Good-looking women were easy to trust, which was what made them such effective liars.

I looked at Tequila. He was digging his fingers into the armrests of his chair.

"Do you know T. Addleford Pratt?" I asked her.

"He contacted me after Larry died. He said Larry owed him some money, and he threatened to get a lien on the life insurance payment. If I have to pay off Larry's debts, I'll have nothing left, and if I fight them, then legal fees will wipe me out anyway. What I've got isn't much of a foundation to build a life on, and I don't know what I'll do if those men take it from me. I think the casino people must have been the ones who killed Larry, unless . . ."

I waited for her to continue, but she didn't. I broke the silence. "What's any of it got to do with me?"

"Let me show you." Felicia began to unzip her handbag, which I must have noticed her carrying when she walked in but had not thought to search.

"Gun!" shouted Tequila, and he leaped forward out of his chair to snatch the purse from her hands. Felicia let out a little shriek and curled herself up in a fetal position on the side of the couch farthest from Tequila.

He pawed through the bag.

"Has she got a weapon in there?" I asked.

"No."

"Then give it back to her, and sit down."

He stammered some kind of protest, but he did what I told him.

She recomposed herself, but tears were now streaming down her face. She reached into the bag and pulled out a top-spiral reporter's notebook, a lot like the one I carried around for my memories.

She flipped about a third of the way through it, and when she found what she was looking for, she gave it to me. At the top of the page, the words *Things I mustn't forget about Baruch Schatz* were written in small, neat cursive script.

"With so many parishioners to keep track of, Larry had to take careful notes, to help him remember what was going on in everyone's lives," she said. "He had dozens of these pads in his desk. I shouldn't be reading them. I'm sure I'm intruding on his confidences. But I lost him so suddenly, and they're all I have left of him."

I looked at what Kind had written about me and handed the notebook back to her.

"All our friends, everyone I knew, was connected to the church," she said. "Now I can't turn to them. My husband trusted you, and I've got nobody else. I need you to find out who killed him."

"Why?" I asked her.

She crossed her long tan legs. "You were sort of right about me needing insurance money. If the murder was related to Larry's job, I'm entitled to a payment of around two hundred thousand from the state workmen's compensation fund. But until we know who killed him and why, I can't make a claim."

I didn't say anything. She uncrossed and recrossed her legs.

"I'll pay you a fair cut of the proceeds if you help me find out what happened to my husband. Please, Mr. Schatz, I need that money to get away from this city and the things that happened here. It's my only chance to rebuild some kind of life for myself."

It sounded like what she was saying could be true. On the other hand, she'd been prowling around outside my house, and in the days since her husband's murder, she'd had plenty of time to come up with a story that would sound plausible, or even compelling.

While I was mulling it, the phone rang.

"Probably my wife," I said to Felicia as I picked up the receiver. It wasn't.

"Howdy, Buck-o," said Randall Jennings. "I heard you made it home safely, so I thought I'd ring you up." This was his way of telling me that he was indeed watching my house. "That's a tight new whip you picked up along the way."

Tequila could evidently tell it wasn't his grandmother by the expression on my face. He was making inquisitive gestures at me. I held up a hand to let him know he should quiet down.

"I don't know what that means," I told Jennings.

"Your car. Your new car."

"Okay," I said. "I get it. You've got an eye on me."

"Well, I just want to keep you safe."

"Good night, Randall." I started to hang up the phone

"Hold up a second, Buck." He cleared his throat. "I called to tell you I hauled your pal Norris Feely downtown to sweat him on the Lawrence Kind thing."

That surprised me. Jennings had made it very clear that he liked Tequila as the killer, and now he was questioning Feely. Either this cop was all over the map or he had some kind of elaborate plan I couldn't see the shape of.

"Folks tell me you used to be a wizard in the interrogation room," Jennings continued, maintaining a friendly tone. "Why don't you come and take a few swings at this chubby little piñata we've got here, for old times' sake."

I had no idea what he was up to. "Are you saying you need my help, Randall?"

"Nah," he said. "But I figured life would be easier on you if this guy confessed, and I know you'll get all pissy if you feel like you didn't get asked to the dance."

He was right about that, although I doubted he had my best interests at heart. I tried to guess what sort of trap he could be setting for me, but I couldn't figure out his angle. That made me uncomfortable.

Felicia Kind agreed to give me a lift downtown, so I left Tequila at the house, with the gold. He was vocal about his distrust of Felicia, and he was angry about getting left out, but he knew we couldn't leave three million dollars unsupervised, and he acquiesced.

I also knew that letting him visit the police department could somehow look incriminating. Jennings's trap might be for him, and his relationship to Yael made him vulnerable. If a prosecutor could establish the mere fact that two unmarried adults had engaged in consensual intercourse outside the bonds of sanctified marriage, that evidence would be enough to get a murder conviction from most Tennessee juries.

The preacher's widow, however, would be very difficult to convict unless the jury saw something as persuasive as video footage of her actually committing the act. At least, she would be difficult to convict unless somebody managed to prove she had been unfaithful to her husband. If a jury heard that, she'd get the death penalty whether she was involved in the murder or not.

"Did you ever cheat on Larry?" I asked her as we cruised down Poplar in her little Toyota.

Her response looked enough like genuine shock and outrage to convince me of her sincerity. She wanted to know how I could dare to suggest such a thing and whether I understood what it meant that she was a minister's wife and an avowed Christian. She told me I was cruel and vicious to even imagine she might be capable of such things. And she said some other stuff about me as well. I didn't take it personally.

I cracked the window, lit a cigarette, and waited for her to calm down. When she quit screaming, I said:

"As long as that's true, you're fine. But if you can be linked to anything that looks like infidelity, you shouldn't get within five hundred feet of the police station unless you are with your lawyer."

"I loved my husband, Mr. Schatz, and I believe in his work," Felicia said, her voice husky and low, still full of anger but without the undertone of fear I'd expect from somebody guilty.

"As difficult as it's going to be, you're going to have to endure suspicion until the truth comes out. When police have a white, middle-class murder and it's not a clear robbery, the spouse is usually the culprit. But if you didn't kill him, we'll get you your money."

"I'm sorry I shouted at you, Mr. Schatz, and I'm sorry I frightened you and your grandson. You're innocent in all this."

But I shook my head. "Nobody's innocent."

Degenerate gambler Lawrence Kind's notes about me:

I like Buck Schatz a great deal, although he seems to dislike me. Buck pegged me as a sinner the moment we met, and because of that, he believes I am a charlatan, a fraud. He's a man trained to rely upon his instincts about people as much as or more than I do, and I take him seriously. Thus, it falls upon me to consider whether his assessment is accurate.

I think that it is not.

Buck associates piety with his own ethos of personal discipline, a worldview that is deeply embedded in ancient Jewish tradition. Because the Jews do not believe in redemption through Christ, they aspire to worldly perfection by compliance with the Halacha, an exacting set of over 600 biblical laws governing every aspect of daily life.

Buck is not an observant Jew, as far as I can tell, but the faith of his people instructs his values. He judges men by how they act and cares too little for what they believe. He expects a pious man to lead the life of a monk, the life of a rabbi.

A holy man, to a Jew, must be a scholar, a thinker, a man of books. But that is not what I am, and not the path that is required of an Evangelical minister.

I'm a man of faith, and a teacher of Christ's word. But I am also a sinner, weak and vulnerable to temptation. I profess to be nothing else, and I preach to my flock on how Christ redeems me regardless of my transgressions, about how I am saved despite my shortcomings.

The evangelist becomes a man of God not by learning or study, but by revelation. My credibility in preaching Christ's word is not tarnished because I have wallowed in the depths of sin; His glory is proven by the fact that I've come out the other side, with His help.

Mostly.

I can't say I don't still struggle. I can't say I don't still slip. But that is His will also, and that is the journey I must undertake. Buck wants to judge me for this, but Christ is with me on the road I walk, and He forgives my failures.

My struggle is God's will, because when my congregants seek my counsel, they need advice not from a scholar, not from a rabbi, but from a man who knows sin and temptation and knows the burden of struggling against it to find a way to Grace.

I preach often about the malefactor, the criminal, who was crucified with Jesus. His punishment was just and deserved, the "due reward of his deeds." But he begged Christ for forgiveness. He said: "Lord, remember me when Thou comest into Thy kingdom."

And Christ promised him: "Today shalt thou be with me in paradise."

Jesus knows our hearts, and He knows we have sinned and He knows we will sin again. We are born of sin, and carry it in our blood and our bones and our flesh. We cannot purge sins through acts; we can only be cleansed by the blood of Jesus. And if we ask for absolution, He will bestow it.

I think Buck can teach us all about discipline and about honesty. He reminds us that we can and should be better than we are. But he has a lot to learn about faith and forgiveness.

I am eternally grateful that, when I stumble, I have Jesus there to pick me up, but I fear that as Buck reaches his end, he will find himself facing the abyss alone.

38

Randall Jennings looked seriously pissed when he saw me stroll into the Criminal Justice Center with Felicia Kind.

"What's she doing here?" he demanded, pointing an angry finger at her.

"I didn't know it was improper for a victim's wife to visit the detective in charge of the murder investigation," she said.

"Back in my day, we treated crime victims with a modicum of dignity and respect," I added. "I assumed that was still the policy."

"That's a bunch of shit and you know it," Jennings said. "You came in with one of my suspects, just to fuck with me."

Felicia gasped and put on the same wide-eyed expression of shock she'd shown me at the house. It was an extremely persuasive facsimile of surprise, and I would have been fooled if I hadn't known it was a lie. I wondered how much of what she'd told me was true. I didn't think she was the killer; I enjoyed looking at her, but she certainly wasn't my favorite suspect. I wasn't about to trust her, though.

"This nice church lady?" I asked Jennings, feigning confusion.

"I had no idea you were thinking in that direction. Isn't Norris Feely under arrest for the murder?"

"Norris Feely is in custody because he is a person of interest," Jennings said.

I scratched my head. "Is that a different thing from a suspect?"

His mustache seemed to bristle. "You know what you're doing to me, you mean old bastard."

But I wasn't doing anything to him as far as I knew. I certainly had no intention of messing up his murder investigation if it was leading to an outcome other than a frame job on me or Tequila. Maybe he thought bringing her to the station could jeopardize the admissibility of some future confession she might make. I didn't see why it would, though. When I was working homicide, concerned spouses of victims routinely visited me at the police station to check in on my investigations. It had never caused any legal problems, even when I ended up having to arrest them. I said something that wasn't quite apologetic and veered the conversation back toward Feely.

"He hasn't said anything helpful," Jennings said. "But he seems to like you. Maybe he trusts you. And I've heard people say you used to be pretty impressive in the interrogation room."

I'd loosened a few tongues in my day, and I had a gift for coaxing admissions out of the weak-willed. But I couldn't imagine Feely cracking easily, and my technique for softening recalcitrant subjects had involved liberal use of a rolled-up phone book.

"I'll see him alone," I said. I didn't want to have to spar with Jennings while I was trying to figure out what was going on with Feely.

The detective stayed outside with Felicia. The two of them had a lot to talk about. I stepped into the sweatbox.

This, at least, was a kind of place that hadn't changed much since I was working. Two steel chairs, bolted to a cement floor, on opposite sides of a steel table, and a door that opened only from the outside. On television, interrogation rooms usually had two-way mirrors so people could watch the questioning. They always had microphones and cameras to record any statements. And maybe interrogations looked like that in places like San Francisco. But Memphis still stuck to the old ways, and this facility was just four solid walls. The process of extracting a confession could be ugly, and nobody wanted witnesses to what happened in that room.

If there was a video or audio recording of the interrogation, the scumbag's defense lawyer was entitled to a copy. Then he could scrutinize the cops' behavior throughout the process, looking for a reason to move that his client's statement be excluded from the trial. So every cop worth his salt knows that the only record of what transpires in an interrogation room should be a signed confession.

I leaned against the table and felt very much at home.

Feely was sitting with his arms shackled behind him, and the handcuff chain threaded through the back of the chair. This pleased me; I didn't want to shake hands with him again.

The furniture had been arranged with a less generously proportioned occupant in mind, and Feely's gut was smushed up against the edge of the table.

"You look uncomfortable, Norris," I said.

"Buck . . ." He smiled, relieved to see me. "Thank God you're here. I'm in a jam."

I lit a cigarette and dropped the pack on the table. "Damn right you are."

I offered him a smoke, but he just sat there looking indignant.

I pulled my memory notebook out of my pocket and laid it

next to the Luckys, open to a clean page. I took my .357 out of the shoulder holster and set it next to the notebook, where Feely could get a good look at it.

"You have to help me," he said. "Randall Jennings is trying to set me up for murdering Lawrence Kind."

"That's one way of looking at it," I said. "But maybe he fingered you because you're the one who killed that poor guy."

His face slackened into what I didn't think was an expression of genuine disbelief. "You can't be serious."

"I can be, sometimes, I reckon." I picked up the .357 and spun the cylinder. "My friend here, though, is serious all the time."

Feely smirked. "Come on, Buck, you're not going to scare me. We're friends. I had dinner at your house."

"Larry Kind also had dinner at my house," I said. "I had dinner with that poor Israeli girl."

"What Israeli girl?"

If a suspect is left to sweat long enough in an interrogation room, some police believe they can actually smell a lie on him. Feely was giving me a nose full of it. He knew something; I was pretty sure. I decided to press him.

"We can place you in St. Louis at the time of the killing. We've got the records. Every place you go is recorded by the GHB."

"The what?" His greasy features arranged themselves in a way that suggested real confusion.

I'd lost the name of the thing, got it wrong. I tried to look nonchalant as I flipped through the memory notebook.

"The GED."

"Buck, I don't know what that means," Feely said.

"The goddamn navigation computer."

"You mean a GPS? I haven't got one of those in my car."

I eyeballed him hard, trying to gauge whether he was telling a lie. If he wasn't, I supposed I'd bungled the bluff pretty well. It served me right for trying to bullshit about things I didn't understand.

"Don't give me that," I said. "I know you were in St. Louis."

Feely squirmed in his chair. "I didn't kill anybody."

That response surprised me. I had expected him to deny leaving Memphis.

"What were you doing there, then?"

"I don't have to tell you that."

Confirmation. He had been in St. Louis. I didn't let surprise register on my face; if he realized he was giving me information I didn't already know, he would clam up. So I sat there looking at him, drumming my fingers on the steel table.

"Look, I'm not your enemy here," Feely said. "If you get me out of here, we can help each other."

"Let's say I was willing or able to do that. What can you do for me?"

Feely didn't have an answer. He looked down at the table and carefully avoided my gaze.

"Norris," I said after a long pause, "the best thing right now is to admit what you did."

"I didn't do anything," he insisted. "Jennings is trying to frame me."

I couldn't totally dismiss the idea that Jennings might be up to something fishy. I had suspected him of trying to frame me and Tequila, and I still didn't understand what he was trying to accomplish by putting me and Norris in a room together.

"Why would Jennings frame you?"

"I can't explain here. He might be listening."

"Nobody's listening to anything, Norris."

"Yes, he is. It's a trap."

It made no sense to trust Feely over Jennings. Despite my

misgivings and my personal animus for the detective, he hadn't done anything that seemed wrong. I knew my grandson couldn't be a killer, but Jennings's suspicions about Tequila were objectively valid. And Feely had been on my short list of suspects even before he admitted he'd been in St. Louis when Yael was murdered. I wasn't ready to let my guard down around the detective; couldn't rule out the possibility that he'd tie Tequila up into some bogus bust. But I couldn't see any proof he was running the case dishonestly, and he seemed to be at least a couple of steps ahead of me on the killer's trail.

"I just wanted to do something for Jim, and to take care of Emily," said Feely. "It isn't fair."

I frowned at him. "If you want my help, you're going to have to come clean about what you were up to in St. Louis."

"The same thing as you, I suppose."

"How did you know Ziegler was there?"

He gave a full-body shudder when I spoke the Nazi's name, and his gaze flitted toward an air-conditioning vent in the ceiling. The guy watched too many movies. "I'm not as dumb as you seem to think I am."

Maybe not. But I had three million dollars' worth of gold in my attic, and he was handcuffed to a chair, so he couldn't be all that smart, either.

He bared his teeth; scrunched up his little ferret face. "You've got it, don't you? I want my share."

I wrinkled my forehead in mock sympathy and slid the pack of cigarettes across the table.

"Where you're going, those are as good as currency," I said.

"Buck, all games aside, you know I got a raw deal here. Help me, please. I want to go home."

But I didn't know how I could help him, even if I had wanted to. And what I wanted to do was let Randall Jennings do his job, at least insofar as he was doing it to Norris Feely.

"I saw you threaten Kind, and you were in St. Louis when Yael was murdered. You're as good a suspect as anybody, and if the detective said you did it, I don't know any different."

"Don't leave me in this place." He was sobbing a little, realizing nobody was coming to rescue him. "Think of my wife. She just lost her father."

"I'll look in on her for you." I had a feeling Emily would be better off without him in the long run anyway. Of course, I might have thought the same thing about Felicia Kind, and she seemed to be having a rough time since her husband's death. But I remembered Kind's father, weeping at the funeral. I had no sympathy for Norris Feely.

"You son of a bitch, you've been setting me up all along," he shouted. "I swear to Christ, I'll get you for this."

"Maybe you should speak to a neurologist," I said. "My doctor tells me paranoia is an early symptom of dementia."

"You're in cahoots, you bastards. I'm not your patsy." His eyes turned upward, toward the vent. "Do you hear?" he shouted at it. "I'm not your fucking patsy."

I stood, scooped up the rest of my belongings, and banged on the door. Jennings opened it from the outside, and I left Norris to scream at the ceiling.

"Did you learn anything?" the detective asked.

"No," I said, looking at Felicia. Her expression was hard to read. "Did you?"

Jennings gave a diffident shrug. "Suppose not."

I sighed. "Guess I'll just collect my pretty blond lady and take my leave, then."

39

"Norris Fucking Feely."

Tequila had been growling about what he was going to do to Feely ever since I'd told him what I learned at the police station. I'd expected him to be angry, but I figured he'd cool down after he'd fumed a bit and gone off to bed; he stayed in my house and slept in his father's old room.

The next morning, though, he was still muttering darkly, and he spent the whole day stomping around the house and inflicting streams of colorful invective on anyone within earshot.

I heard about how he wanted to pop Feely's fat head like a zit and about how he wanted to punch Feely in the belly until the tubby little fucker puked blood. I heard about how he could beat Feely to death with a shovel and then use the shovel to bury the body in the woods. I heard about how he wanted to take things slow; put in some quality work with a fish scaler and a screwdriver on the motherfucker's fingers and toes and then cut some things off the face before moving in toward the vital bits.

Rose and Fran had been around to hear some of these things,

and they'd found it all very upsetting, but Tequila wasn't paying any attention.

"That's not the kind of stuff you should be saying when you are a suspected psycho killer," I told him.

He couldn't take the hint. "Feely is the psycho killer. That's why I am going to peel his fucking face off, shove a candle up his ass, and turn his skinless head into a macabre jack-o'-lantern."

"He's not under arrest for the killings. He's merely detained as a person of interest."

Tequila scratched his head. "What the fuck is a person of interest?"

I sighed and dropped myself down on the sofa. "It means nobody is sure whether he did it or not. I don't know what the hell is going on, Billy. We have three million dollars' worth of gold in the attic, there's a killer who may still be on the loose, and the only thing keeping Feely from telling the police about the treasure is the fact that he still thinks he can take it from us."

Tequila told me some things he'd like to do with meat hooks and acetylene torches. He told me what a razor blade could do to a human eyeball.

I felt sorry for everyone who hadn't been blessed with grandchildren.

"Can you help me work this out?" I asked. "I thought you were supposed to be helping me, and I feel like I'm alone with it now."

"I'm so fucking pissed off about Yael."

I crossed my arms. "Well, instead of acting like an ass, why don't you try to figure out who killed her?"

"Because I don't know how."

"You can start by telling me a story about how and why Feely might have done it. It's a good first step, before you go peeling faces off of skulls."

"Isn't it obvious?"

"Pretend it isn't," I said. "And start from the beginning."

"Okay," he said. "Feely wants to kill the minister. He thinks Kind is muscling in on his piece of the treasure, right?"

"It's your story."

"Okay, Feely told you that he didn't want Kind getting a cut. You told him there was no treasure. He was upset when Kind showed up at the dinner party; he made explicit threats."

I nodded.

"Then he confronted Kind in the church and killed him."

This was a problem for me, and I told Tequila so. I was willing to believe a lot of things about Norris Feely, but the idea that the man was adept at hand-to-hand combat strained credulity. Lawrence Kind, pacifist Christian that he was, would still have been stronger and quicker than Feely. Yael would have been, also. Although Feely easily had eighty pounds on the girl, most of it was fat, and she was toned and hard and trained by the Israeli army.

"Maybe Feely caught her by surprise, hit her over the head," Tequila suggested.

Sure; lots of maybes and no way to get concrete answers, since I didn't have access to the coroner's report. Jennings might let me see it; maybe he was sincere about wanting my help on the case. But I didn't understand what he was up to, and he was not a friend. It seemed a bad idea to ask a favor of him if I didn't understand the ramifications.

The real nut of it was, Feely could have been responsible for both killings. He had no alibi for either, and his presence in St. Louis at the time of Yael's murder moved him right to the top of my list of suspects. But I was still far from convinced of his guilt.

In any case, even if Feely was innocent, his exoneration would refocus Jennings's attention on Tequila, and Feely would probably start plotting to steal the treasure as soon as he got out of jail.

I was happy to let the bastard cool his heels downtown while the system sorted things out.

"If you don't think it was Feely, who else could have done it?" Tequila asked. "I think Felicia might have been involved. She didn't carve him up herself, but a woman that good-looking always knows a couple of guys who are willing to do things for her."

Tequila didn't tell me a lot about the women he dated, but I could tell by his tone that he'd been worked over by someone beautiful he thought had loved him. To his eye, the widow was clearly a user and a manipulator. He brought his prejudices to bear on the question, but that didn't necessarily mean he was wrong. I'd watched Felicia Kind lie to Randall Jennings, and she was utterly convincing. I would be a fool to trust a single thing she'd told me, no matter how honest it sounded.

"What do you think about T. Addleford Pratt?"

"Why would he kill Kind and then try to come after us for the treasure, when he could have just taken whatever Kind might have got from us?" Tequila asked.

"Killing Kind meant he could try to get Felicia to pay him out of the life insurance recovery."

"Okay, but why would he kill Yael?"

"Maybe to make it look like we killed Kind, or to threaten us, so we'd give him the gold."

"What is the point of doing that, if he doesn't let us know it was him?"

He was right. Killing Yael would not pressure us to pay Pratt off unless he came out and told us he'd done it. And we had no reason to believe he'd been in St. Louis anyway.

"How are you feeling about the Israelis?" Tequila asked.

That theory was looking a lot weaker. Yael's death seemed to indicate that she had not been working with Yitzchak Steinblatt and Avram Silver, but there was no way to be sure. Maybe they got rid of her after she completed her role in the scheme: one less person who could expose them, and one less person to split the gold with. I suggested this to Tequila.

"I don't buy it," Tequila said. "Silver seemed like a whiny loser when we spoke to him. I don't think he's some kind of a murderous puppet master. And our only basis for suspecting old Yid's Cock is the fact that he is a large man."

"An extremely large man," I said.

"I'll give you that. The motherfucker looks like some kind of pro wrestler from the shtetl. But a spy is supposed to be inconspicuous, and that guy is about as subtle as a goddamn bulldozer. I think Steinblatt is exactly what he says he is, and Avram Silver is a doofus, and this whole Israeli preoccupation of yours is bullshit."

I lit a cigarette and thought about that for a minute. Steinblatt showed up in Memphis soon after we spoke to Silver, on the same day Kind was murdered. He also had the considerable physical strength that Kind's murder would have required. I was hunting a killer, and the big Russian looked the part. Maybe some ACLU types would call that profiling, but when there's a guy who looks like a killer, he usually is one.

The thing that made this unusual was that even though so many people seemed to have means and motives to do the crime, none of them seemed to intuitively fit as the killer. Murder, contrary to widespread belief, usually doesn't make for much of a mystery. In the stories and on the television programs, cops are always trying to decipher opaque motives and people are never what they seem. But real murder is mean and dumb and unsubtle, and pretty much everyone a detective meets is exactly what they appear to be. If scumbags had the brains or the imagination to manage convincing deception, they wouldn't have to be scumbags.

"Mom told me that Steinblatt is going to be speaking about Israel down at the JCC tonight, to the Jewish Federation," Tequila said. "It might be worth hearing what he says. Maybe we should go."

That would at least give me a chance to see if he looked at all like a genuine flack for the Israeli government.

"I'll take your grandmother," I told him. "You're not going. I don't want you embarrassing me in front of people I know."

40

Tequila gave us a lift to the Jewish Community Center, and despite his protests, he didn't stay for the speech. I wanted him at the house to guard the treasure, and he'd already upset his grandmother enough with the things he'd been saying. I was getting worried about him; even if he'd had his head on straight, it looked like we were dealing with more trouble than we could easily handle. My detective's instinct had been whispering to me all day, but I couldn't understand what it was telling me. I felt sure something bad was about to happen, and I couldn't figure out what it was or where it would be coming from.

I needed my grandson's help to stand any chance of getting ahead of this thing, but I couldn't trust his judgment anymore. Even when he wasn't sobbing or fuming, I could hear emotion welling behind his voice. The kind of cool, flawless logic he'd used to dismantle the LSATs and the bank manager would have been a useful tool in our situation, but his thinking was obviously clouded. And, I was scared of putting him in harm's way. The lousy little jerk was all I had left of my son.

In the meantime, I hoped Steinblatt would be persuasive enough as a Diaspora liaison that I could write him off my list of suspects. I sure didn't want to wake up to find him standing over me with those huge hands of his.

The JCC was crowded. People who were elderly and Jewish found that Memphis offered very little to do on an average Saturday night, so most of them had come out for Steinblatt's speech and for the free refreshments the Center always served at these events. A sizable crowd of people we knew were kibitzing in the lobby.

Rose had insisted on getting rid of the wheelchair, even though it hurt her to stand up and sit down. She was walking with assistance from a steel cane with four rubber feet on it.

"Everybody is looking at me with my cripple cane," she said. "This sure isn't something Fred Astaire would carry around."

I smiled at her. "If it's any consolation, I feel just like Ginger Rogers right now."

"Oh, hush up, Buck."

But folks were looking; she was right about that. Health problems were big news among our contemporaries, since most of our social calendar revolved around burying one another.

Esther Katz spotted us from across the lobby and shambled over to say hello. She used to play gin rummy with Rose, but then she started getting confused and had to be put away.

"I heard you were in the hospital." That Esther had heard it wasn't surprising. That she remembered it, though, was nothing short of remarkable.

Rose nodded.

"Is it serious?" Esther's face pursed with concern.

"What business is it of yours?" I asked.

"Well, I just wanted to know if I should ask my daughter-in-law to make her noodle kugel."

Rose's expression darkened. "What does my health have to do with that?"

Esther started to speak and then realized what she was about to say. Jews customarily bring food when they make condolence visits to a grieving family; she was asking if Rose was planning to die.

Suddenly cognizant of the impropriety of such a question, Esther was left without words; she stood there with her jaw hanging open. I thought she looked like a baby penguin waiting for its mother to vomit some fish guts into its mouth. Then I thought I should probably stop watching so much of the Animal Planet channel.

"The kugel is awfully thoughtful of you, Esther," Rose said, gently touching her friend's hand. "We were planning to just pick up a bag of day-old bagels on the way to yours."

I may have made a few wrong decisions in my life, but I damn sure married the right woman.

We chatted, more or less amiably, with various friends and acquaintances for a while longer before the crowd began gravitating into the social hall to hear what Yitzchak Steinblatt would have to say about Israel.

Rose and I found our seats. On the stage at the front of the room, there was a podium with a microphone, three chairs, an American flag, and an Israeli flag. Two of the chairs were occupied by the director of the Center and the president of the Jewish Federation. The third, empty chair was presumptively for Steinblatt.

The president looked at her watch and then whispered to the director, who nodded. Then he stood, adjusted his pants, and moved behind the podium.

"Good evening, ladies and gentlemen. I spoke to our guest a short while ago, and you're in for a real treat tonight. Yitzchak Steinblatt is a thoroughly warm and engaging person, and we're thrilled that the state of Israel has sent him here to spend some time with us."

He spent a couple of minutes making the sales pitch for donations to the Federation, an organization that had been squeezed, like many Jewish charities, by investment losses related to the massive Bernard Madoff Ponzi fraud. The local Jewish women's group had to cancel a trip to visit Israel because the organization's funding fell through.

Of course it went without saying, the director told us, his face a grim and solemn mask, that there would be no government programs for the Jewish community. I whispered something funny to Rose, something about the Holocaust. I must have said it sort of loud, because people sitting around us turned to give me dirty looks.

The community, the director continued, would have to bail itself out. All of us were hurting, and he assured us he knew that, but *tsedakah,* charity, was not a luxury, and it was most crucial, and a bigger mitzvah, to give during hard times.

He paused and looked at his watch.

"Uh, Yitzchak should be almost ready to begin his presentation."

The president of the Federation stood up, and the director covered the microphone with his hand while the two of them whispered to each other.

Then she walked backstage.

"You've all been very patient, and if you'll indulge us for a moment, we have a very pleasant evening ahead."

The big, slippery Israeli had ditched town, I knew it. Or worse, he was at my house, killing Tequila. I'd known something was wrong with the bastard from the start.

The Federation president came back onto the stage and spoke to the director. She looked upset.

The two of them went backstage. The audience began to get noisy.

"What do you think is going on?" Rose asked me.

I tried to reassure her, but I knew she could tell how nervous I was getting.

Then the house lights came on, and a young man in a golf shirt with a JCC logo on it came in through the back door of the room and started calling my name.

"Detective Schatz, can you come assist us for a moment?"

"No," I shouted back, and people started laughing. But Rose poked me with one of those sharp elbows she's got, and I hauled myself to my feet and began to help her stand up as well.

"Mrs. Schatz, perhaps you should keep your seat for the time being," said the golf shirt man.

"Buck, what's happening?" she asked.

"Don't worry," I assured her, automatically. "Everything is fine."

I didn't believe it, though.

I walked back out to the lobby, and the JCC director met me there. The golf shirt went back into the social hall and extracted a guy from the audience who I knew was a doctor but didn't know much else about.

"We appreciate your help," the director told us.

I looked at the doctor, and he seemed to be as confused as I was, a fact I found kind of comforting.

The director ushered us down a hallway that ran behind the social hall, around to the backstage area. He was talking the whole time, with the fast, nervous inflection of a man on the edge of shock, telling us that he'd never had a situation like this and hoped we'd know how to handle it.

The Jewish Federation president was slumped next to a door leading to one of the dressing rooms. It might have been the fluorescent light, but her skin seemed to have taken on a distinct greenish pallor. The doctor and I looked at each other and then looked at the door. I reached for the knob, paused for a moment, and pulled out a wad of Kleenex I had in the sleeve of my sweater so I could open the door without leaving any fingerprints.

The first thing I noticed in the room was the smell: a wet, coppery stink, like a summer breeze coming off an abattoir. Hanging from a metal hook on the wall that might normally have held the costumes for the Chanukah pageant was a carcass that was the right size and just about hairy enough to have recently been Yitzchak Steinblatt. But the body was so mangled, it would be difficult to identify him without getting a lot closer, and I wasn't going into the room, because the floor was slick with blood.

The killer had hung Steinblatt by his feet. The hook was mounted at a height a child could reach, so Steinblatt's head, shoulders, and arms were resting on the floor. That meant the killer wouldn't have had to lift Steinblatt's full weight, but getting him up there still would have required a pretty significant effort from a fit adult male.

Even more impressive, Steinblatt must have been alive when the killer hung him up, because there was arterial spray all over the walls, and arteries do not spray unless the heart is still pumping.

"Hung him upside down and slit his throat," the doctor whispered.

"Apparently, this killer has a sense of humor," I said.

The big Jew had been slaughtered kosher.

And just as with the other murders, the torso was cut open and the entrails were spilled out all over the linoleum.

"Can you fix him?" the director asked the doctor. "Can you perform CPR?"

"I don't," the doctor stammered. "I can't."

"CPR only works when the patient's lungs are still in his chest," I said.

The doctor nodded. "Um, yes."

"What should we do?" asked the Federation president.

"Has anyone been in there? Has anyone touched anything?"

She told me nobody had.

"Good," I said, and I pulled the door shut. "Call the police and don't let anyone touch anything until they arrive."

She waved a hand to indicate her assent. "What do we do in the meantime?"

"I schlepped out here tonight because I thought there would be some free cake."

Her eyes were sort of glazed over. "Yes, we had planned for refreshments after the presentation."

"Good," I said. "How about you cut me a piece of that? And fetch me a Diet Coke as well. Do you want anything, Doc?"

The doctor gave a sort of half shrug. "I could eat."

"Attaboy," I said. "Get Doc some cake, too."

"And a Sprite, if you've got one," he said.

I lit a cigarette. The JCC was about the only place I generally followed the no-smoking rule, but these were extenuating circumstances.

I looked around as the director and the president beat a quick retreat from the murder room. The hallway we were standing in ended with a door marked EXIT. The killer had butchered Steinblatt and then walked right through that door and out to the parking lot. The body was still warm, and the perp was probably halfway across town.

I found Rose in the lobby among a crowd of Jews, gossiping about what might have happened to cause the cancellation of the speech.

She looked at me and then looked with disapproval at my cigarette. "Are you going to tell me what's going on?"

I glanced around to make sure nobody was listening, and then I leaned in close to whisper in her ear:

"Yid's Cock got clipped."

The homicide forensic techs were doing whatever they do at a crime scene, under the supervision of the local Lubavitcher rabbi who had come to make sure that every bit of flesh and drop of blood was collected for burial in accordance with Jewish law.

Even the detectives had been shocked by the mess the killer had made, and the young rabbi was the only one who did not react visibly. He told me he'd performed this grim task at the scenes of terrorist bombings in Jerusalem when he was a yeshiva student.

Randall Jennings looked thoughtfully at the flayed corpse of Yitzchak Steinblatt.

"Norris Feely has a pretty ironclad alibi for this one," he said.

"He's still in your jail?"

"Yeah, but he's about to get sprung."

"He could have an accomplice."

Jennings chuckled a little. "He could be the accomplice."

I nodded. "You're thinking T. Addleford Pratt is behind these, then?"

"No, I'm not."

The two of us stared at each other for a long minute. I knew what he meant.

"That ain't how it is, Randall."

"I can't rely on your word, at this point. Your grandson was acquainted with all three victims. Nobody else who might be suspected of killing Lawrence Kind had any connection to this guy, or to the girl in the hotel. And I've got Buck Schatz and his grandson at the scene of every one of these. I've been making my life a lot harder than I ought to, giving you the benefit of the doubt. But if you look at this objectively, there's only one answer that makes sense."

"My grandson didn't kill anyone."

"Can you account for his whereabouts at the time of this murder?"

"He dropped me and my wife at the front door at around seven. Then he went home."

"How do you know he went home?"

"I just know."

"Put yourself in my shoes, Buck. How do you make the facts we know fit together?"

I didn't say anything.

"Lawrence Kind comes to your house in the middle of the night. This isn't an ordinary sort of social call, I don't expect. Maybe you quarrel. The next day, he's dead. Your grandson has no alibi."

"Kind had a lot of enemies."

"The girl in St. Louis was visiting from out of town. She didn't have any enemies; didn't even know anyone except your grandson. And she gets the same kind of knifework, same disembowelment."

"The killer followed us, maybe."

He frowned. "Why would a killer follow you to St. Louis to butcher your grandson's one-night stand in her hotel room?"

For the gold, I thought. For the goddamn gold.

But what I said was: "I don't know."

"Exactly. And now we have this guy. And look at this scene. This victim was killed the way Jewish dietary rules dictate an animal must be slaughtered. Who would know about that, except for a Jewish killer?"

"Anyone," I said. "It's common knowledge."

"You think Lawrence Kind's Tunica loan sharks know the rules of Jewish ritual butchering? You think whatever dropout Orange Mound hit man Felicia Kind might have hired to kill her husband would know something like that? And why would they go to the trouble to kill Yitzchak Steinblatt?"

This seemed obvious. "To frame Tequila."

"Why would anyone frame your grandson?"

I didn't say anything, so he continued.

"I look at this crime, I look at all these crimes, and I see this killer was smart. All Steinblatt's blood went out of him, onto the floor, onto the walls. But there's no blood in the hallway, and nobody saw anybody running around covered in blood. The perp probably wore a smock or a coverall, and brought a change of shoes, and put the bloody stuff in a plastic bag at the door, so he could walk out clean. That's the way a detective's genius lawyer grandson would commit a murder. And at the previous two killings, we saw the same thing. There were bloody, horrible messes at the scenes, but no bloody footprints or drippings leading away."

"I know Tequila didn't do it. He was at my house when Steinblatt was killed."

"How do you know?"

"I called him right after the director showed me the body, to tell him what had happened."

"On your home line?"

I thought about it for a minute. "No, on his cell."

Jennings frowned. "So he could have been anywhere."

"Could have been. But he was at my house."

"Even if he was, your house is less than a five-minute drive from here. He could have gotten back before anyone even found the scene."

He was right. I grunted at him.

Jennings sighed. "Look, the kid lost his father, and that's a terrible thing for somebody to go through. And, you know, some people have a loss like that, and they never get right again."

He was trying to goad me into an emotional response. "We don't need to talk about this."

"Point is, a man goes through something like that, maybe he could snap. And from where I'm standing, that's the only story that makes sense, unless you know something you ain't told me."

I could come clean about the gold, give it up to Jennings and throw some suspicion back onto the other people. But there had to be some way to get out of this mess without losing the treasure. I just couldn't think of one.

"Are you gonna charge him with it?" I asked.

"I damn sure want to talk to him. I'll wait until tomorrow, as a professional courtesy. I trust that you will not let the kid lam it. Bring him downtown by lunchtime, if you want to save him the embarrassment of a perp walk. Otherwise, we will be looking for him. There's a lot of evidence."

I grunted. "It's all circumstantial." But I had seen plenty of convictions on circumstantial evidence.

He patted me on the shoulder, but I brushed his hand away.

"You might want to use this time to lawyer up," he said.

Something I don't want to forget:

Tequila could have been at home the summer Brian was killed, but he stayed up at his college. Ostensibly, he was doing some internship for credit, but mostly he wanted to horse around with his friends at the fraternity house. He wanted to spend his afternoons at the swimming pool and his evenings making love to some young girl he was seeing at the time.

One night, Tequila called home; his father was outside talking with a neighbor and didn't come to the phone. It was no big deal, they'd talk the next time. Fifteen hours later, he was on his way home for the funeral. Jewish people are quick about covering up their dead.

I remember he sobbed all the way through the memorial service. Sobbed at the graveside. It was his task to drop the first shovelful of dirt on his father's casket. He did it, and then he ran off to throw up in the cemetery parking lot.

For the next week, shiva visitors came in and out of the house. Rose and Fran and I sat there to meet them, and Fran's parents were there, too. Tequila spent most of the week locked in his bedroom.

He left only to go to synagogue, twice a day, at seven A.M. and seven P.M., to say Kaddish, the mourner's prayer.

For a parent or a child, a Jewish man must mourn a year, and it is a son's duty to go to minyan and exalt God's name. Tequila would rather have been raging against the heavens, and while he dutifully obeyed the commandments, he seemed to take profound personal offense at the traditions that had saddled him with such an obligation. To my knowledge, Tequila did not step foot in a synagogue ever again once he'd completed his mourning duties.

After the services, he would come back to his mother's house sullen and angry and press through the gauntlet of condolence visitors so he could shut himself back up in his room. The idea behind shiva is that friends come out to support the bereaved in their time of need, but Jewish people tend to gravitate to wherever there is free food, and the house inevitably fills with strangers. It becomes more of a burden than a consolation.

On the third day, somewhere between the door to the house and the door to his bedroom, he overheard somebody saying something he didn't like. Now, reverence for the dead has never been a strong suit among the Schatzes, but we usually have enough decency to make wisecracks only when the grieving are not within earshot. And maybe Tequila was looking for an excuse to take something out on somebody.

So Tequila punched the guy until he fell to the floor. Then he kicked the guy until he stopped trying to get up. And then he went into the kitchen and started looking for a knife. That's when some friends intervened and dragged Tequila off someplace to cool down while other people got the injured man out of the house.

Despite whatever conclusions Randall Jennings might have wanted to draw, I knew my grandson was a good kid. But if I had looked at the situation dispassionately, I'd have been forced to admit that the detective's position wasn't unreasonable.

42

I called Tequila to get him to come pick us up. His cell phone rang six times and went to voice mail. I tried the house phone and nobody answered.

We hitched a ride home with some friends. The front door was securely locked, the burglar alarm was engaged, the purple Volkswagen was still in the driveway, and Tequila was gone.

I carefully checked all the windows and could find no signs of forced entry. I was not strong enough to climb the stepladder to the attic to check on the gold, but it didn't look to me like anyone had been up there. I called Tequila's cellular again: no answer. I called his mother. She didn't know where he was. I checked every room in the house. No note or message from him. No sign of a struggle. My .357 was missing.

I sat on the couch. Possibly Jennings had lied to me and sent officers over to pick up Tequila while I was still at the crime scene. They would have found the gun on my nightstand and bagged it as evidence.

Maybe Tequila had seen the hammer coming down and had

decided to flee. But I was sure he was innocent, and that didn't seem like something an innocent man would do.

It was also possible that the real killer had taken him. Although nothing had been disturbed in the house, none of the other victims had struggled. Making Tequila disappear would be the logical last step of a frame job on him.

The idea that the killer would proceed here immediately after killing Steinblatt made a lot of sense. Nothing scuttled a frame job on an innocent man like having the fellow mucking around trying to vindicate himself. Since Tequila vanished the same time Steinblatt got carved up, it would look to an observer like Tequila had done the job and then fled. The police would consider his disappearance an admission of guilt and would pursue no other leads.

Tequila could go into a shallow grave, and the investigation into the murders would stop until some jogger or somebody's dog found the body. By then it would be too late to piece together solid evidence against another suspect. I comforted myself with the idea that Tequila would probably stay alive, though, at least until the killer got hold of the treasure. Unless he already had it; there was no way I could check the attic.

I dialed Tequila's cell again and got no answer.

Rose didn't know about the girl in St. Louis and didn't know Tequila was now a murder suspect, so she imputed nothing sinister in his absence. I decided not to alarm her. But I sat up in the living room, watching Fox News and hoping he'd come back.

Sometime after midnight, I fell asleep on the sofa. I woke up around three, when a black Chevy Malibu pulled into my driveway.

43

Wiping sleep from my eyes, I padded into the darkened kitchen and leaned over the breakfast table so I could peer through the window.

The Chevy rolled to a stop in front of my garage. I could see the back of it, and it looked like it had a yellow license plate, which meant it was from Mississippi. I could not make out the number.

The door opened and the silhouette of a man climbed out of the driver's side. The only light was from a streetlamp at the end of the driveway, and my vision was kind of fuzzy, so I couldn't tell who the driver was, even squinting.

Despite the near darkness, though, I could see he was holding a gun in his left hand. I wished I had my .357.

The Chevy's trunk popped open, and the driver roughly hauled a second man out of it and dropped him hard on the ground. The man from the trunk was bound or shackled around the wrists and ankles.

The captive tried to struggle, but the driver cracked him over the head with the gun and dragged him around the front of the car toward the garage.

I figured the captive must have been Tequila. The driver was probably Pratt. The debt collector must have kidnapped Tequila out of the house, taken him someplace, and beat him until he admitted we had the gold. Now he was back to take it from us.

I picked up the phone and started to call Randall Jennings. But then I realized that if the police showed up, my grandson would be caught in the middle of a standoff between police and a cornered man. My faith in the competence of the cops was less than total, and I didn't know if they could safely defuse a hostage situation. It seemed foolish to think that I could do a better job myself; I was infirm, unarmed, and confused. Even negotiating a swap of my grandson for the gold seemed to be a task beyond my capacity. But escalating the situation by involving police would be extraordinarily dangerous.

I went out the front door, closing it as quietly as I could, and walked across the damp lawn in my slippers.

On close inspection, the Chevy in the driveway looked a little different from the one that had chased us in St. Louis. I distinctly remembered that Chevy having black windows, but the one in the driveway had ordinary transparent ones.

This car also had an Ole Miss souvenir license plate on its front bumper; the pursuer in St. Louis had not had a license holder on the front of the car. I tried to think of a reason why the killer might have replaced all his windows in the last couple of days and couldn't come up with one.

I walked around to the garage, where the driver had dragged his captive, and I saw T. Addleford Pratt. But he was the one lying on the floor, bound up with duct tape. Tequila was waving my gun in Pratt's face.

"What the hell is this?" I asked.

"I'm trying to get a confession out of this son of a bitch," Tequila told me.

"I didn't do nothin' to nobody," said T. Addleford Pratt. His rotten brown teeth were smashed, and his nose was bent sideways and kind of flattened. The white part of his left eye was full of blood. I was impressed, momentarily, before I realized how much trouble we were in.

"What have you done, Billy?" I reached my hand toward him, and he gave me back my gun.

"As soon as you called and told me Steinblatt was dead, I knew Pratt had to be the killer. We told this asshole that Steinblatt was connected to the treasure, but Norris Feely and Felicia Kind didn't know anything about any Israelis. So I called a cab and went out to Tunica to find the son of a bitch, and it turns out he's driving the same car that chased us around St. Louis."

"I ain't never been to St. Louis," Pratt howled.

"You picked him up in Tunica?"

"Yeah. I caught him leaving the casino."

I did the math in my head, and it didn't seem to work. "Steinblatt was killed less than twenty minutes before I called you. If Pratt was in Tunica, that's a solid alibi. He can't be the killer."

Tequila kicked Pratt hard in the stomach. "He did it, the son of a bitch. Tell him you did it."

Pratt moaned.

"Did you murder Lawrence Kind?" I asked.

Pratt spat a mouthful of blood onto the concrete floor of the garage. "Fuck, no."

"Felicia Kind said you tried to get her to pay you out of her life insurance."

"Dammit, I try to get ever'body to pay out of ever'thing. That's muh fuckin' job, you asshole."

Tequila raised a leg to stomp Pratt again, but I signaled him to hold off.

"There was no money to collect on before you killed Kind, and after he was dead, there was money to collect from the life insurance."

"No, you got it wrong. The casino is a creditor of the dead man's estate. The wife is the beneficiary of the life insurance. Since the insurance money never passes through the estate, we can't get a piece of it."

I looked at Tequila. "Does that sound true?"

"I don't fucking know," he said. Way to go, NYU Law School.

"Look, I am an accountant. I handle delinquent accounts." Pratt paused for a moment to let out a snuffling moan. It sounded like something inside him was filling with fluid. But when he started talking again, a lot of the redneck inflection seemed to have drained out of his voice. "First, I identify that the debtor is late on his payments and I put a stop on further gaming credit. Then I call the debtor and listen to excuses. I threaten legal action, I send out a couple of letters, and see if I can shake anything out of 'em. When they don't pay up, I send an e-mail to my boss, telling him that I think he should write off the debt, or that he should pursue legal action."

"You told us you work in the muscle business," I said.

"Yeah. I bet I said a lot of shit. I was trying to cow you into handing me payment, at least partial payment, on a debt that's legally unrecoverable. There are lots of stories among gamblers about broken legs and crushed fingers. About holes in the desert outside Las Vegas. It don't hurt, in my line of work, to keep people scared. Folks in this part of the country are the kind of sanctimonious Christians that don't think casino debts ought to get paid, so it's a lost cause, most times, trying to get what we're owed in court. If the losers stay scared, they won't try to draw credit they ain't good for, and they won't go deadbeat on what they owe us."

"Bullshit, bullshit, bullshit." Tequila's eyes were welling up. "People get killed over gambling debts all the time."

"Not by us, they don't," Pratt insisted. "The Silver Gulch Saloon and Casino is licensed and regulated by the state of Mississippi. If we looked for a single second like a criminal enterprise, the state would yank our right to operate without hesitation. We ain't gonna jeopardize the whole damn business by committing murder over the piddly-shit debt Lawrence Kind owed us. And I sure ain't gonna kill nobody, 'cause it ain't my ass on the line over the loss. I didn't approve any credit for Kind. I just shook down whoever I thought might be shakable when the deadbeat turned up gutted."

"Grandpa, the man drives a black Chevy Malibu. He's got to be the killer."

"F'chrissake," said Pratt. "If I was some kind of nefarious homicidal fuckin' kingpin, would this little dicksucker here have been able to kick the shit out of me, and shove me in the trunk of my own damn car?"

What Pratt was saying sounded, to my ears, like the truth. "The world is full of Chevys," I told my grandson.

What I was thinking was that Tequila could have killed Steinblatt and then gone straight to Tunica to pick up Pratt. But I tried to banish such thoughts from my mind. I knew my grandson. I knew, absolutely, that he hadn't killed those people.

Certainly, there were other plausible scenarios, Pratt or Feely or Felicia might have a personal alibi, but any of them might have some sort of accomplice; two of them could have been working together, or somebody might be using some kind of contract killer. Hired muscle didn't usually do jobs in a messy psycho killer style, but if the money was right, most things were negotiable.

But even if Tequila was innocent of the murders, he had committed a pretty wide assortment of crimes in his apprehension of Pratt: kidnapping, grand theft auto, and assault, at least. And he'd taken Pratt across state lines, which subjected him to federal charges. And he'd used a gun, which meant he could be hit with an additional federal weapons charge. He was looking at three or four decades of jail time.

And as long as the real killer was still loose, and as long as we had Heinrich Ziegler's treasure, the people I loved would be in danger. I had to make the safe play now. And I had to protect Tequila.

I sighed. "You remember when you asked me if I ever framed a man up to close a case in a way I liked?"

"Yeah?"

"Well, I never exactly did that before. But it looks like I'm about to. Go haul the gold down from the attic."

Something I don't want to forget:

After I left the death camp at Chelmno, I found a dank little tavern in the basement of an old building in Lodz, and I settled onto a wobbly stool to drown my dark mood in sour, cloudy vodka.

There was only one other barfly in the place, a stoop-shouldered Pole who carried years of hard living in deep creases on his face. He looked at me for a while, his milky yellow eyes glowing like phosphorus in the lamplit room. I ignored him, but he came over to speak to me anyway.

"Amerikaner?"

I nodded without turning my head toward him.

"Good on you, then," he said in English. "I hate the Germans. They are full of lies."

"They're full of something," I said.

"I am Krzysztof," said the drunk.

"Buck."

"Ah. Book. I like this. Is fine American name. Like cowboy."

"Sure."

"Germans don't have such names."

"Reckon not."

"Germans come with big promise. Work for us, Krzysztof. Be a police. And I go to work for them. Now, what am I? Peasant farmer again, like before they came, only now, much worse. Nothing will grow, not even potato. So many marching boots and tank treads, strip the good earth. You have word for this?"

"Topsoil?"

"Yes. Topsoil stripped away. Fields are fallow. I have little money, and I spend it to drink. Perhaps later, I will starve. Things are very bad."

"Be thankful you ain't a Japanese," I said.

"Yes, or a Jew," said Krzysztof, and he laughed. "I was police, at the Jew camp nearby. Very fine, the Germans promise. Pay is good. Plenty to eat. When you want woman, you take. Then they decide to send the Jews to Treblinka, and all goes away."

"You were a guard up at Chelmno?"

"Yes, until damn Germans took it from me. Now, things could not be worse."

But things got worse for Krzysztof a half hour later, when I took him outside and beat him until his face was mush and his nose caved in and his mouth was a ragged, gasping hole.

I left him lying on the street, his blood running down through the gaps in the cobblestones, and I skipped town before the local authorities caught up to me. A few days later, I booked passage home. Became a police. And now, what am I?

44

Randall Jennings was sitting at my kitchen table, looking at two hundred pounds of Nazi gold. Tequila was standing by the doorway with his arms crossed.

He'd wanted to hold back at least a couple of bars, but I knew that we needed our story to be as close to the truth as possible, and as long as we had anything, the killer would be after us. So despite Tequila's objections, all eight bars were resting on the table.

T. Addleford Pratt was on the floor, curled in a ball, bleeding. His hands and feet were still wrapped in duct tape.

"If you want to know why Kind was murdered, this is it," I told Jennings. I'd explained to him who Ziegler was and how he had escaped from Europe with the treasure. I told him why we were in St. Louis and gave him a version of the story about how we acquired the gold that didn't involve stealing from a bank.

"Jim Wallace knew about the treasure all his life, but he was ashamed of letting Ziegler escape, so he never told anyone. He started talking about it when he was on his deathbed. He told me, and Norris Feely and Lawrence Kind."

Jennings peered at Pratt and then at the swastika stamps on the gold bars. He rubbed at his eyes. He looked tired; he'd been off duty, and I'd called him at home.

"How does this guy fit into the story?" he asked.

"This is the debt collector for the Silver Gulch Casino in Tunica. Lawrence Kind owed him money and promised him a cut of the treasure against gambling debts."

"And he's the killer?"

"I don't know," I said. Which was sort of true. "We caught the son of a bitch snooping around, trying to break in."

"That's a lie," Pratt shouted.

"You got a right to remain silent, asshole," said Jennings.

That clammed Pratt up. He seemed bright enough not to say anything else without his lawyer present, which was fine with me.

"Anyway," I said. "We heard this guy scrabbling around outside, and Tequila threw him a beating. But, you know, we were on edge after what happened to Yitzchak Steinblatt, and we didn't know if he was armed until we had him subdued."

"And what did Steinblatt have to do with this mess?" Jennings asked.

I told him about Avram Silver and about how Steinblatt's arrival coincided with my call to Silver and with Kind's death. I explained how we'd suggested to Pratt that Steinblatt was connected to the treasure. I realized, for the first time, that Steinblatt's death, and Yael's death, too, had been my fault.

"The Israelis had nothing to do with anything," I said, shaking my head sadly. "They died because the killer associated them with us."

Jennings seemed to turn this over in his head for a few minutes. "I have to hand it to you," he said. "I did not expect you to come up with a story that would get your grandson off the hook, but I guess that will do it."

I figured as much. No prosecutor on earth would have taken the case to trial after I'd stacked up three million dollars' worth of reasonable doubt on the kitchen table.

"He's innocent, like I said."

"I need him available for questioning, though."

"He'll be going back to school in New York in a couple of days," I said.

Jennings rubbed his mustache. He didn't like that but couldn't do much about it. "He better be down here double quick if I want him."

Tequila helped put the gold bars in the backpacks and loaded them into the trunk of Jennings's car. Then he went back into the house to sulk. He let the door slam behind him.

Jennings had cut the tape off of Pratt and put some real handcuffs on him. He put a hand on the back of the debt collector's head and guided him into the backseat of a brown unmarked police vehicle.

"That rotten little bastard doesn't even appreciate what you did for him," Jennings told me, jerking his head toward the house to indicate he was talking about my grandson. "You could have kept the treasure and let him take the fall for the killings."

"He's all the family I've got. Somebody's got to carry on the Schatz name."

"I hadn't figured you for the sentimental type."

"Yeah, well, sometimes I'll surprise you like that."

Jennings patted me on the shoulder and climbed into his car.

I lit a cigarette and stood there on the lawn, watching my fortune ride off down the street.

It seemed like I'd put myself through too damn much to have the treasure slip through my fingers. I felt like I'd been beaten or outsmarted somehow, and I didn't like it much.

But I figured I'd gotten my money's worth for the gold; it had bought Tequila out of the trouble Pratt or whoever had gotten him into. And it got me out of a full-contact game that I was too old and too weak and too confused to play any longer.

I took a drag on my Lucky Strike, and I turned to go back into the house. That's when I felt something like an angry horsefly hit me low on my left side and whiz through me. It took me a long moment to realize that I must have been shot.

There was nobody around, but somebody with a rifle could have hit me from pretty far away. Norris Feely must have come straight here after Jennings cut him loose and had been waiting all night, somewhere out in the darkness, for a clean look at me.

I felt hot screaming pain as my body realized what had happened, and I knew I was going to fall down. At that moment, my mind could barely even process the terrible significance of the injury I'd already sustained. I was completely preoccupied with what would happen when I hit the ground.

If a guy my age falls and cracks his head, that's a fatal injury. I'm probably not strong enough or quick enough to cushion a fall with my arms, and since my bones are somewhat brittle, my skull would break like an eggshell.

That's what happened to Katharine Graham, the publisher of *The Washington Post*. She was one of the most powerful people in a city full of powerful people; she toppled Richard Nixon. And she died when she tripped on an uneven sidewalk. I didn't want to go out like that.

I could feel myself beginning to go into shock. My shirt was drenched in blood, and I could feel the stuff soaking my under-pants. The blood thinners protected me from strokes, but when I bled, I bled a lot and didn't stop.

I bent my knees as far as I could and sort of sat down, catch-ing as much weight on my arms as they would bear. Then I care-fully laid myself on the lawn. Having succeeded in getting to the ground without causing additional damage, I was now free to safely bleed to death from the gunshot wound.

I thought about shouting to Tequila for help, but I remem-bered how Nazi snipers would wound a man and then leave him lying in the open, screaming for assistance, so they could kill any-one who tried to rescue him. Feely could still be skulking around out there, waiting. I couldn't risk getting my grandson killed; couldn't endure that kind of loss again, even for the few minutes I had left to live. I kept my mouth shut.

My hands were going numb, so I reached into my pocket for my memory notebook, but it wasn't there. I must have left it in the house. I had my cell phone, though; I'd forgotten about it. I pressed my emergency speed-dial button.

"Nine one one," said a voice on the line.

I gave my address and told her I'd been shot. Then I dropped the phone on the lawn without bothering to hang it up. Where I was going, I wouldn't need my anytime minutes.

The grass underneath my body was soft and fresh, like it always was in the springtime, like it had been when I was young, like it had been when I'd tasked myself with taking care of it, and like it would remain, even though I wouldn't be around any longer. There was some kind of metaphor there that Tequila might appreciate: the gold riding off down the road, the old man bleeding out onto the indifferent sod, the world going on as if none of it had happened. A lesson for him to learn, like that professor had been talking about on the television. It wasn't much consolation; mostly I was just angry. But I was too weak to holler about it, so I closed my eyes.

I think I might have heard the sirens, but I don't remember much after that.

46

When I woke up, I was someplace dark and I felt hot. So I assumed I was in hell. As things turned out, though, I was still in Memphis.

More specifically, I was in the geriatric intensive care unit in the MED. As my eyes adjusted to the darkness and my initial panic dissipated, I could see the blinking monitors next to my bed and hear them beeping. I could see the television mounted high on the wall. I could see a window with venetian blinds over it and a little bit of light streaming through them. And I could smell hospital, piss and death. That meant I wasn't much deafer or blinder than I had been, and my brain seemed to still be mostly functioning.

I took a careful inventory of myself to assess the damage. There was an oxygen line in my nose, but no feeding tube in my throat, so I had probably not been out for longer than a day or two. I had both of my arms and all of my fingers. An intravenous line was plugged into me, taped to the back of my right hand. It itched a little. I had a catheter in me, which also itched. I really, really hated hospitals.

I could still feel my feet and wiggle my toes. I tried to raise and lower each leg, to see if I'd shattered a hip, which was a big concern. Because of my age, I couldn't survive an invasive surgery like a hip replacement, so that kind of fracture meant permanent confinement to a wheelchair. Both my legs lifted, which was a relief, but when I raised the right one, my side hurt so bad that I screamed in pain, which was embarrassing.

The noise woke Rose, who had been asleep in an armchair next to the bed.

"What's wrong, Buck?" she asked, concern etching lines in her face that were even deeper than the usual.

"I must have forgotten I got shot," I told her.

I hiked up my hospital gown and inspected the wound. There were about twenty sutures in the front, to the right of my navel, and the wound in the back felt like it was about the same size. Somebody once told me how a fully jacketed rifle bullet can shear right through a human body, and at that moment, the fact seemed pertinent.

I could vaguely remember having half woken sometime recently. I recalled staring through a drug haze at a man wearing a white coat over surgical scrubs standing at the end of the bed. Not our regular doctor.

"You're very lucky. Massive trauma injuries like this are extremely dangerous and routinely fatal in patients who are on anticoagulants," the surgeon had told me. "And elderly patients can decompensate quickly when they experience a severe injury. You would have died if they hadn't brought you to the hospital with the finest goddamn vascular surgeon in the southeastern United States."

"Elderly than who?" I had asked, pointing an accusatory finger at him. Then I'd passed out again.

"Am I going to die?" I asked Rose.

"Yes," she said. "Just not right now. You should try to stop getting in the way of bullets, though."

Her advice was sound, but it annoyed me nonetheless.

"Buck, I've spoken with the doctors, and they say you are going to have a harder time getting around, even after you recover. I think it's time we talk about our living arrangements."

"I'm going to get out of this place, and I am going to go home, and things are going to be the same as they have always been," I said.

She crossed her arms. "No, they're not. Not this time."

I rubbed at the IV line where it went into my hand. "What have you done?" I growled.

"I've met with some people, and I've put down a deposit on an assisted living condo at a place called Valhalla Estates. There's room for your sofa and there's full premium cable with all your channels, right in the apartment. They've got parking for residents, so you can keep your Buick, and they will sell our house for us and credit it against our expenses."

"We can't go to Valhalla," I said. "That's heaven for Nazis."

I didn't want to give up the ungrateful lawn and the paper at the end of the driveway. I didn't want to give up my coffee and oatmeal at the kitchen table with the sun streaming in through the windows. I didn't want to give up Brian's old room and its shelves lined with the books I'd read to him when he was a boy.

"I don't want to go any more than you do, but what am I supposed to do?" Rose asked me. She wasn't just giving me the piss now, there was real anger and sadness in her voice. "They say it's going to be hard for you to get upright from a lying-down position. For months, at least, and maybe forever. I can't lift you out of bed."

"I can manage."

"I sure don't see how. And that little wound goes all the way through you, through every layer of you, and that surgeon had to stitch every one of those layers up. So as long as you're healing, you could tear all that stuff back open, and healing is going to take a while, because of the blood thinners. You need to be supervised by a nurse."

"Baby, there's another way." But I didn't really believe it.

"There's no magic treasure we can use to bargain our way out of this, Buck," she said. "And even if there was, I'm not sure there's a bargain we could make. We can't take care of ourselves anymore, and there's no getting around that."

I tried to think of something else to say, but there wasn't anything, so I kept my mouth shut. Rose took my hand and squeezed it. We stayed like that for a while.

Something I don't want to forget:

Tequila came to visit a while after that. He had an overnight bag full of my things he'd brought up from the house. I looked inside, but I wasn't very interested in pawing at relics from a life that was over.

"What am I going to do with these in here?" I asked, pulling out a pack of Lucky Strikes.

"I don't know, but you always have them. I didn't think you would want to be without them."

I put the cigarettes on the tray next to my bed and found my memory notebook in the bag.

"Thanks for bringing this."

"I really fucked things up, didn't I, Grandpa?"

"No," I told him. "Everything had already come apart when you took Pratt. Jennings was going to charge you with killing Kind and Steinblatt. I'd have had to give up the gold to get you off the hook anyway." All my anger had been drained out of me, along with most of my blood.

"I still didn't handle myself the way I might have hoped."

"You learn from that."

He was silent for a moment, and I let it hang there. Then I said: "You know how you thought the treasure hunt was a search for meaning or a way to define my legacy?"

"Yeah," he said. "But maybe it was a mistake to try to graft symbolism onto straightforward things."

"No, I think you were right. There's a reason I went out there after Heinrich Ziegler. But it wasn't for the reason you thought. You see, Ziegler is Death. In 1944, I faced him down in the rain and the mud, and I knew he was Death when I stared him in those cold, savage eyes of his. And I went looking for him again, because I had to go hunting for it. I had to face it on my feet; I couldn't stand just waiting for it to find me. I had to hold it accountable for what is happening to me and your grandmother, for what happened to your father. Heinrich Ziegler was the closest thing I ever saw to a rider on a pale horse, and when I found him, he was just used up and emptied out like the rest of us."

I'd seen them, the sad cases, sinking into the cushy sofas in retirement homes, mulling their missed opportunities, wondering how they ended up there. If we'd seen it coming, we'd have got out of the way. Bleeding in the mud in 1944, I'd had an opportunity never to look into the city's rotten soul, never to shovel dirt onto my son's coffin, never to watch myself and my beloved Rose wither. All I had to do was give up, but I was too damn pigheaded, so I went ahead and lived another seventy years. And ended up getting shot in the back on my own lawn by a soft and silly man.

"Yeah," Tequila said. "But what about the gold?"

"It's funny, you know. You said you never believed it was real, and maybe you were right. There was a box of gold bricks, sure, but whatever it was I thought I needed wasn't in that bank. We went to St. Louis chasing a lie we told ourselves. All we hauled out of that vault was death."

"This can't be how it ends up, with you in the hospital, and the gold gone and Yael's killer still on the loose."

"Every story has the same ending," I said. "We just stop telling most of them before we get to it."

"And they lived happily ever after," said Tequila.

"That's a nice thought," I told him. "It would be nice if it was true."

47

I woke up sweating and disoriented in my hospital bed sometime in the night. My side was throbbing despite the painkillers the IV was pumping into me. My palms were sweating and my eyes itched. I felt like I was being watched, but the only other figure in the room was Tequila's silhouette, in the chair next to the bed.

I squinted. Tequila's silhouette was broader and taller than it was supposed to be.

"Evening, Buck," said the voice of Randall Jennings. "Sorry to wake you."

"I was up anyway," I told him. "What are you doing here?"

He moved his chair closer, so I could see his face in the low light coming in through the miniblinds on the window.

"I heard you got popped, and wanted to see how you were doing."

"Looks worse than it is," I lied, gesturing at the wound. "In and out. Just flesh, mostly."

"The word downtown, around the CJC, is that old Buck Schatz is indestructible."

"I don't know about that," I said. "An inch to the left, and it would have missed me. An inch to the right, and the doc says it would have shredded my guts. Somebody told me once that it's better to be lucky than good. I figure I'm maybe half and half."

He exhaled and his shoulders hunched toward me a little mournfully, or at least it looked that way in the half-light of the darkened hospital room. "I suppose the legends are always bigger than the men who make them," he said.

I nodded. "And I ain't as big as I used to be, either."

"Our mutual friend Mr. Pratt was neither lucky nor good. Poor guy didn't survive. The doctors worked real hard to save him, but they took him off the ventilator a little while ago."

"I don't understand," I said.

"He succumbed to his severe head injuries. Blunt force trauma." Jennings pointed demonstratively at his skull.

I made a series of rapid calculations. "Where is my grandson?" I asked.

The detective let out a theatrical sigh. "He's downstairs, in the back of my car. This gives me no pleasure, but I've got to charge him on Pratt. There's nothing else I can do, under the circumstances."

"That can't be right," I said. "Pratt was hurt when we gave him over to you, but not fatally."

Jennings shrugged. "Well, what can I tell you? Head injuries can be kind of funny. Sometimes they don't seem as bad as they are until the brain starts hemorrhaging, or whatever. I'm no doctor. All I know is the man started having some kind of seizure in my car, and he was unconscious by the time I got him to a hospital."

"No," I said. "It doesn't make sense. I've seen what it looks like when a man is beat to death. We may have roughed the son of a bitch up, but we didn't smash his head in."

"Why are you trying to debate this, Buck?" Jennings asked.

"The man is dead. They're putting him through autopsy. How do you argue with that?"

He leaned forward and squeezed my shoulder. "Don't worry about Tequila too much, Buck. I'm sure the D.A. will let him plead to manslaughter, and he'll be a free man inside three years. Under the circumstances, the prosecutor might even drop the charges, or the judge might suspend his sentence. Even if he spends a couple of years in jail, he'll get his life back, more or less. Nobody will hold it against him for getting rid of the fellow who butchered all those nice people."

"Yeah," I said, trying to convince myself it would work out okay. "Yeah."

It was my fault. I'd pulled Tequila into my Nazi hunt, because I couldn't run from my real problems without help, and now the poor kid was tangled up with all those corpses and facing prison.

"I want you to know, even though you and I have had our disagreements, it doesn't make me happy to be doing this. If you ask me, Tequila is a hero. But doing police work in a town this dirty is like wading balls-deep in a river of shit. The only way to keep yourself clean is to do things by the book."

That was something I knew pretty well. I grunted my reluctant assent.

"We're not going to trick the kid into making a damaging statement in an interrogation room or anything like that. Pratt was an evil bastard, and Tequila comes from a good police family. He will have the best chance we can fairly give him," Jennings assured me.

I shrank sadly into my hospital bed as I told the detective how much I appreciated his help arresting my grandson. My side was hurting, and I was wondering how to go about getting some more drugs.

"Of course, it could go down another way," said Jennings. And it might have just been the shadows playing off his face in the darkened room, but his expression seemed much less gentle, although his tone was unchanged.

"What do you mean?" I asked.

"I might decide I have to charge him with all three of the Memphis killings, and let St. Louis charge him for the girl. Then the two departments can take turns raking him over the coals until he makes an admission unhelpful to his cause."

"I don't understand," I said. I thought I was beginning to see how it fit together, but I wanted to hear him spell it out.

"Let me make it easy for you." Jennings grinned magnanimously at me. "Tequila saw Kind brace you for money, and that's a motive. He was also the last one to see the girl in the hotel alive. And I have witnesses who recall the two of you having an unfriendly altercation with Steinblatt at Kind's funeral. On top of that, I caught him red-handed in the act of bludgeoning Pratt. Now you told me an interesting story about how Pratt did the first three killings. Maybe I like your grandson for all four of these murders. You see, Buck, depending on how I stick the facts together, William T. Schatz either stopped a serial killer, or he is one."

The pain in the bullet wound was white hot. I could feel each individual stitch cutting into my flesh. At least I was fully alert now. I felt coiled, like a spring. But I knew that feeling was a lie my body was telling itself. I had never been more fragile or feeble, and the detective's cool monotone contained an unmistakable threat.

"What is it you want here, Jennings?"

"I've already got what I want. Now, I'm trying to make sure I get to hang on to it."

"The gold."

"There you go. I think all this unpleasantness can get explained without anyone having to mention any Nazi treasures. People kill each other over so much less, sometimes even nothing at all."

I sighed. "Didn't you say the only way to keep clean was to do things by the book?"

He laughed. "I said doing police work in this town was like wading balls-deep in a river of shit. There ain't nothing clean in a river of shit, Buck. And I got bills to pay."

"River of shit," I repeated. I squinted in the darkness to get a better look at him, and my detective instinct, my unconscious danger alarm, started screaming inside my skull. My doctor told me paranoia was an early symptom of dementia in the elderly, but I didn't think senility was the thing setting me on edge. "And Norris Feely?" I asked.

Jennings leaned forward in his chair. "It seems pretty clear he's the one that shot you. We'll say it was a dispute over Jim Wallace's assets. He'll shut up about the gold if I threaten to charge him for murdering Lawrence Kind."

His pieces all fit. But the problem was, the pieces of this thing seemed to fit any way I stuck them together. Everyone had the means, the motive, and the opportunity.

On television, the killers always make mistakes and the innocent are always vindicated, but most real murder cases are circumstantial, and circumstance doesn't always point in the right direction. Facts were of less importance to Jennings than hammering together a story that could stand up to reason. Truth was a malleable and relative thing.

"You'll just pin most of the crimes on the dead guy, and Tequila and Feely will shut up and cop to the lesser charges when you threaten to hang a murder beef on them," I said. "And when your story becomes the official truth, the gold just vanishes. It works out well, except it doesn't explain who killed those people."

Jennings scratched his head. "It was Pratt, wasn't it?"

"You believe that?" I asked him.

"Why shouldn't I? The story makes sense. It's good enough." He paused for a moment, pretending to be confused. "Didn't you tell me Pratt did all the killings? You're the legendary Buck Schatz. I trust you."

Jennings had a point. I couldn't very well play the hard-nosed truth seeker when I'd very recently been trying to frame the thing on the debt collector.

But greater sins were in play here than a few judicious lies, and Jennings was looking to palm the money off the table while moving the chips around.

What I was thinking was that it was a five-hour drive from Memphis to St. Louis, not including stops. Jennings said the St. Louis police had told him we were checked in at the same hotel where Yael was murdered. But there was just barely enough time for him to get from Memphis to St. Louis between noon, when the housekeeper found Yael, and five-thirty, when Jennings met Tequila in the lobby. The St. Louis cops would have had to contact Jennings immediately after they discovered the body, and Jennings would have had to drive the whole way with a blue light on top of his car and the pedal mashed to the floor.

Possible, maybe. But more likely, Jennings was in St. Louis ahead of the murder. And, damn him, I knew what a man with a fatal head injury looked like.

"We didn't beat Pratt to death," I said. "He wasn't dying when we left him with you."

"I don't know why you keep coming back to this, Buck. The guy is dead, I promise you."

I pictured Jennings sticking Pratt in the backseat of his Cavalier and then rolling off down the street. But when he got to the corner, maybe Jennings didn't turn and head toward Poplar

Avenue. Instead, he shifted the car into park, and he reached beneath his dash. Maybe he had a scoped hunting rifle hanging under there.

He'd have crouched on the wet grass, glancing around to make sure there were no witnesses. Then he would have braced the stock of the rifle against his shoulder, and his elbow against his knee, and squeezed off one shot.

I pictured him opening his trunk, throwing the rifle onto those four heavy backpacks, and reaching in to pull out a tire iron or maybe one of the gold bricks. I pictured Jennings caving Pratt's skull in.

I sat up straight in the bed and tried not to grimace in pain, even though my side was screaming. "I ain't arguing with the fact that Pratt's dead. But it wasn't us that killed him."

Jennings was silent for a moment, and then a slow smile split his face, and that pretty much confirmed it for me.

"I am disappointed you didn't figure it out sooner. You didn't quite live up to the legend," he said. "But then again, you are much harder to kill than I expected you to be."

There was only one reason for him to stop trying to deny it.

"I reckon you're here now to finish the job."

"Reckon so, Buck." He rubbed at his mustache again. "If you were in my shoes, you'd be doing the same thing."

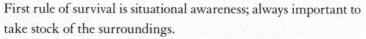

48

First rule of survival is situational awareness; always important to take stock of the surroundings.

I was sitting in a darkened room with a man who had killed at least four people and had come to kill me. I had a bullet hole in my side that was stitched up, but kind of oozy and hurting like a son of a bitch. I was on painkillers for that, and the drugs had dulled my reflexes, which weren't all that sharp to begin with.

The memory notebook and a ballpoint pen were lying next to me on the end table, with all the pills I was supposed to take.

And I knew, somewhere, in that notebook, I'd written what Gregory Cutter had said over Lawrence Kind's coffin:

"In the end, we know we will each come face-to-face with that Enemy, when we are totally alone, in the dark, when we are weak and afraid."

He'd been right about that.

"You can shout now, if you want," said the Enemy. "I don't mind. Nobody will hear."

That sounded true. This was an intensive care ward, so I

knew people were coming and going throughout the day and night, crying and screaming in the rooms and in the hallways, coding out against the protests of squealing monitors. I'd heard none of it; when that sliding glass door sealed itself, the room became a cocoon of silence.

"Used to be, they kept the patients separated by curtains so the doctors could hear all the machines beeping," Jennings said. "They remodeled a few years back. Now it's pretty close to sound-proof, so you people don't have to listen to each other dying. If you have an irregularity, your monitor will send a text message to the physicians' iPhones. Pretty amazing."

"I don't need to scream," I told him. Couldn't have if I'd wanted to. My mouth had gone all cotton-ball dry.

My eyes flicked toward the button next to my pillow that would call a nurse. But Jennings saw it, too, and he wagged a finger at me.

"Buck, there's an easy way and a hard way to do this thing. If there is an extra corpse in this room when I'm done here, I am going to add that murder to your grandson's tab."

With nobody around to say anything different, he could make it stick, too.

"I ain't planning to call a nurse to come save me," I said. My voice was barely a whisper, more of a rasp.

"Good," Jennings said, nodding. "Wouldn't do much for the Buck Schatz legend, would it?"

I glared at him. He reached into his jacket pocket and pulled out a syringe.

"You let me put this into your IV line, and that's the easy way. What's in here won't show up on your toxicity screening. Won't show up in your autopsy. You'll drift to sleep and that will be the end of it; an old man dying of natural causes. There's dignity in that, and peace. Best possible death I can imagine. But if you try to struggle, I'm going to get the knife out and make a mess. Ain't no point in wrestling the needle into you when you'll just bruise up like rotten fruit and everyone will know it's murder anyway."

"Is there any possible way to not die?"

He shook his head. "You and I both know that if you leave here alive, you'll be coming for me. You and I can't cut any deal. I can't stick anything to you that will shut you up, except this needle. As long as you're alive, I'll have to watch my back. Am I wrong, Buck?"

He wasn't. Somewhere inside my skull, my primal detective instinct was bellowing a battle cry. But there was also a weary part of me that didn't want to face months of painful recovery, didn't want to face Valhalla Estates, didn't want to face degenerative cognitive impairment.

Jennings put his hand on mine, touching the spot where the intravenous line was stuck in the vein. "So, how do you want to do this?"

"How long have I got to decide?" I asked, pulling my hand back.

"Take your time. I got nowhere to be."

We sat in silence for a few moments, staring at each other. I coughed noisily.

"When did you find out?" I asked him. No negotiations. No deals. No tricks. Just two professionals, talking.

"What? About the gold?"

"Yeah."

It couldn't have been news to him when I handed it over. He'd already killed three people for it by then. He must have known about it almost as long as I had. I thought he was out of the loop; I hadn't even suspected him.

"Norris Feely was tailing you the day you drove down to the CJC, the first day I met you. He came sniffing around after you left, trying to find out what you were up to. He spilled pretty much everything to me, right there."

Goddamn Feely. I hadn't even started watching my back until after my conversation with Avram Silver; hadn't known there was a reason to.

"Then you lied to poor Norris about the treasure, right in his face, at his father in-law's funeral." Jennings sucked on his teeth, making a reproachful, clucking noise. "Cold, Buck. Real cold."

Feely must have believed Kind and I were squeezing him out. So he'd gone back to Jennings for help finding the gold. They had been trying to get to it ahead of me.

"And all the while, you and the preacher were having your late night strategy sessions. It seems a little unfair of you to ambush poor Norris at that dinner party."

The way I remembered, it was me who got ambushed by the dinner party. But the point seemed largely moot.

"So you killed Kind because you thought he was working with me to get the gold?"

"We figured you wouldn't be able to chase it down on your own, so if we eliminated the reverend, you'd just go away."

"Tequila," I said.

"You have no idea how close he was to getting the treatment," Jennings said, drawing a finger across his throat and then downward in a zigzag diagonal line over his belly. "But then we found out where the gold actually was, and decided we might need to keep y'all alive for a bit."

"You found Avram Silver," I said.

"I never heard of Avram Silver until you told me about him."

That didn't make sense. I asked him how he found out the Nazi was in St. Louis.

"We punched the name 'Heinrich Ziegler' into the police database," he said. "The feds investigated him for war crimes years ago, and never ended up charging him with anything, but their files were in the computer and all the information came right up."

The same information he'd refused to look for when I tried to get him to help me out.

"Have I mentioned that you're an ass, and I don't like you?" I asked.

"You have no idea how happy it makes me to know that is the last time I will have to hear you say that," he said, smiling at me. "Anyway, I sent Feely out to the house in St. Louis that Ziegler owned before his stroke. The neighborhood has gone to shit since he left, and half the street was foreclosed, so the place was empty. Norris went in and broke up the walls and floors with a sledge-hammer. He even rented a backhoe and dug up the lawn. He didn't find a goddamn thing."

"That's why Norris wasn't at the Kind funeral."

"Probably," Jennings said. "Who gives a shit?"

I grunted.

"So when the gold wasn't hidden in the house, we guessed he'd either buried it someplace off his property or stashed it in a safe deposit box. And either way, we couldn't get to the gold without getting to Ziegler, and we had no pretense to get into a room alone with him. So we decided to stand back and see if you could get any information from the guy. Seems you had a pretty easy time of it." He wagged a finger at me. "Nobody ever suspects the elderly."

"And you figured that between chasing us in your black car after we left the bank, and threatening to arrest us for the murder you committed, we'd tell the truth and hand you the gold."

He nodded. "I expected you to spill it right there in the hotel parking lot. The kid started crying as soon as I told him about the girl. I didn't think it would take much. But you didn't budge an inch. And then you disappeared somewhere along the highway, and turned up in a different car. That was clever. I didn't know what you'd done with the gold, so it was like I was right back where I started."

"So you locked up Feely, your partner. Why?"

"I was never going to split the gold with him, and I needed him to take the fall for killing Kind. I was planning to bump him off and set you up for it."

That was why he put us in that interrogation room together. Feely had imagined that Jennings was watching what was going on in that room, eavesdropping on our conversation. But the room was a sealed box. Nobody could see what happened in there, and that was the whole point. If I had showed up at the police station alone or with Tequila, I would have gone into the room, and Feely would have come out in a rubber bag. With no proof to the contrary, Jennings could have blamed the gun-toting, senile loose cannon for killing the suspect. I'd spoiled the frame by accident when I showed up with the reverend's widow; she'd seen me leave Feely alive. And since that didn't work, Jennings killed Yitzchak Steinblatt to frame Tequila for the murders.

"How could you do those things to innocent people?"

Jennings laughed. "Memphis will top a hundred and sixty murders this year. We're probably going to edge out Detroit and Newark to be the most violent city in America. A couple more killings don't make a difference on top of all that. Hell, maybe carving up somebody like Lawrence Kind will get people upset about crime, and the city will have to find some extra resources to throw at the police department. But either way, I'm through busting my ass trying to clean this town up. I'm cashing out."

"Max Heller and I didn't see eye to eye on many things, Randall, but he'd be just as disgusted with you as I am. You sold out your own ideals, and nothing is worth that. You'll regret it, if you live long enough."

"If I do, I'll dry my tears with my big-ass piles of money, and then I'll cheer myself up by pissing on your grave. Speaking of which, how do you want to do this?"

I sighed. "I guess I don't want to make things any worse than they have to be for my family."

I reached over to the tray next to the bed with my right hand, the one with the tubes coming out of it, and I picked up my memory notebook. I gripped it tightly and brought it in close to my chest.

"Will you do me just one favor, Randall?" I asked.

He frowned. "Depends on what it is."

"This notebook, right here, is where I write down things I don't want to forget. This is my life, sort of, and I'd like for my grandson to have it. I sure don't want it to get thrown away or bagged up in some evidence locker after I'm gone."

Jennings mulled that over for a second. "So you want me to give it to him?"

I nodded. "It would mean a hell of a lot to me."

"No secret messages in here, are there?"

"That's not my style," I told him.

He frowned. "You're going to have to excuse me, Buck, for not trusting you."

"You can read it if you want to," I said. "But keep it safe and see that he gets it."

"That's your life, there, in that little book?"

"Yeah," I said. "The parts that matter, at least."

"Shit, man. That's pretty sad."

I glared at him. "It is what it is."

"Okay," he said. "I'll take it. But no promises."

He stood up out of his chair and leaned over me. He reached out his hand.

"I sure hope I don't ever get old like you," he said as he grabbed the notebook.

I didn't let go, though. I yanked my memories toward me as hard as I could, which wasn't very hard. But he was off balance, and I'd managed to surprise him. He fell across me, catching himself on his right arm.

His face was barely six inches from mine, close enough that I could smell coffee on his breath, even with the oxygen tube in my nose.

I stared Death right in the eye.

And I smiled, because in my left hand I had an obscene, non-regulation Smith & Wesson .357 Magnum, and it was pressed against his ribs.

"I wouldn't worry about it too much," I told him.

From this range, I didn't need to be able to hold my arm steady. From this range, I didn't need to be able to control the recoil. From this range, I couldn't miss. So I didn't do anything except raise a wall of noise; sound a clarion call of protest; bellow with rage at the enveloping shadow. And even though my ears were ringing from the blast, I'm pretty sure I heard Randall Jennings's guts splatter against the wall behind him.

Tequila had brought the rod up from the house along with my other things, along with cigarettes and my notebook. He knew I didn't feel comfortable without it.

And I'd been sleeping with it under the pillow, for two reasons:

The first was that, goddamn it, I'm superstitious. I hate birthdays, and I really fucking hate hospitals. When folks get scared, they cling to what makes them feel secure, and I'm no different.

The second reason was General Dwight D. Eisenhower.

History remembered Eisenhower for crushing the Axis and for becoming the thirty-fourth president of the United States. But what I remembered about him was that he told a frightened young soldier what to hang on to when all else was lost.

For sixty-five years I followed the general's orders, and when I faced my Enemy in the dark, when I was weak and afraid, I wasn't alone. Not entirely. When Lawrence Kind met death, he had Jesus with him. I had Smith & Wesson.

Jennings was still holding himself up with his right arm; his left still clung to a corner of my notebook. He tried to speak, but all that came out of his mouth was a froth of pink bubbles, because his right lung was mostly pulp.

"Sorry, Randall," I said. "But if you were in my shoes, you'd be doing the same thing."

Jennings let go of my notebook and started clawing at his armpit beneath his jacket, trying to get his sidearm out of its holster. But I just pressed the .357 against the right side of his jaw and I squeezed the trigger, and then his left eye and the top part of his head were gone, and the body collapsed on top of me.

Dropping a two-hundred-pound corpse into my lap is kind of like hitting a wet loaf of bread with a sledgehammer. Even with the painkillers, it hurt something awful, and I wasn't strong enough to roll the body off me. Through the blinding pain, I could barely even perceive the warmth and wetness around my legs and ass as Jennings drained into the sheets.

I reached behind me to press the nurse-call button. Since my legs were pinned under the body, I had to twist, and I popped all my stitches. The dark room went white for a moment, and I figured my valiant heroism had been to no avail; I'd probably seen my last sunrise. It would be okay, though. Tequila would be smart enough to figure out what had happened. He would be able to exonerate himself and, less important, Feely, who didn't deserve to take a murder rap.

I yanked the oxygen line out of my nose and threw it as far as I could. Then I picked up the pack of Luckys from the tray next to the bed. I shook out the last cigarette, stuck it between my lips, and lit it.

I took a deep pull and held on to the smoke. I figured this one might have to last me.

The nurse on duty, a middle-aged white woman, showed up about five minutes later, a silhouette in the doorway of the dark room.

"What's the problem, Mr. Schatz?" she asked.

"I seem to have made a mess here," I told her.

"Oh, that's nothing to be embarrassed about," she said with a little giggle. "It happens all the time. We'll get you cleaned right up."

She flipped on the light. Randall Jennings was lying on my bed, one unblinking eye staring at the nurse out of half a face. The white bedsheets were soaked black with blood. The wall behind Jennings was looking vaguely abstract expressionist, an explosion of dripping red with bits of pink and black stuck in it. On the wall beside me was a sunburst of brain matter with more blood and white skull fragments to accent the brownish-gray stuff.

The nurse screamed.

"Yeah, I know," I said, stubbing out my cigarette. "No smoking in the hospital."

49

Davy Crockett had the Alamo. Wyatt Earp had the O.K. Corral. Jack Kennedy had PT-109. John McCain had the Hanoi Hilton. I got the geriatric intensive care unit. And the YouTube.

I'd never even heard of the YouTube before I got famous on it, but apparently it was some kind of Web site where people could watch strange and stupid little videos on computer screens, and it was very popular. This was what young people were spending their days doing instead of working.

Here's what happened: I was lying on my back, ripped open and bleeding, and the doctors were running another transfusion into me. They had hosed off most of the blood that wasn't mine, and somebody lifted me onto a bed with wheels and rushed me down to the operating room.

The anesthesiologist was holding a mask over my face and telling me to try to breathe naturally. The best vascular surgeon in the southeastern United States was getting ready to sew me back up. I told him that I enjoyed moderately strenuous activities, like shooting bad guys, and that he should do his job right this time so I'd hold together. The surgeon told me I wouldn't be doing anything strenuous for a while, because my right leg was broken in two places and I would be in a wheelchair for at least several months. Then I passed out.

In recovery, hours later, I was shaking off the haze of anesthesia, hurting through the painkillers, and trying to figure out whether I'd lost some kind of argument. That's when the lady from the local news and her cameraman came to visit.

"You look like you've had a bit of a rough night, Mr. Schatz," she said, pointing a microphone at me.

"You should see the other guy," I told her.

She smiled. "How did it feel when you realized that the man in your hospital room had come to kill you?"

I shrugged, which hurt. "Familiar."

That seemed to confuse her a little bit, but I was sleepy and didn't have the energy to explain it.

"Look," I said, "I just got out of surgery."

She made some kind of gesture to the cameraman. "One more question, Mr. Schatz. How did you manage to stop a rampaging serial killer?"

She could look at the coroner's report and see how I'd stopped him. I watched plenty of news on television and I knew what she was looking for, though. This was the story about the plucky old man who wasn't letting age slow him down, and I was supposed to dispense some kind of vaguely spiritual or inspirational wisdom for the television audience. But I knew I would not be shitting unassisted in the foreseeable future, and I didn't feel very plucky at all.

What I said was: "I shot him in the face with a .357 Magnum revolver. That usually does the trick."

That went out on television, and I figured I wouldn't hear any more about it. But I was wrong, for reasons Tequila had to explain to me. I'm still not entirely sure I understand what happened.

It seems the local news channel put the video on its Internet site, and somebody took that video and put it on the YouTube. Within forty-eight hours, over a million people had seen it.

Then somebody went and found the old newspaper stories about all the other people I'd killed while I was a cop, going back fifty years. Whoever did it must have gone to the library to find that stuff, into the microfilm. I think it was Tequila, but I could never get him to confess.

The result of this strange, anonymous project was a second video on the YouTube that featured text excerpted from the newspaper articles flashing on the screen, alternating with photographs, creating a three-minute recap of my police career, set to some kind of noisy guitar music. This one, too, hit the top of the "most viewed" list.

Other popular videos on the YouTube include, incidentally: a baby that smiles, some kind of bug-eyed rodent, a sneezing panda bear, and a retarded kid trying to disco dance. So by becoming famous on the Internet, I was joining truly illustrious company.

After the second video came out, the "Buck Schatz joke" became very popular. Tequila said this was like the joke about Chuck Norris kicking somebody in the head or the joke about the walrus with the bucket. I had never heard either of these jokes. He tried to explain them to me, but they didn't make any sense. I don't think people Tequila's age understand what a joke is.

The "Buck Schatz joke" combines two observations: that I am very old and that I have killed a lot of people. So, for example, one basic version might be:

"Do you know why there aren't any more Tyrannosauruses?"
"Why?"

"Buck Schatz."

This joke had numerous constructions, crediting me for every-thing from the disappearance of the lost city of Atlantis to the capture of Saddam Hussein.

"When I was your age, we read James Thurber," I told Tequila.

"Well, we've made a lot of progress since then," he said.

The "Buck Schatz joke" bled over into real television around the time I departed the hospital and ascended to Valhalla, the un-discovered country from which no travelers return. Or, at least, to Valhalla Estates, a lifestyle community for older adults.

Rose had rented a three-room apartment for us, and our stuff was already there when I left the hospital. I went without com-plaint; I didn't have much of a choice. With the busted leg, I needed someone stronger than my wife to help maneuver me be-tween the wheelchair and the bed, or between the wheelchair and the toilet.

The house was empty for the first time in sixty years, except for the workmen who were tearing down our wallpaper, which was out of fashion, and tearing up the carpeting, because there was hardwood flooring underneath. The old place would soon be ready to go on the market, which meant it would look like we had never been there. And the grass would go right on turning green in the springtime.

I never went back home.

So, I was sitting in the common room on our floor, in my wheelchair with a blanket over my lap, when I heard them talking about me on Fox News. I remember it was The O'Reilly program.

"I've got two words for all those liberals on Capitol Hill who want to take away our gun rights," O'Reilly was saying .

I hoped the two words would be "Second Amendment."

"Buck Schatz."

Oy gevalt.

Something I don't want to forget:

"It just isn't right," Tequila said. "This isn't the way it's supposed to end."

"How do you mean?"

"We went to all that trouble, and all we got was hurt."

The Memphis City Council had pushed through a special resolution diverting Ziegler's fortune to something called the executive discretionary fund. There was an urgent need to build a new guesthouse behind the mayor's mansion. Tequila was trying to get a lawyer to sue the city on our behalf, but they all told him we had no right to the gold. It was the kind of situation that disappointed me but didn't surprise me.

"I don't see your wheelchair," I said.

He pulled out his Internet phone and poked his finger at the screen for a couple of seconds, an excuse to avoid looking at me. I could tell he was thinking about the Israeli girl and about Brian. "Fair point," he said. "But still."

"The bad guy got what he deserved. The hero saved the day. Things turned out well enough." Nothing could compensate the loss of my independence, but I took a kind of grim satisfaction in having disposed of Randall Jennings. Putting him down gave me back my sense of myself, a thing I'd been missing since Brian died.

But Tequila hadn't found the catharsis he'd come looking for, and maybe that was my fault. I understood, at least to a degree, what it was that he needed. But I didn't know how to give it to him. He was right: we were hurt. And he'd have to come to terms with it, somehow. But I didn't have my life ahead of me, and it was easier for me to just not talk about it. Whatever he needed to face, he'd have to deal with alone. It shouldn't have been that way. But things are rarely the way they ought to be.

"I kind of thought I was the hero," he said.

"Yeah, well, that's a common mistake."

50

They buried Randall Jennings a few days after I moved from the MED to Valhalla. I decided to attend; always believed in making my peace after I killed a man. Tequila had already returned to New York, but Felicia Kind gave me a ride.

She would be getting her workmen's compensation settlement, thanks mostly to me solving her husband's murder. So she owed me one. She told me she was getting set to leave town. Under the circumstances, that didn't seem like a bad idea.

She offered me a piece of her payday; I think she felt bad that I lost my treasure. But I turned down Felicia's money. She'd need it to set herself up someplace away from here. Rose and I would be okay. We could last quite a while on the proceeds from the house, and my physical therapist said I'd be walking again after a couple of months of healing. I would need a cane, but I'd be able to get around on my own and I could use a toilet or a shower without help. And I got one of the handicapped parking stickers for the Buick, which was a nice little perk. All things considered, I was glad Jennings was dead and I wasn't.

My vanquished foe drew an even smaller crowd than Jim Wallace; I guess that comes with dying disgraced. No church would host the memorial service, and since Jennings had murdered a clergyman, none of God's folks would read a psalm over him. So the half-dozen mourners stood graveside, and I was stuck looking over the coffin at the wife and teenage daughter of the man I'd shot, and at a guy about my age I figured was his father. They stared back at me with eyes full of hatred I knew I'd earned. Jennings had twenty-five years on the force, but dying dirty meant he forfeited his pension. They were facing hard times.

Only one cop showed up to mourn the dead man: Andre Price, the young colored officer I'd spoken to at the CJC the day I met Jennings. He was wearing neatly pressed dress blues, and his cheeks were drawn and tense as he looked at me, as if his whole body were straining to contain some outburst of emotion.

Andre read a eulogy, and I focused on writing it in my notebook to avoid meeting the dirty stares getting thrown my way by pretty much everyone in attendance.

"They say Randall Jennings turned dirty at the end, but he worked clean for all the years I knew him," Andre said. His voice wavered a little as he spoke.

"When I was fourteen years old, some of the neighborhood scumbags found me, told me I should do some slinging for them, on the corner. They turned out kids to deal for them on the street and in the schools. Once they got pulled into the life, the only way most of them kids ever got out was in the back of a meat wagon. But I was only there maybe twenty minutes before Randall, who was riding the beat at that time, grabbed me around my neck and threw me in the back of his squad car. And I know he could have taken me into booking, and I would have gone away to juvie, and Lord knows where I'd be today if he had."

He paused for a moment and dabbed at his eyes with a hand-kerchief.

"Instead, he took me to my grandma's house, and he told her what I'd done. And boy, she gave me a whuppin'. But I never went back out on that corner. Randall Jennings showed me mercy. Randall Jennings saved my life. And whatever else he did, I know he was doing Jesus's work the day he rescued me. All the folks who didn't come out here to see him buried, the folks who won't come out to pray with his family, they don't remember the things he did for this city, and for so many of us. But me, I'm not going to forget."

I had no reason to disbelieve a word he said, Jennings had been clean, as far as anyone knew, until he found out about Nazi gold, so in a way, the whole mess was my fault. I mean, really, I guess, Feely was the one who told him most of the details, but Feely rode in my wake. At the very least, I was the harbinger of Feely.

I remembered, when Brian died, I went to speak to the rabbi at our synagogue. He told me that God tests us and that loss was one of those tests. He told me to remember the story of the Garden of Eden and how the snake had tempted Eve to eat from the Tree of Knowledge. The Christians, he explained, believed the snake was the Devil, something older than the world and evil; intent on un-doing God's plan. But Jews had no Devil; the snake was just a snake. And he was there in the Garden because God made him; God put him there.

"Randall always said doing police work in this town was like wading waist-deep into a river of filth," Andre said. I remembered Jennings phrasing it differently. "I guess, after twenty-five years watching the scumbags take whatever they wanted, watching the businessmen and real estate developers take whatever they wanted, watching the politicians take whatever they wanted, Randall fi-nally succumbed. It ain't an easy thing, walking away from what you desire."

Maybe Jennings was the Devil, or maybe I was the snake. Maybe I'd tempted him off the path of righteousness. But likely as not, he was just a mean son of a bitch who never met anyone meaner than he was, until he met me. But Yitzchak Steinblatt had said something that seemed true, about the folks who turned sick, who got to like killing too much, and Jennings would have been one of those whether there was Nazi gold or not.

Either way, I supposed, it had ended up how it ended up. Like Tequila had told me, dead was dead. So, to Valhalla with Buck Schatz, and to hell with Randall Jennings. The old man I figured was Jennings's father was sobbing loudly. The detective's widow looked at me, and her lower lip was quivering. Felicia Kind's hand squeezed my shoulder, reminding me not to feel sorry for these people.

"You're an ass," I told the box. "And I don't like you." It was the last time he'd ever have to hear me say it.

We watched Jennings go balls-deep into the ground, and then everyone dispersed, and the young, pretty blonde helped me out of my wheelchair and back into the car.